Soledad
Dark Republic Book One

D.L. Young

For Stephen

AUTHOR'S NOTE

For those of you familiar with my short fiction, you may notice some similarities between this novel and one of my short stories, "The Reader." Those similarities are not your imagination, nor are they coincidental.

When I wrote the original story, I felt like there was a lot more there, that I was just scratching the surface of something larger. And as much as I love "The Reader," writing it as a five thousand-word story felt a bit like trying to stuff an elephant into a Mini Cooper. So I went ahead and made it into a novel.

If you've read the shorter piece already, don't worry. The novel is different enough that you won't feel like you're watching a TV rerun. *Soledad* is much broader in scope with a bigger cast of characters and a more expansive world.

Enjoy the story.

D.L. Young
Houston, May 2016

CHAPTER 1

Motherfuck it, I'm done.

That's what it's come to, I decide, as I sit here in the dirt under the desert sky, clear and dark and full of winking stars.

Let Guzmán find someone else to do his dirty work. Let someone else be the foundation he builds his castle on. Let someone else be his slave.

I've had enough. I'm finished with Guzmán, finished with all the lies.

It's a shitty world and people are the shittiest thing in it. And three years is a long time to wallow in that reality, seeing what others can't, learning nothing except that human beings are self-serving, cruel, untrustworthy. They'll screw you over without a second thought, beat you senseless over a scrap of bread. No, that's being too generous. They'll ruin you just because they can. Or maybe for fun. I once saw a man hack another man's arm off with a machete to test the sharpness of his blade.

What a fine species we are.

And we lie. Jesus, how we lie. Before I ended up here, I never would have guessed how much. Men lie about how many women they've slept with. Women lie about loving their husbands. Children lie about stealing candy. Everyone lives in a constant state of bullshit-spinning. They lie about everything, all the time. To friends, to family, to strangers, to themselves. Especially to themselves.

People lie, they're dangerous, and they can't be trusted. And tonight, for the who-knows-how-many-eth time, that's exactly what I'm supposed to go and prove.

"¿Estás lista ya?" I start at Lela's voice behind me, asking me if I'm ready.

"Almost," I answer without turning around. She's asked me the same question every minute for the past quarter of an hour.

"They starting to eat, Soledad," Lela says, switching to English, as if this will make me more reasonable. "Need to go now."

"When I'm ready." I feel the hierba slowly starting to creep up on me, tendrils growing through my mind. Lela's voice starts to change, vibrating with a tangible frustration and urgency I hadn't noticed a minute earlier. The hierba's bitter taste lingers on my tongue. I take a mouthful of water from my bottle, swish it around, spit it onto the sandy dirt.

"That's a waste," Lela scolds. "You should no waste water in the desert."

I turn and look up at her towering over me, her giant silhouette bathed in moonlight. Shaved head, muscled arms, and twin shotguns strapped over her shoulders. A vision from some nightmare.

I stand and brush the dirt off the back of my trousers. Around Lela's neck her Virgin of Guadalupe pendant hangs by a frayed rope.

I point to the pendant. "You're going to lose that thing if you don't replace that rope pretty soon."

Lela grabs my finger, her enormous hand making mine look like an infant's. "You touch that, I kill you."

There's an almost undetectable quiver in the wrinkles

around her eyes, the barest lilt in her voice. Everything around me is suddenly vivid, like a black and white image blinking into full color. I see more, hear more, feel more. The hierba has taken hold.

"You're lying," I say, pulling my finger out of her grip.

Lela smiles, her silver teeth gleaming. "You right, I lying." Then she grabs me by the arm and jostles me toward camp. "And that means you ready. Vamos."

*　　*　　*

Lela and I weave our way through the maze of tents. Children scurry about, kick up clouds of dusty West Texas dirt while their parents cook over campfires. Cast iron pots filled with beans and stews, large flat irons covered with tortillas. My mouth waters, stomach growls.

Lela seems to sense where my attention's gone. She pauses next to one of the campfires, where a large, round-faced woman with long braids piles a fresh batch of tortillas into a basket.

"Buenas noches, señora," Lela says. "¿La molesto con una tortilla?"

"Claro," the woman answers. She smiles and hands a tortilla to Lela, who then passes it to me. The woman's expression changes as she recognizes me. Fear glows from her face like the incandescent halo around a light bulb. *New to camp*, I think. The new arrivals are always wary of me. Guzmán's bruja, the one they'd heard about, the witch who can look into someone's eyes and see their soul.

Lela thanks the woman and we walk on.

"Want some?" I ask, tearing off a piece.

Lela shakes her head.

The warm tortilla fills my mouth with the taste of roasted corn.

"I've got all the gear ready for you," a voice behind us says. I turn and see Rafa, grinning at me. He's the very image of puberty, all elbows and knees, pimpled face, hands and feet that look too big for the skinny frame that's stuck somewhere between boy and man.

"Muy bien," I say, turning back around, trying to ignore the longing I see in his face. His adolescent lust, as awkward and obvious as a hard-on tentpoling his pants.

It's your own fault, Sol.

It's not the smartest thing I've done, sleeping with Rafa, but there you are. Endless monotony can drive you to try any distraction.

He follows behind us like a dog with hopes of a treat.

As I swallow the last bit of tortilla, we turn a corner and the food tent comes into view. I stop and sigh.

Lela walks a few paces ahead, stops, and turns. "Come on," she says, returning to my side. She places her hand on my shoulder and presses me forward, insistent. "Time for work."

The food tent is the largest structure in camp, its towering peak propped up by an old telephone pole. Thick, taut ropes staked deep into the ground hold everything in place. They throw parties here during all the major holidays: Dia de los Reyes Magos, Dia de los Muertos, even some of the gringo ones like Thanksgiving and Fourth of July. Hundreds crowd under the tent, packed tight, drinking and dancing until dawn. Hundreds more spill out into the camp. You can't get an hour's worth of sleep for all the fucking noise.

"Wait here," Lela tells me and walks ahead to the tent. She peeks inside the door flap and comes back. "He facing this way," she says, pivoting her shoulders to show me the subject's orientation. "The gringo with the colita."

Lela and I move to the side of the tent, leaving Rafa behind. I pull back the flap that's disguised to look like a fold in the tent's canvas, then I slip inside. The narrow, concealed space between the outer and inner walls of the tent has a short ladder leading up to a small platform, the secret spot where I'll spend the next couple hours, observing the visitor. I climb the ladder and step onto the platform, where there's a small table and a three-legged stool. On top of the table sits a pair of headphones, and next to them a plate of steaming cabrito, tortillas, and a mug of water.

I lean over the outer edge of the platform and whisper to Lela's shadow. "Gracias por la comida."

I sit on the stool, my belly pressed against the table. There's hardly any room to move, but I've long since grown accustomed to the cramped conditions. In front of me, there's a wide pane of one-way glass. On my side, I can see everything going on inside the food tent. From the other side, diners see only what looks like a framed mural, a Diego Rivera replica depicting peasants with rifles, waving banners that read Tierra y Libertad. Land and freedom.

Inside the tent, I see a dozen of Guzmán's men, mostly inner circle types. Shifty-eyed advisers and grizzled muscle men. They all wear the same loose-fitting garments: white cotton shirts discolored by desert dust and sand, camel brown pants. They're a kind of uniform: the simple, functional garb of the desert-wandering rebel, little changed since the days of Pancho Villa, who led his bandit revolutionaries through this same godforsaken land some two and a half centuries ago.

Some of the men mill about, but most are already seated at the long wooden bench-style tables. Pepe the cook hovers around them, scooping large spoonfuls of beans from a small pot. His son, little Pepe, maybe six or seven, follows close behind handing out tortillas. The meal's only just started. In a little while they'll bring out some kind of meat, maybe a stew or cabrito. I've got maybe fifteen minutes before the hierba's effect starts to peak, so I take some time to eat.

After I finish, I grab the headphones, cup them over my ears, and flip the switch. Good sound, not much static. I turn the knob through positions one through ten, testing each of the tiny microphones hidden in the tables.

I remove the headphones, turn around in the stool, reach down and tap Lela's shoulder through the canvas outer wall. "Lista," I whisper. Then the shadow of her head nods slightly, her signal to Rafa, who's hanging around nearby, that the gear's working fine and he can tell Guzmán's men inside the tent that I'm ready to go.

I turn back around, put the headphones on again, and settle in to start the read.

The subject sits at a table, scoping everyone out, a half-eaten tortilla in his hand. Conspicuously gringo among the brown-skinned men, he's tall and lean, his blond hair pulled back into a ponytail. Lela gave me the data dump on him earlier in the day. It was a story I'd heard countless times: he had the deal of a lifetime, a huge moneymaker, and to bring it to fruition all he needed was access to Guzmán's manpower and resources. Blah blah blah, the deal would pay Guzmán back ten times over, guaranteed. They all use that word: guaranteed. *I guarantee it*, they say, as if the word actually had meaning. How many of these pitches have I heard? A hundred? Two hundred? More? Cattle ranching, narcotics production, natgas conversion plants, drone factories, fish farms in Galveston Bay, trade deals with the Chinese or the Brazilians. There seems to be an endless supply of these would-be big shots, these bullshitters and fast-talkers who come here to the desert, drooling at the chance to do business with Guzmán. Maybe one out of twenty has a legit deal.

Scrub brush, coyotes, and hustlers. In the West Texas desert, one finds these in abundance.

I watch and listen as Pepe serves the stew. Everyone is seated now, eating and chatting in the low, controlled tones of serious men. Blond ponytail attempts small talk with one of the bodyguards. He's no dummy, blond ponytail. I can see that right away. He knows it's bad manners to talk business before the meal's finished. Most of the gringo hustlers make the mistake of going straight into their pitches.

I close my eyes for a moment, then open them. I feel the hierba's effect peaking, so I lean forward and take a few deep breaths, relaxing my mind like Mama taught me to. I feel my awareness expand like a lens opened to its highest aperture, letting all the light in.

The first thing I sense is a deep skepticism emanating from Guzmán's men. They don't trust blond ponytail. Their suspicion hangs in the air, heavy and thick, a cloud of unseen smoke. I see all the tiny physical giveaways I normally wouldn't notice, those things the brain files away as irrelevant, unworthy of the conscious mind's attention: furtive movements of hands, small changes in body posture, minute facial tics. But with Mama's training and the help of the hierba, I can see everything. Hear everything, too. Fear and nervousness, confidence and joy, love and hate. There's nothing they can hide from me right now, not even the things they hide from themselves. Mama taught me to see it all.

Mama. I try not to let the memories distract me.

There's an unnatural strain in the men's voices. I hear their distrust like someone else might notice an out of tune key on a piano, ringing untrue. I lose myself, seeing these men, hearing them, reading them like a book written in a language only I can understand. A book of lies and deception, one I wish I'd never opened.

I focus on blond ponytail. "Whitetail," he says, drawing out the word into three syllables. *Waht-tay-el.* His Southeast Texas accent rings clear and unmistakable in my headphones. "Can't hardly find whitetail deer no more. Last season we sat a week in a blind, and nothing. Stalked a week more, nothing. My granddaddy said before Secession, he got him eight-point bucks every season."

When the man across the table ignores him, he turns to another sitting next to him. "How's the deer hunting around these parts?"

Blond ponytail's neighbor doesn't look up from his bowl. He shrugs and says, "You're eating coyote stew.

What do you think?" Nods and chuckles from around the table. Blond ponytail forces a smile.

They finish the stew and Pepe brings the café de olla. The smell of roasted coffee beans and cinnamon fills my nostrils.

I watch and listen, concentrating on blond ponytail as he starts his pitch.

"I've been in the natgas business all my life."

Lie.

"My chemists get the highest gas conversion in all the Republic."

Lie.

"Payback on this here deal's six months, nine tops. I guarantee it."

Huge lie.

He's in his element now, building lie upon lie, relaxed and smiling, bullshitting everyone around him. Such a comfortable, practiced storyteller. One of the best I've ever seen. Effortlessly he spins a spider's web of deceit, weaving strand after strand. A small exaggeration here, an intentional omission there, a complete fabrication when he really wants to pique their interest. Two years ago I might not have picked up on him so quickly. That's how good he is. He even starts to win over some of the men, making them laugh, nod their heads. I sense the cloud of doubt dissipating. Not that it matters.

Sorry, blondie, but it's not their opinion that counts.

I sit there, watching and listening for another half an hour, as the gringo slowly digs his grave, one lie at a time.

When I've seen enough, I switch off the headphones, place them on the table. I stand up, stretch my back, and ease my way down the ladder.

I slip through the false fold and step outside, where Lela's still standing guard. The cook's son stands next to her. The boy looks up at me with big eyes, full of expectation.

"I'm done," I tell Lela. "Tell Guzmán I'm ready."

Lela pats the boy on the head and says, "Vete, niño." Little Pepe takes off at a run. He hops over a pair of legs sticking out from an old Jeep, someone making repairs, and knifes his way through an obstacle course of campfires, cooking pots, and families relaxing in the cool night air. He turns a corner and disappears from sight.

I enter the food tent with Lela, and we sit at the far end of the table, away from everyone else. Dinner is over and blond ponytail anxiously looks over at us, unsure what our sudden appearance might mean. He fidgets and bites his nails as he waits for Guzmán's arrival. I let my gaze linger on his face a few moments. Underneath his anxiety he's still confident, the fool. Even as the walls are closing in on him, the cocksure bastard still thinks he'll make the deal. I steer my eyes away from him.

A minute later Guzmán bursts through the door flap and everyone stands. Two bodyguards follow close behind, shotguns in hand. The security detail always strikes me as redundant, even comically unnecessary. At two meters tall and pushing what has to be a hundred and twenty kilos, Guzmán's bigger and meaner-looking than any of the guards.

"Don Flaco!" blond ponytail shouts. "Wonderful to see you." He smiles broadly and takes a couple paces forward, his hand extended. A bodyguard steps in front of Guzmán and racks the slide on his shotgun. The gringo stops cold and lowers his hand. His face melts into confusion.

Guzmán eyes the stranger carefully. He strokes the black stubble on his wide anvil of a chin, contemplating. Then he turns to me. "So what about this one?"

Out of the corner of my eye I see blond ponytail shifting his gaze between Guzmán and me. His confusion blooms into panic. Beads of sweat break out on his upper lip and forehead.

He deserves what's coming to him, I tell myself, this silver-tongued scam artist. Given the opportunity, he'd slit every one of our throats without a second thought if there was something in it for him.

At this point I usually turn away, so I can't see or sense the subject. It's an ugly thing to watch, the way a person's face changes the moment they realize they're going to die. Some panic and try to run, some beg for mercy. Others nod and look to the ground, unsurprised, as if some long-expected bad news has finally arrived. It's a hard memory to shake afterwards, even when some crooked thief has more than earned it.

All I have to do is shake my head, like I've done so many times before. One small gesture from me and they'll drag him kicking and screaming out into the desert and shoot him like a dog.

"Dime, niña," Guzmán says, his voice rising a notch. "¿Sí o no?"

Lela nudges me with her elbow and I snap back to the moment. Every pair of eyes focuses on me in anticipation. Some fear me, some respect me, some want to fuck me. The tent blares with the unspoken din of Guzmán's men. How I wish I could turn it all off.

I look at blond ponytail. Vain, greedy blond ponytail. The last remnants of his confidence ebb, then disappear altogether. He finally seems to understand what's happening.

Fuck it.

I turn to Guzmán and nod. "He's fine."

"Muy bien," Guzmán says. "I'll meet with him in the morning." Then he turns and leaves, followed by his security detail.

It fills me with a strange kind of satisfaction, the way Guzmán believes me, how completely he takes me at my word. Makes me wish I would have lied to him long before now.

But it's nothing more than a reprieve for blond ponytail, a stay of execution. When they figure out his deal is a bullshit scam, they'll shoot him in the head and dump him in the desert. A meal for coyotes and vultures, like all the others who dared to pull one over on the great and powerful Guzmán.

And then after they take care of him, they'll come for me.

CHAPTER 2

It's long after midnight and I'm still awake. I sit on my cot, running my finger back and forth over the tracker scar on my forearm.

Outside, camp is quiet, peaceful. The canvas walls of my tent ripple gently in the cool breeze. The guard outside my tent starts to snore. I see the shadow of his head droop, catch, then droop again, like a lazy fisherman's pole.

"Despierta, güey." I see Lela's large shadow towering over the seated guard, her hand reach out and slap the back of his head. The dozing man jolts awake with a curse.

She pokes her head inside the tent, sees me awake. "No sleeping yet?"

I shake my head. She enters, looks around, nods. "It's nice, your new tent. More room for your books." Then she taps her boot on the floor. "And wood better than dirt, yes? Not many have wood floors."

I stare at her dully. "Lucky fucking me."

Lela furrows her brow. "Don Flaco wanna see you."

I blink. "Guzmán? Now, why?" A twitch of worry twists my stomach.

"No sé. Just told me to come for you. Vamos."

I lie down on the cot. "Tell him I'm sleeping." I roll over, my back to Lela, mind racing. He's never called for me this late before. "Or tell him the hierba made me sick. What's so important it can't wait until morning?"

Lela grunts in frustration. The floor vibrates with heavy boot steps as she approaches the cot. "I carry you like a baby. That what you want?"

I glance back and wrinkle my nose at her. "You wouldn't dare, you big ape. Hey, what the hell?"

She's reaching under my legs with one hand, under my shoulders with the other, lifting me. I wriggle free and sit up. "All right, all right, Christ. Let me throw a jacket on."

*   *   *

Guzmán's "office" is an unassuming tent where he holds court with his inner circle, planning raids or divvying up spoils from the latest captured town. It's cramped, cluttered with several chairs, none of which match: a faded red recliner with yellow foam bursting from rips in the sides, a pair of dented aluminum stools, an old wooden rocking chair. I sit in the corner on one of the stools as Guzmán and his top military man, Chavez, stand hunched over a large map of the Republic spread out over a wobbly folding table.

I fidget on my narrow perch. No one has said a word about why I've been summoned. My thoughts turn anxiously to the lying gringo.

A scattered mess of papers covers much of the table, and a few have fallen to the dirt floor. A dozen or so black and white photos line the tent's walls, fastened to the canvas with pins, portraits of Mexican revolutionaries torn from ancient books and magazines. Zapata, Juarez, and Guzmán's favorite, Pancho Villa. Among the old photos are several pencil drawings, gifts from the camp's children, depicting Guzmán riding a horse, shooting a gun, flying in the air with a cape like a superhero. The back wall of the tent is covered by an enormous bookcase, three meters wide and taller than a person. In contrast to the haphazard mess of the rest of the space, Guzmán's library is organized with meticulous care. There's an entire shelf of history books (the biggest section), arranged alphabetically by author, and smaller sections on economics, natural gas production, and science.

Every few minutes Chavez, a brute of a man with narrow slits for eyes and silver-streaked hair, throws me a dirty look. At the moment he's looking down, tracing a big circle on the map with his finger. "We took the town much easier than expected."

Guzmán rubs his chin thoughtfully. "You call losing two dozen men easy?"

"We thought we'd lose much more, don Flaco," Chavez says.

"Good news, then."

Chavez glances over at me. "Can we speak on these matters privately, don Flaco?"

Guzmán's right hand loathes me, calls me a bruja, a witch. If it were up to him, I'd take the same walk into the desert that blond ponytail should have taken earlier.

Chavez. The hulking, flat-nosed peasant who wanted to kill me the first time he saw me. *Bad luck to have a witch with us*, he said, when they brought me to Guzmán's camp, starving and half-dead. He took out his gun and pleaded with Guzmán. *Let me do it*, he said, right in front of me like I wasn't there, like I was some dangerous animal that had wandered into camp, a rattlesnake that had to be taken care of.

Three years on, I think he likes me even less. But now it's more about professional jealousy than backwoods superstition. It kills Chavez that a half-gringa bruja has wormed her way into the inner circle, that I have Guzmán's ear. Not that I ever wanted it, of course.

"Don't worry about her," Guzmán says, waving his hand. "Unless you're lying to me, of course. Then maybe you *should* worry."

Chavez shifts his weight from one foot to the other and clears his throat. "Don Flaco, I would never tell you anything but the truth."

"I'm glad to hear it, compadre." I catch a glimmer of a cagey smile under Guzmán's thick mustache. He knows the hierba has long since worn off, knows I can't tell for certain if Chavez is lying any more than he can. But of course *Chavez* doesn't know that.

It's typical Guzmán: keep everyone around you off balance, unsure of their standing, worried about what you might do next. Even with Chavez, the loyal bulldog who's been part of Guzmán's inner circle longer than anyone, complete candor is as rare as a desert thunderstorm. Guzmán once told me the best boxers always keep their opponents guessing. Too many Mexican fighters didn't understand this, he said. They went straight forward, flat-footed, throwing hook after hook, willing to take two punches to give one. All offense, little strategy. And when they finally came across a skilled fighter, they got picked apart round after round, broken down like a dumb bull whose horns can never find the matador behind the cape. Feints, unpredictability, and deception were as important as a strong punch.

"So how much do we have now?" Guzmán asks. "What are the gas techs telling you?"

Chavez moves his hand over a portion of the map. "Now that we have Odessa, twenty-five percent, más o menos. We have most of the Permian Basin now."

Puta madre. Twenty-five percent. A year ago he had maybe half that. Two years ago he hadn't even taken his first town.

I imagine billions upon billions of cubic meters of natural gas deep in the ground underneath Odessa, underneath all the West Texas towns and territories Guzmán has taken in the past year. A quarter of the natgas fields in all the Republic under his control. How rich did that make him? How powerful? How the Bullock family must seethe whenever they hear his name, this dirty desert rebel who once only nibbled at the edges of their empire.

"What about the conversion plants?" Guzmán asks.

"Ten midsized ones in and around the city," Chavez replies. "The Bullocks' people torched two of them. The rest they wrecked before they got out of town, but the gas techs say they'll be up and running in a couple weeks."

Guzmán strokes his stubble. "They only had time to burn a couple. So they left in a hurry."

Chavez nods. "That's what it looks like, don Flaco."

"Leave any bots behind?"

Chavez shakes his head. "We've haven't found any. Only a few spare parts in the conversion plants."

"Drones?"

"Nothing so far. The airport outside the city has a few control rooms, but the hangars were empty."

For a moment neither man speaks, both studying the map like a chess board, their eyes darting back and forth, considering possibilities.

Guzmán asks, "How far to Dallas from here?"

"It's far, don Flaco," Chavez replies quickly, as if he's been expecting the question. "Five hundred and sixty kilometers."

"Too far." Guzmán looks up from the map. "That's what you want to say, yes? You think it's too far."

Chavez pauses, then nods. "Sí, jefe."

Guzmán scratches his chin and frowns. "So you think I should stay here? Is this your military strategy? Wait for them to come to me? Start playing defense?"

Chavez takes a deep breath. "We've taken so much in so little time, don Flaco." He speaks carefully, slowly. "Just to hold the territory we've gained takes a lot of manpower. We're stretched thin. To think about taking more, at least right now..." His mouth tightens into a straight line and he shakes his head.

Guzmán grunts in disapproval.

"I'm not saying we stay here forever," Chavez says, "but a few months would let us—"

"A few MONTHS?" Guzmán booms, his voice a sudden crash of thunder. "We've got them on the ropes, compadre. Why give them time to recover? We have to move *forward!*" He punctuates the last word by striking his fist on the table. Its legs buckle and papers scatter.

For a long, uncomfortable moment Guzmán says nothing, papers slowly drifting to the floor as he stares down his military chief. My heart races and I fight down a surge of animal fear telling me to run out of the tent. The crazed, simmering look on Guzmán's face would have most people pissing themselves right about now. It's a stare I've seen break down a roomful of hardened men, reducing a pack of snarling wolves to harmless sheep. I watch Chavez, grudgingly giving the man credit as he stands firm. He may be a backwards peasant from Michoacán, but there's not a cowardly bone in his body.

The silence lingers on like slow torture, then finally the temperature on Guzmán's face comes down a few degrees. "You're too careful," he sighs. He motions toward the photos pinned to the wall. "Look at those men. Zapata, Villa, Juarez. Were they careful? Were they happy to take a few towns, count their money, and then wait around for the perfect moment to move on? Never. They pressed forward when everyone thought they wouldn't. They marched to the east when the easier path was to the west. The gringos chased Villa and his men around this very same desert for *five years* and they never caught him. You know why? Because he didn't play it careful. The careful men never make into the history books, compadre."

I glance at the history section of his library, at the volumes dedicated to the Mexican revolution. *Wait, five years?*

Guzmán strokes his chin, smiles. "Let's get another opinion." He tilts his head in my direction. "Reader Soledad, what do you think? Should I stay here and wait for the stars and planets to line up before making my next move, or should I carry on?"

Chavez turns and glares at me. The unexpected opportunity to needle him lifts my spirits. I shrug indifferently and say, "Best defense is a good offense. That's what they say, isn't it?" I let the barest hint of a smirk raise left the side of my mouth. Chavez's faces boils over with rage. If looks could kill.

Guzmán bursts out with laughter, slamming his palm on the table, sending more papers flying. "You see? Even she understands. Now, go get some sleep, compadre."

Chavez's face contorts as he tries to compose himself. "Bueno, jefe," he says. "Buenas noches." He turns, shoots me one last go-to-hell look, and leaves.

As soon as Chavez exits, Guzmán sits and waves me over. He studies the map as I nervously take the seat across from him, his brow furrowed like he's working out some complex equation.

"Old Chavez has a special hate for you," he says without looking up.

"That's strange, because I really like him."

Guzmán chuckles.

"Nine months," I say.

"Nine months what?"

"That's how long the gringo army hunted Pancho Villa. Nine months, not five years."

The tips of Guzmán's mustache curl upward as he smiles. He looks up from the map. "Some say nine, some say eleven. Depends which history you read." He reaches down to the floor, fishes around inside his bag, and pulls out a pipe and a fist-sized bag of tobacco.

He shifts his gaze to some point beyond me, outside the tent. "Old Chavez is right about being careful," he says, removing a fat pinch of tobacco from the bag and packing it into the pipe. "You see how he looked me in the eye? Didn't flinch, didn't even blink. That's a loyal man for you, Reader Soledad. That's the kind of man you can count on."

"Count on to shoot me in the back," I mutter, instantly regretting it. Guzmán frowns at me as he strikes a match. The sudden flare of orange illuminates his face, light and shadow exaggerating his features, stretching them out of proportion. I shift uncomfortably in my chair. *You and your mouth, Sol.*

Guzmán watches me but doesn't say anything as he moves the flame slowly back and forth over the pipe, inhaling with careful, measured puffs. A smoky, sweet aroma fills the tent.

"Old Chavez knows," he says, "there are times for taking risks and times for being careful." He motions toward the old photos. "Those clowns on the wall, they never knew the difference. Villa died at forty-five, did you know that? And Zapata never even reached forty. Reckless fools, the both of them. The things they might have done if they hadn't been so careless." He tosses the match to the floor, mashes it into the dirt with his boot, and gestures toward the bookcase. "Count up all the wise men in those books, and you'll find five times the number of fools."

Those clowns on the wall. I look over at the photos. Hard men with weathered skin and sharp eyes stare back at me. Heroes of the common people, still celebrated and revered in songs and stories. Guzmán often quotes these men in his speeches, eliciting cheers from his followers. He sports the same wide mustache as Zapata, the same crisscrossed bandoleers. And like Villa, he openly keeps half a dozen mistresses, fathering who knows how many bastard children. Until this moment, like everyone else in camp, I'd bought the idea that these revolutionaries were his role models, his spiritual forefathers.

Guzmán chuckles as if he knows exactly what I'm turning over in my mind. "I know, I know," he says. "Sacrilegio to say such things, no?" He blows smoke rings from his mouth, then grins like a kid who's been caught stealing cookies. "But people need a story they can believe in, don't you think?"

After a few moments, I realize I'm staring at him with my mouth open. It's an odd feeling—like an unexpected shove in the back—especially for someone with my abilities. I can't recall the last time someone's actions or words surprised me. When you can see what I see, everyone's an open book, a story with disappointing characters and a bad plot.

I grapple for composure, telling myself I really shouldn't be surprised. Guzmán's always been careful with what he revealed to me about himself, going to great lengths to make sure I don't see him the same way I've seen so many others. While I'm under the influence of the hierba, he never shows his face for more than a few moments, and even then he rarely makes eye contact with me. And he shrewdly keeps the camp's only supply of hierba under his personal lock and key, doling it out to me in small, single-use quantities, and only when he needs a reading.

Still, even without the hierba, after three years in his service and countless hours alone with him, I thought I'd seen every side of the man. *A story people can believe in.* A *story.* A vague, deflated feeling settles over me, which I quickly dismiss as ridiculous. What does it matter if he's an enlightened folk hero or simply a greedy, land-grabbing opportunist posing as one? Either way, he's still the jailer holding the keys to my cell.

Guzmán leans back and puffs thoughtfully on his pipe. "So how's your new tent? Comfortable, no?"

"It's fine, gracias."

He nods. "It's the least I can do after how much you've helped us." He looks me over carefully. "How are you feeling these days, Reader Soledad?"

"Fine." I wonder where he's going with this, why he called me here. *Does he know about the gringo?* I decide he doesn't. The price for betrayal is quick and brutal, even for his inner circle. I've seen it, I know. If he had any idea I'd crossed him, I wouldn't be sitting here having a chat. I'd be facedown in the desert with two rounds in my brain.

So he doesn't know…yet.

He takes a long draw on the pipe; the tobacco glows and crackles softly. "I wonder," he says. "You see so much death, maybe too much. It's a hard thing, to see it like you do, up close and ugly."

So let me walk out of here if you're so concerned about my state of mind.

"Your soldiers see a lot more than I do," I say.

Guzmán nods. "Yes, but that's different. They fight and kill because they want to, because they believe in what we're doing."

Must be nice to have a choice, I nearly say, but I keep my mouth shut.

A thin wisp of blue-black smoke rises from his pipe, snakes upward, and dissipates into nothing. Guzmán glances down at my arm, sees the diamond-shaped tracker scar. He looks like he wants to say something else, but then stops himself.

"After your next read," he finally says, "I'll give you a break. A nice long one."

It's the same thing he said last time, and God knows how many times before that. *I'll give you a break.* Whatever trace of sincerity the phrase might have once carried has long since vanished. Now it only feels cruel, like someone pressing their thumb into a bruise you'd forgotten was there, the pain coming back sudden and fresh. I don't want to hear it anymore.

I say nothing, waiting for the moment to pass. It never lasts long, this flash of bogus generosity or slave owner guilt or whatever it is. After a few moments, Guzmán's face inevitably hardens, becoming once again the stone mask of a man who's all business, who'll get what he wants and God help you if you stand in his way. The kind of man who, deep down, doesn't remotely mind killing an innocent, or even hundreds of them, if it expands his territory, adds to his growing legend, wins him more fawning concubines. The kind of man who doesn't mind having a slave, even as he pretends for a few moments that he does.

And slaves don't get breaks.

Ernesto "Flaco" Guzmán is full of shit, and I don't need the hierba to see it.

CHAPTER 3

The next morning a sharp poke on my shoulder wakes me. "Come on, levántate." I pretend I'm still asleep. Lela pokes me again, harder. "Fresh air and coffee, this is what you need."

I crack one eye open. The diffuse orange light of a desert dawn pours into my tent through the open door flap. A tangle of hair covers my face and Lela hovers over me, her pendant hanging out from her neck as she leans forward. The dark-skinned Virgin of Guadalupe swings back and forth over my head.

"*Sleep* is what I need," I mumble, turning my back to her and pulling the blanket over my head. "Don't you have morning mass to go to or something?" As if on cue, a church bell rings first call in the distance.

"I go two times tomorrow," she says, tugging on my arm until I roll back over. "Let's go. You don't stay in bed all day." She pulls the blanket down off my face. "No more of that, entiendes?"

I sit up, groggy, and rub my eyes. A metal mug sits on the bookcase at the foot of my cot, coffee steam wafting lazily upward. I smooth my hair back, yawn, look over at Lela. She stands with her arms crossed, a determined look in her eyes. I sigh and reach for the coffee, too tired to argue.

I think it's Tuesday, but I'm not sure, and I'm only vaguely certain the month is July. All the days blur together, each one a repeat of the last, a never-ending road to nowhere I'm forced to shuffle along in invisible shackles. Ugly thoughts to wake up to, but there you are.

The coffee warms my insides. I stand and stretch, feeling the gritty sand under my bare feet, the sunlight waking my skin with the gentle heat of a desert morning.

Lela frowns at me and throws the door flap closed so no one can see my nakedness. Such a prude. I recall the first time she saw me naked. It was after a reading and the hierba's effect was still lingering. I sensed a strange awkwardness in her face and voice. Not sexual, just a…discomfort I couldn't understand. Later I learned that Lela had grown up in the remote wilds of Chiapas, where gringos were rarely seen. My brown eyes and hair—the Mexican features from Papi's side—must have looked normal to her, but the fair skin and narrow nose—the Anglo part of me from Mama's side—struck her as alien, odd.

She grabs my clothes from the chair. "How many days you wear these?"

I shrug and take another gulp of coffee. She smells the shirt, makes a face, and tosses it to the floor. Then she rummages through my foot locker for a clean shirt and pants and flings them onto the bed.

She looks me over, assessing me in the same way I've seen her puzzle over a broken-down truck motor. A disapproving crease marks her forehead as her brow furrows. "You're too skinny," she says, pointing at my ribs. "I can count your costillas. You need to eat more."

I look down at my body. Solid, muscular, but definitely not skinny. Of course next to Lela, with her thick bones and slab-like massiveness, who wouldn't look thin?

Before she can nag me again, I get dressed. Lela never

lets me sleep off the grogginess that always comes after a dose of hierba. She has an early riser's annoyingly unshakable faith in the restorative powers of strong coffee and a brisk walk in morning air.

We leave the tent. All around camp families are going about their work, starting small fires, getting breakfast going. A few (early risers like Lela) have already finished packing up, adding their folded-up tents to a growing pile on the bed of an eighteen-wheeler. By noon, a dozen truck beds will be stacked high with abandoned tents.

I've watched the same scene repeat itself in town after captured town, maybe a dozen times now over the past year. Guzmán's forces take the city, and afterwards whoever wants to stay in the newly captured town is free to do so. Many take the opportunity, happy to exchange the nomadic, tent-dwelling life of a desert revolutionary for the stability of solid walls. Administrators divvy up the available buildings, and long-forgotten shops, restaurants, and schools are transformed into residences.

The local townspeople are left alone, neither persecuted nor displaced from their homes, which never fails to surprise them. In Bullock-held towns and territories, which still make up the vast majority of the Republic, Ernesto "Flaco" Guzmán is depicted as a terrorist, a bloodthirsty madman bent on destruction, leading an army of insatiable killers in the West Texas desert. In the days after a town falls to Guzmán, locals huddle together, hidden and terrified by stories of rape and mass executions.

Eventually, hunger or curiosity drives them from their hiding places, and they emerge, squinting in the bright sunlight, incredulous at the steady buzz of ordinary life humming all around them. Carpenters hammering away, subdividing an old factory into apartment units, food sellers setting up their portable carts, children playing soccer in the streets. For most, the sudden change takes some getting used to. For generations, life as they'd known it had been an ever-worsening mess of poverty and scrambling desperation under Bullock authority, whose local soldiers did little more than collect bribes and protect the clan's natural gas infrastructure—extraction towers, processing plants, distribution pipelines and trucks.

By the time the locals come out of their hiding places, Guzmán already has a police force keeping order, administrative institutions installed, and trade routes between cities secured. After a few weeks the locals' loyalty is won over, and don Flaco goes from the feared marauder to beloved liberator. The man who expelled the Bullocks and their corrupt authority. In every town, I've watched it happen. And in every town, hundreds of new volunteers take up arms to join Guzmán's cause, inspired to help him liberate the next town, and the one after that.

Of course, it's not like they're suddenly rich and happy. Just a bit less fucked than they were before. The townies all make the same mistake: confusing a change of jailer and a more comfortable cell for freedom and liberation.

I drink my coffee and watch a long line of camp residents, maybe a couple hundred in total, as they make their way toward Odessa, half a kilometer away. Mostly families, their arms loaded with bags and bundles and children. Some push their belongings in wagons fashioned from ancient, rusting shopping carts, the original wheels replaced with thick, knobby tires better suited for desert use. An old school bus, windowless and dented and riddled with bullet holes, slowly trudges through the sandy dirt, its gears grinding, carrying the old, the sick, and those too weak to make the short walk into town. A church bell rings second call from somewhere inside the city, resonating long and low in the morning air. Some quicken their pace so they can make it in time for the morning service, to give thanks to the Virgin and pray for blessings in their new lives.

Lela nudges me forward. I feel her eyes on me. She's watching me more carefully this morning. I wonder how long it'll take them to figure out that I lied about blond ponytail. Not for a while, I hope. Not before he's ripped off Guzmán for a small fortune. The thought of it makes my stomach flutter. Maybe the gringo will even get away with it, manage to make it out of Guzmán territory alive, back to whatever desert hole he crawled out of to come here. A robbery *and* a clean getaway. That would be the icing on the cake. And then when they come for me, I'll laugh and laugh and the only way they'll stop me is with a bullet in my head.

Everywhere around us, families bustle back and forth, packing up their belongings, breaking down tents. The morning air chirps with children's questions.

"Is that our new home over there, Mama? Can I take my teddy bear, too?"

"Are they going to give our tent to another family?"

Parents answer back as best they can.

"Yes, nena, a real home with a real roof."

"Of course your bear can come. It wouldn't be a home without your osito, would it?"

We come across a young mother squatting in front of her toddler, holding the little girl's hands. The child cries and shakes her head back and forth, inconsolable. The mother wears her hair in shoulder-length braids, the same way Mama used to. Though she's younger, her hair is streaked with gray at the temples like Mama's was. A familiar ache begins to twist my stomach.

"I don't wanna leave our tent!" the child cries, tears flowing down her cheeks. "I don't wanna go!"

The mother pulls the child to her chest and kisses her on top of the head. "Ay, niña, all your friends will be there. Lalo and Gabi and Claudita. You'll miss your friends if we stay here in camp."

I stop and watch them.

The woman gently moves the child to arm's length so the girl can see her face. She lowers her head and looks at the child through the tops of her eyes. "You're a big girl now. You don't have to be scared. We'll be safe here. You can trust your mami."

We'll be safe here. You can trust your mami.

And just like that, the memories of my worst day come flooding back.

*   *   *

That day.

It started out like any other: normal, routine, boring even. Mama woke me up early so I could help with the outside chores before it got too hot. It usually took her a few attempts to rouse me—I was never an early riser—but not that day.

I sat up and stretched. "You think they'll be back today?" Papi had promised he and his apprentice Abner would try to finish their measurements quickly so they could get back in time for my birthday.

Mama puckered her lips in doubt. "He hasn't sent a message, so don't get your hopes up."

The survey site was a full day's trip to the west: a couple hours in the Jeep, then several more on foot. Papi always called Mama on the satphone when they were getting ready to come home. If he hadn't called yet, that meant they wouldn't arrive until tomorrow at the earliest.

"Did you try calling?"

"Twice already this morning," she replied. "But you know how he is. Your papi never answers when he's busy."

I sighed, disappointed.

Mama kissed my forehead. "Don't worry. I'm sure they'll be back in time for your birthday." She got up and opened the shades. I blinked as light filled the room, dust motes floating in the air. She took a sip from her coffee mug, gazing out at the endless flat grasslands of the Panhandle.

"Can I have a sip?"

Mama stared into the distance. "I told you a hundred

times, Sol. When you're seventeen you can have coffee."

"I'll be seventeen in two days. And besides, Papi lets me."

At this Mama lifted her eyebrows. "Well, your papi's too easy with you. Always has been." Then she turned to me. "All right, come on, let's get up. Lots to do today."

After she left the room, I reached under my pillow where I'd hidden the hierba and stuffed the thick, rubbery leaves into my mouth. The plant's bitter taste coated my tongue as I got out of bed and dressed. On my way out of the house, I quietly slipped past the kitchen so Mama wouldn't see me chewing.

Outside the dew on the soft grass was wet and cool under my feet. Still half-asleep, I chewed the leaves while I watered the vegetable garden, then I collected peppers and tomatoes for lunch and dinner. After that I swept the front porch and fed the chickens. I always left the goats, those smelly, obnoxious goats, for last. As I went to the shed to fetch a bundle of hay, they pranced around their pen in anticipation, making ugly bawling noises that sounded like a person howling in pain. I grabbed a bale and tossed it over the fence into their pen. The noise thankfully stopped as they shoved their noses deep into the yellow bale, chewing greedily.

I brushed hay off the front of my shirt. It was still early but the sun was already warming the back of my neck. The diffuse light of morning was gone, replaced with a bright, endless prairie sky, pale blue and empty, without even a wisp of a cloud. I looked toward the west, the direction Papi and Abner had gone four days ago. I'd watched and waved as the Jeep grew smaller and smaller, until it became a tiny speck and then disappeared over the horizon.

It was our third summer in the Panhandle. Before coming here, we'd lived a nomadic existence. Papi's job—surveying natural gas fields for the Bullocks—kept us constantly on the move; we never stayed in one place more than a few months. There was always a new assignment, another field to survey, another careful calculation of the Bullock clan's wealth. Eventually they assigned Papi to the Panhandle, a coveted post for a surveyor. Papi said it was his reward after all those years of paying his dues on the road. In the southern Panhandle several massive gas fields converged, and keeping track of their volume required almost constant measuring and remeasuring. It was the kind of job that allowed you to have a house instead of a temporary apartment, allowed you to live a settled life. And other than quick trips to set up and troubleshoot equipment (which never lasted more than a few days), there was very little travel. Simply put, it was a really good gig.

With each passing month, the movable life we'd led in the past grew more distant in my mind. And dimmer still were my recollections of Dallas, where we'd lived until I was six or seven, before Papi started surveying. All I remembered of Dallas were scraps of my youngest memories, like flashes of an almost forgotten dream. Elegant, well-dressed people, tall buildings, robots everywhere. More robots than people. Everything shiny and clean, so different from the rest of the Republic.

Our little clapboard house on the plains wasn't much to look at, old and sun-worn and cramped, and it was the only building for miles in any direction. But it was cozy and warm on cold nights and it felt like a home. The grassy prairie of the Panhandle stretched as far as the eye could see, featureless except for the occasional lonely copse of mesquite or cottonwood trees. It was a quiet, remote existence, like the four of us were pioneers from some bygone era. When Papi and his apprentice Abner weren't out on a survey, they took turns teaching me about science and history and mathematics. The house was full of books. I loved the musty smell of their yellowed pages. I spent countless hours curled up in my bed, reading about everything from the fall of Rome to geology to linguistics.

I left the goats to their meal and went inside. When I

entered the kitchen I stopped, the smells hitting me all at once. Fried eggs, toast, coffee. Mama stood at the sink, rinsing out a drinking glass. I smelled her too. A hint of perspiration mingling with the flowery perfume of her hair rinse. Other smells wafted through the open kitchen window. Prairie grass and topsoil. The musky scent of the goats.

Then the familiar euphoria began to tickle the edges of my mind.

For anyone else, hierba's just a bitter-tasting desert plant, but for those us with the gift, chewing the weed changes us, alters how we see people and the world around us. It heightens perception, expands awareness. The plant flips a switch in us somehow, enabling us to see the complex hidden language of facial tics, breathing rhythms, body posture, the countless physical giveaways the conscious mind normally ignores.

Over the last year, Mama had been teaching me how to use this awareness to spot lies. A powerful reader herself, she'd recognized the gift in me when I was little. *True seeing*, she'd said, tapping my forehead and smiling, promising me when I was old enough she'd teach me how to read people the same way I read my Dr. Seuss books.

Mama turned to me and wiped her hands on her apron, then motioned toward the plate of eggs on the table. "Eat your breakfast before it gets cold."

I sat, pierced the egg with a piece of toast, and took a bite. The yolk-soaked bread lessened the hierba's bitterness. "Can we have a lesson after breakfast?" I asked, chewing.

She sighed. "I'm very busy today."

"You said that yesterday."

"Well, I was busy yesterday too."

I took a drink of water. "Come on. We haven't had a lesson in two months," I protested.

Mama turned away. "Oh, Sol. I don't think it's been *that* long."

"Yes, it has."

When she didn't respond, I grunted and continued eating. For months we'd had 'liar liar' lessons two or three times a week. She'd taught me what to look for, all those involuntary telltales that were invisible to everyone else, and over time I'd become a proficient lie detector. Neither Mama nor Papi nor Abner could get a single white lie past me, no matter how hard they tried. After a while spotting deceptions became routine, even boring.

Then one day I'd noticed something else, something *new*, as Papi sat across the kitchen table from me, doing his best to keep a poker face while he told me some whopper.

I had a hard time making sense of what exactly I saw in Papi's face. It wasn't the kind of thing you could put into words, these bits and pieces of feelings and impressions that I sensed. After that it had happened again and again, every time I chewed hierba for my lesson. I'd see things in Mama's face and Abner's too. Sometimes I'd understand it—a glimpse of joy or doubt or worry—but most of the time it was gibberish, like a book written in a foreign language.

When I finally told Mama about it, she looked at me for a very long time before she spoke. "There are some readers who can see more than just lies." She sat across from me, her face serious. "Seeing lies is one thing, but seeing the *truth* is something else entirely. Do you understand?"

I nodded, though at the time I wasn't sure what she meant. "Can you do it?" I asked.

She shook her head.

"So you can't teach me more about it?"

"I'm afraid not, Sol." She placed her hand on top of mine. "I'm sorry."

After that our lessons became less frequent, which frustrated me. I wanted to learn more about this strange new ability, understand it, try to develop it. But Mama seemed to lose interest, postponing our lessons or putting them off with thin excuses.

I finished my eggs and as Mama picked up my plate, I grabbed her arm. "Mama, why don't you want to teach me anymore?"

She shrugged. "It's not that I don't want to. I'm just not sure I have anything left to show you."

I gazed up at her, suddenly noticing something in her face. Something I'd never seen before. I sensed a strong…*dread.*

She turned toward the sink and I blurted out, "You don't like it here."

Mama whirled around. "What did you say?"

"You don't like this place. You hate living here, don't you?"

Mama leaned down and looked at me critically, tilting her head to one side. "You sneaky young lady. I thought I noticed some of my hierba missing."

My cheeks flushed. "I thought if I took some, you'd have to give me a lesson."

"You little stinker," Mama scolded. Then she placed a napkin on the table and tapped it. "All right, out with it."

I'd spit most of it out after feeding the goats, but there were still a few leaves tucked between my gum and cheek. I fished them out with my finger and placed them on the napkin.

"Do you really hate it here?" The thought stabbed at my heart. I loved our house on the plains.

Mama considered the question, then forced a smile. "Hate's a strong word. I grew up in Dallas, you know. Life out here in the wild isn't easy for a city girl."

Her hand rested on my shoulder for a moment, then jerked away. Mama's eyes widened as she looked past me, out the kitchen window. "My God, what do they want?"

I whirled around. Through the window I saw Papi and Abner, walking slowly toward the house with their hands clasped on top of their heads, followed closely by a group of armed strangers on horseback. There were maybe a dozen of them.

Mama grasped me by the arm and pulled me toward the back of the house.

"Mama, what's going on?" I scrambled to keep my balance as she dragged me down the hallway. "Who are those men?"

She yanked open the back door and shoved me outside. A splintering crash came from the front of the house as someone kicked in the door.

"Run and hide, run and hide!" Mama shouted, her face twisted, eyes frantic.

I froze. From the kitchen angry shouts and dishes crashing to the floor.

Mama grabbed my shoulders and spun me around, away from the house. "Get out, go! Hurry!" She shoved my back and I stumbled forward.

Panic seized me. I couldn't think, couldn't open my mouth to argue or beg Mama to come with me. I did as I was told, sprinting to a thicket of cottonwood trees a couple hundred meters behind the house.

I dropped down behind some bushes and lay with my belly to the ground, my breath shaking the fallen leaves in front of my face. My mind raced, scattered. Should I go back? Wait here? What was happening inside? I wanted to get up and run back to Mama, but my legs wouldn't move.

It felt as if I'd been lying frozen for an hour, but it had likely only been a couple minutes when the freelancers found me in the thicket, shaking and terrified. One of them tied my hands and feet and threw me over his horse. I craned my neck around toward the house.

Two of the freelancers came out the front door. One of them, a short fat man, walked over; the other stood on the porch holding a rifle.

The short man approached me. Without saying anything he shoved his fingers into my mouth, and I gagged as he forced my mouth open wide. His face was so close I could see the little red veins in his eyes. He inhaled deeply with his nose, smelling my breath. Then he let go of me and smiled. "Hierba."

I spit out the dirt taste of his fingers. In a low voice he asked, "You one of them readers? One of them who can see lies?"

I was too terrified to answer. He slapped me, then whispered in my ear, "You tell the truth and no harm'll come to your people. You got my word on that."

I looked over at the house, at the man on the porch. I didn't know what to do, what to say.

"Y-yes," I sputtered, barely able to speak. "I can see lies, read people. Please, don't hurt them."

He turned and signaled his partner standing in front of the house, who then walked inside. Three shots rang out, sending electric shocks through my body. I screamed for Mama and Papi. The men around me laughed. The tinny echo of the gunshots bounced around my head. It felt as if time had stopped.

The short man announced, "We won the lottery, boys. This one here's gonna make us rich." His companions cheered and fired shots into the air.

They robbed whatever they could carry from the house and took me with them. Later when they set up camp in the desert, the short man boasted about how he'd worked it all out. He took sick pleasure in recounting everything to me: how he had Mama and Papi and Abner on their knees, and right as he raised the gun to the back of Mama's head he noticed the napkin with the hierba on it lying on the kitchen table. He recognized the weed he'd seen so much as a boy growing up in the desert, recalling what his kinfolk had said about the plant, how there were people who could use it to tell lie from truth.

He asked whose it was. Mama and Papi didn't answer, but he could tell by the way they looked at each other that he'd hit on something. Then he smelled the leaves, still wet with my saliva, and checked their breath. He had the nose of a hunting dog, he bragged, tapping the side of his nostril. When he sniffed me out, he knew he'd hit the jackpot.

That first night with them, he forced me to chew some hierba he'd taken from our house, holding a cocked gun to my temple and demanding I prove what I could do. He asked me question after question until he was satisfied. I cried and trembled, waiting for the bang after each answer, but somehow I managed to pass his test.

After a nightmarish month traveling the western desert, the freelancers sold me to Guzmán for their biggest payday ever.

*   *   *

Tears blurring my vision, I turn away from the mother consoling her child. It's too much: all those faces beaming and full of hope, ready to start their new lives together. It's a cruel reminder of my place in the world, of everything I don't have. Everything I lost. I break into a run, away from camp and families and Lela and gringo swindlers and most of all from Guzmán.

"Adónde vas?" Lela barks from behind me.

I nearly fall, stumbling into a gully overgrown with Indian Grass. Hands outstretched, I scramble up the side, nearly blind, my cheeks wet and salty. I run for the desert, crazed. Before long I feel Lela's hands on my shoulders, grabbing me and pulling me back with such force my legs kick out in front of me. She grips me in a bear hug from behind, her arms like two iron vises. I flail around uselessly, cursing her. Then I reach down with my mouth and sink my teeth into her forearm until I taste blood. She doesn't scream, doesn't react at all. Finally, I stop squirming. I open my mouth and release her, blood oozing from teeth marks in her arm. A coppery taste fills my mouth.

Lela slowly lowers me to the ground, sets me down. I sit with my head drooped, arms hanging lifeless, legs splayed out on the desert floor like an abandoned marionette. My face is a hot mess of tears, snot, and dirt.

Lela watches me, towers over me.

"No more reading for a while," she finally says.

I look up at her. She's taken out a rag, wrapping it around her bloody arm.

"You don't make the schedule," I say.

"I tell don Flaco you sick."

"Sure you will."

Lela stands there, says nothing for a moment. Then she says, "I tell him you sick, okay? He believe me."

I narrow my eyes. "You'd lie to him?"

Her face is serious, sincere. But then so was Guzmán's last night. I wipe my face with my sleeve. She helps me up and we head back to camp.

As we walk, in the distance a group of men load up a pair of Jeeps on the far side of camp. The shocks sag with each heavy bundle, and a couple of the men inspect the vehicles, kicking tires, pulling out dipsticks to check oil levels. One of the Jeeps slowly rolls forward, and several men hop in. The vehicle then accelerates and heads out into the desert, passing within a hundred meters of us. It's a new Jeep, not worn and broken down like most of the others in camp. I don't recognize any of the men.

"Where are they going? Town's the other way."

"I don't know." Lela shrugs. "Come on."

The Jeep disappears behind a cloud of kicked-up dust. Back at camp, someone hops into the driver's side of the second vehicle. I stop for a moment, squinting as I put my hand against my forehead to block the morning sun.

"Who are those people?" I reach my hand out toward Lela. "Hand me your binoculars, would you?"

"Let's go," she says quickly. "No time for this."

"Just give them to me."

"Vamos, me muero de hambre," she insists. "We gonna be late for breakfast."

"Jesus," I complain. "One quick look." I reach down to

her belt, where her binoculars hang. She slaps my hand away.

"What the hell?" I shake the sting from my hand.

The second Jeep follows the same path as the first one. As it gets closer to us, Lela tugs hard at my arm, nearly pulling me off balance. "Ya vamos."

"What's the matter with you?"

I yank my arm back and glance over at the passing Jeep.

And I see him.

Abner.

Abner Cunningham, my father's apprentice, sits in the Jeep's passenger seat, not twenty meters away. I drop to my knees and time stops.

Abner.

He's supposed to be dead. Shot by the freelancers that horrible day. Shot and killed with Mama and Papi.

But he's alive.

CHAPTER 4

The Jeep is far past us before I can breathe again, before a coherent thought finally breaks through the chaos swirling in my head.

Go after him.

A burst of energy surges through me. I spring to my feet and sprint toward camp.

"¿Adónde vas?" Lela shouts. My eyes dart around frantically, searching for a vehicle I can steal.

It was him. Shorter hair, three years older, but definitely him.

At the edge of camp I see an old truck with the roof sawed off and no doors. It'll do.

Seconds later I'm at the truck, panting. Nearby a family mills about, folding up their tent, stacking their belongings onto a wheelbarrow. They notice me and I try to appear cool and calm as I look in the truck's front seat. A tornado of questions whirls through my mind.

What's he doing here? How is he alive? And if he managed to survive, what about Mama and Papi? Did they send him to find me?

I look down into the truck's cab, see the key in the ignition, then I hop into the driver's seat and start the engine. I glance back at the family to see if they're reacting, if it's their truck I'm stealing. They're still packing, uninterested in me or the truck. As I'm watching them I hear the vehicle's motor sputter and die.

I turn back around to see Lela removing the key from the ignition.

"What are you doing?" I try to snatch the key from her but she's too quick. She drops it in her pants pocket. I scramble out of the Jeep and lunge for her pocket. "Give me that!" She knocks my hand away.

"Give me the key, goddammit! Do you know who that was?"

Lela shrugs. "Some hombre importante from the Bullocks."

"That was *Abner*. Abner Cunningham. My father's apprentice. I've told you about him."

She ponders my words, furrows her brow. I feel Abner getting further away, disappearing into the desert.

"Just give me the key." I reach again but she jams her hand into her pocket, blocking me. "Por Dios, Lela, dame la pinche llave!"

She shakes her head. "No."

Away from camp, the dust cloud kicked up by the Jeeps dissipates and settles. A blinding rage overcomes me. I curse Lela and kick a deep dent into the truck's side panel, knocking a tire iron off the back bumper onto the ground. I pick it up and take a swing at her. She dodges and I miss completely, spinning wildly and stamping my hand on the ground to keep from falling. Then she rushes me and I swing up as hard as I can, both hands gripping the cold steel.

Something hard slams into the side of my head and the world flips sideways. As everything goes black, something Guzmán once told me about boxers flashes across my mind. They say you never see the punch that knocks you out.

*   *   *

"What happened? Is she going to be okay?"

The darkness recedes to the sound of Rafa's voice. My head throbs and I open my eyes, squinting at the sudden brightness of the day. I'm on my cot with Lela and Rafa standing over me.

Rafa kneels down, his face twisted with concern. "Hey there," he says softly, "are you all right?"

"I told you she fine," Lela says. "Now go."

Rafa ignores her. "Come on, try to sit up."

I prop myself up on my elbows and the world sloshes around me dizzyingly. "How long was I out?" I mumble.

"I don't know," says Rafa. "I saw her carrying you in here. Jesus, I thought you were dead, Sol." He places his hand on top of mine.

"Give me some room to breathe, will you?" I pull my hand back.

"Sure, sure." Rafa backs away, looking a bit hurt.

"Vete ya, niño," Lela insists.

"Screw you," Rafa snaps without looking back. In the next moment Lela's hand wraps around his upper arm, lifting him to his feet. He yanks away from her grip.

Lela stares him down and places her hand on her hip, right above the butt of her holstered revolver. "You leave now."

Rafa glances down at the gun. His expression fades, shoulders slump. He looks over at me, sheepish. "Anything you need, you let me know, okay?" Then he exits the tent.

Bits and pieces start to come back to me. New Jeeps driving northward into the desert. *Abner.*

I swing my legs over the side of the cot and rub my temples. A hammer pounds the inside of my skull. My tongue is dry and sticky, and the taste of Lela's blood lingers.

"Why'd you stop me?" I ask, wincing. The sound of my voice makes the pounding worse.

"You not supposed to leave camp."

"What's Abner doing here? What's he doing alive?"

Lela shakes her head. "He come with some people from the Bullocks. I don't know nothing else."

I inhale deeply through my nose, trying to clear my head. Then I look up at her, study her face. Without the hierba I can't be sure if it's a lie or the truth or something in between.

An image of the two Jeeps fixes itself in my head, shrinking as they get farther and farther from camp. I feel Abner slipping away.

"We have go after him. I have to find out what happened."

"Don't matter what happened," Lela says sharply.

It takes a moment for me to process what she's said. "What?"

"It don't matter what happened."

I stand up. My legs wobble and the tent lurches sickeningly. I take another deep breath to steady myself. Something inside me begins to simmer.

"*Not matter?* If Abner's alive, my parents might be alive too." I glare upward, my head barely reaching her chest. She folds her arms. A mouth-sized crimson stain on a bandage marks the spot where I bit her.

"Why they no come and look for you? If they alive, they would come looking, no? Three years and nobody comes."

"Maybe that's exactly what he was doing. Maybe they sent him." Again I picture the Jeeps, fading and disappearing into the desert. "Por dios, Lela, I have to find out…"

A new thought strikes me as Lela stands there, her massive arms crossed, her face grim and wooden. I narrow my eyes at her. "What do you know? Tell me."

She doesn't answer. The simmer rises to a boil. "What do you know about Abner, about my parents?"

"I don't know nothing."

Lie or truth? Her face betrays nothing. Christ, I'd give

anything for a fistful of hierba right now.

For a long moment she doesn't say anything, then finally she motions out toward the desert. "Out there nothing for you. No hay nada. Here you protected. Here you safe."

The rage inside me boils over, explodes. "Safe? Protected? Are you fucking insane?" I roll up my sleeve, revealing the tracker scar on my forearm. "Are you forgetting how I came here? I didn't just walk up to camp like all these refugees, starving and desperate with nowhere else to go. I was *taken*."

I shove my forearm into her face, hold it inches from her nose. "Guzmán bought me like a goddamn sack of beans. You forget that? I'm a fucking slave."

Lela looks at the tracker scar, then turns her head away.

"I never wanted to be here in the first place," I sneer, "you goddamn illiterate indita."

She winces at this, backs up a step. "Ya sé."

The tent swirls around me and my knees buckle. I collapse onto the cot, lightheaded, my vision blurring.

"Voy por el doctór," Lela says. I can barely hear her over the throbbing of my head.

"Get the fuck out," I spit, squeezing my eyes shut.

She leaves the tent, telling the guard she's posted outside that she'll be right back.

I roll over, turning my back to the guard. *Abner alive. How? No, it doesn't matter how. He's alive, that's what matters. Against all odds, he's alive.*

And if he's alive…

Dare I think it? Dare I torture myself with the hope that they're out there somewhere, alive and well, living a life without me? And what if they are? Do they think I'm three years dead, killed by the freelancers? Or maybe they've heard the rumors about Guzmán's witch and they suspect I'm alive, and they sent Abner to find out?

And what of Abner? Lela called him an important man from the Bullocks. How could an important man from the

Bullocks drive in and out of the heart of the enemy's camp with impunity?

I clench my jaw against the pounding in my head, against the questions torturing my mind. Nothing makes sense.

I grit my teeth, clench my fists.

Answers. I want answers.

*　*　*

Some minutes later, Lela returns with Doctor Felipe, an old man with bushy white eyebrows and a careful, meticulous way about him. The agonizing pain in my skull has lessened to a dull headache. The doctor asks me to sit up, then gingerly moves my hair away from the spot where Lela hit me, his shaky, ancient fingers finding a large bruise but nothing more. She must have pulled her punch, I think, or maybe hit me open-handed. I'd seen those sledgehammer fists of hers crack the skulls of men twice my size. Every so often some stupid, drunken fool will goad her into a fight, determined to prove her reputation is a bullshit exaggeration. They always learn the hard way it isn't.

Next the doctor holds up his finger and moves it back and forth; I follow it with my eyes. He purses his lips and nods. "Muy bien, muy bien," he murmurs to himself. Lela watches from the tent's door flap. The doctor checks my reflexes and, strangely, asks me to stick out my tongue. After a long look, he stands and declares me fine, recommending bed rest for the remainder of the day. Then he leaves Lela and me alone.

She shuts the door flap and watches me. She seems anxious, uncomfortable in a way I've never seen before, with or without the hierba. Twice she starts to speak, but then stops.

I fix my eyes on her. "I'm going after him."

Lela shakes her head. "No good come of it."

"You know something, don't you? Tell me."

"I don't."

"Would you say that if I'd just chewed some hierba?"

She looks at me crossly but doesn't answer. "No good news for you out there," she repeats. "But all this don't matter. I don't let you go. Don Flaco don't let you go."

Her face hardens again as she folds her arms across her chest, impenetrable. I stare at her, suddenly hating her more than Guzmán.

There's no 'let me go' to this. I'm not asking permission.

I'm getting the fuck out of here.

CHAPTER 5

I keep trying to convince myself it's not a question of whether I *can* do it or not.

If I want out of here, I *have* to do it. I have to take a life tonight.

I lie on my cot, a prisoner of doctor-ordered bed rest, waiting for my moment. Time has slowed to an agonizing crawl. Over and over I picture Abner's Jeep disappearing over the horizon, vanishing into the distance along with his secrets.

But the guard outside the tent is still awake, so I have to lie here and wait and try not to let my own thoughts drive me crazy. I don't know the hour, but it's long past midnight, probably close to sunup.

Inside my head there's a ticking clock, tormenting me with a morbid countdown. Each passing second moves me closer to the moment when they'll figure out I lied about blond ponytail. Maybe it'll be a week from now, or maybe tomorrow. But as soon as they figure out his deal's a scam, that'll be it for me. No matter how valuable I might be to him, Guzmán wouldn't think twice about sending me out to the desert. His hard-fisted reputation is far too important, not to mention his ego. He'd never risk being seen as weak or biased or anything that might hint at vulnerability. Not the don Flaco I know.

A handful of hours ago I wouldn't have cared, wouldn't have minded an end to this life of endless lies. In fact I would have welcomed it. But now everything's different.

And if I don't get out now, tonight, under the cover of darkness, Abner's trail will go cold, his tire tracks swept clean by the desert wind.

So it's now or never, I tell myself, watching the guard's shadow against the tent wall, fluttering like a ghost in the firelight.

Minutes later I finally hear it: the sound I've been waiting for. The guard begins to snore.

My stomach contracts into a nervous ball as I picture what has to happen next. It won't be like after a reading, where all I do is nod my head and walk away and someone else does the dirty work. My role's always been the judge, never the executioner.

Abner's Jeep growing smaller, disappearing.

Get up.

Quietly, I get out of the cot and pad over to the bookshelf. I find the copy of *Moby Dick* and open it. A hollowed-out cutaway of pages hides my secret stash of hierba, a fistful of leaves I've accumulated over months, pocketing small amounts with each reading. Never knew what I might need it for, still don't, but I'd rather take it with me than leave it here. I stuff the bag of hierba into my pants pocket.

Next I pull out *Great Expectations*, where another cutaway hides a hunting knife. I remove it from the book, feel its weight in my hand. The serrated blade catches and reflects the dim light inside the tent.

Behind me the guard snores.

I pull on my boots, careful not to make any noise, and tiptoe over to the tent's door flap. My heart beats wildly as I pull back the flap and see the sleeping guard, his head down, shoulders slumped.

Do it. I try to disconnect my mind from the task at hand, try to imagine I'm watching someone else step through the door flap, knife in hand, creeping up behind the guard.

I glance out into camp and see no one milling about. The knife handle's already moist with sweat.

My heart thuds against the inside of my chest. I take another step forward, then strike.

In one motion I cover the guard's mouth with my free hand, pulling his head against my chest, and with my knife hand I plunge the blade deep into the front of his neck, under the Adam's apple. He jolts awake, then begins to struggle as I saw the knife back and forth, ripping through arteries and muscle, popping connective tissues. Frantic, he claws at my knife hand, but with the slickness of the flowing blood, he can't get a good grip. My other hand muffles the gagging, gurgling sounds coming from his mouth. I lean backwards and heave us both into the tent, upending the guard's chair as blood spews everywhere. He lands on top of me, crushing the air out of my lungs. I let go, wriggle out from under him and stand up, gasping. His hands are at his neck and he stares up at me with wide, terrified eyes. His mouth moves but no words come out. Blood pumps out from between his fingers, and a pool of it spreads out on the floor beneath his head, black like motor oil in the darkness. I squat, reach under his arms, and drag him further inside the tent.

I turn away from him as he bleeds out, hustling myself out of my blood-soaked clothes and into some clean ones. Behind me, the sounds of gagging and thrashing slow, then stop.

I leave the tent, the guard's pistol tucked into my pants, my mind blaring with the horror of what I've done.

His name was Eduardo and he'd been my night guard for the last year. Fat Lalo was what everyone called him, and he never seemed to mind. He had three kids, all under five years old.

I feel sick. I find a fire barrel and vomit all over the ashes and charcoal. I wipe my mouth and look around, paranoid and conspicuous, like a prisoner making a jailbreak. It's still dark and there's no one about. Camp is quiet, empty.

I find Rafa sitting outside his tent, fiddling with a portable power generator. Next to the generator is a bucket filled with natgas pellets. Rafa takes one out and examines it, rolling the small, coal-colored cylinder between his thumb and forefinger. He doesn't notice me as I approach.

"Hey," I say, clasping my hands behind my back so he doesn't see them shaking. So much adrenaline's pumping through my body, it's difficult to stand still.

Rafa looks up, surprised to see me. My stomach flutters as I wonder if I look different, if somehow he can see what I've done in my face.

"What are you doing up so early?" He glances around. "Where's Lela?"

I answer with a shrug. "What are you working on?"

He nods toward the bucket. "Got these from one of the conversion plants in town. Just testing them."

"And…?" I shift back and forth on my feet.

Rafa tosses the pellet into the bucket and shakes his head. "Seen better, seen worse. Gas density varies from plant to plant. Depends on who's in charge, how tight a ship they run." He stands. "How's your head?"

"It's fine. Can we talk?" I tilt my head toward his tent. "Alone?"

He glances around, then spreads his arms out, palms up. "Can't get more alone than this."

"Not here. *Alone*. In private."

He looks over to the tent, then back to me. "Sure," he says, though I can see he's wondering what's going on.

Inside, his tent is a mess of machine parts and tools. A disassembled robot hand lies in one corner, a jumble of metal fingers and tiny servomotors. A small work lamp in the corner illuminates the space with dim white light.

I sit next to Rafa on the cot. It's the first time I've been in his tent. He smiles awkwardly, looks uncomfortable, a bit nervous. Which is exactly how I need him to feel.

I push my sleeve up, show him the tracker scar. "I want you to turn this off."

He looks at my arm, knits his eyebrows. "Deactivate your tracker? Why would you want to do that?"

"I'm leaving camp."

Confusion twists his face. "Leaving camp?"

"Yes."

He shakes his head slowly. "You know I can't help you do that."

I tell him about seeing Abner, what I think it could mean, hoping it changes his mind. Rafa lost his own parents in a territory feud.

"If you thought your folks were still alive," I plead, "wouldn't you do anything to find out?"

He ponders my question for a moment. "Are you sure it was him?"

"A hundred percent. If I don't go now, the trail's going to get cold."

He shakes his head. "Sol, if someone finds out I helped you…" His voice trails off.

I lean close to him, place my hand on his thigh. "Rafa, please."

He stiffens, looks down at my hand. "I can't," he says, his voice shaking.

I glance out the tent's door flap. Still dark outside, but not for much longer.

Just do it.

I reach over and close the door flap.

"I need your help," I say, unbuttoning my shirt. He watches my hand work the buttons. His mouth slowly falls open. I drop my shirt on the floor and reach my hand between his legs. He's already hard.

Rafa doesn't move as I lean in and brush my lips

against his cheek. "Can't you help me?" I whisper. He takes a deep, quivering breath as I slide my hand inside his pants. I put my lips on his, slipping my tongue into his mouth. I press my chest to his body, leaning on him, forcing him back onto the cot. He doesn't resist, saying nothing as I remove his pants, then mine, and climb on top of him.

I reach back and work him inside me. Rafa moans and rolls his head back. I grind against him. I feel his resistance crumbling, his spirit breaking, like a horse beaten by a cruel trainer. I grind harder. There's no tenderness, no romance in it. I feel as if I'm battering him into submission. It's strangely intoxicating, watching him fade, feeling his surrender. Sudden waves of pleasure shoot through me and I come hard. My mouth waters.

I lean down and press my forehead to his. My hair dangles down like a curtain around our faces. "Go with me," I whisper. "I want you to go with me."

Rafa's head gently bobs up and down as I move his body with my hips. His eyes are wide and round and scared.

"You know what he'd do to me," he says. "What he'd do to *us*."

I hear the clock in my head, ticking down. I rock my hips faster, taking his face into my hands and kissing him. "Come with me, Rafa."

I whisper things: how I can't go without him; how he's the only one I can trust; how much I care about him. Any lie I can think of that'll break the last few strands of his resolve.

He squeezes his eyes shut and his legs stiffen as he explodes inside me. He squirms and moans so loud I have to cover his mouth.

Then he goes limp and his entire body seems to deflate. I lie on top of him as he catches his breath.

Watching his face, I can see the answer in his eyes, even in the tent's low light.

He nods and says, "I'll go."

Good. Things break in the desert, and the kid can fix anything.

I force a smile and kiss him, but my mind's already elsewhere, thinking about the next tent I have to visit. Outside a purplish haze has replaced the dark of night.

I have to hurry.

*　*　*

I work my way toward the center of camp, where they have tents set up for visitors. I try to stay out of sight, ducking between tents, hiding behind trucks. My improvised disguise is a battered old baseball cap and a jacket that's way too big for me, both from Rafa's clothes trunk. I pull the cap's lid low over my eyes.

Blond ponytail may be a lying piece of shit, but he's got talents I'll need out in the open desert. Maybe letting him off the hook wasn't such a bad call after all.

The first streaks of orange appear, low and ominous in the eastern sky. A few people are already up and about, getting fires started and setting up for breakfast.

Hurry.

I glance around, counting three guards seated at their regular stations. There's a dozen or so other chairs sitting empty. *Good.* Guzmán and his entourage aren't around, as I'd hoped. They're staying in town, as they normally do right after a city's taken. They'll spend the next few days assigning housing for new settlers and dealing with the hundreds of logistical headaches that come with a newly conquered town. All day they'll work, then at night they'll throw fiestas de liberación, where don Flaco—lusty fucker that he is—boozes it up and samples the local ass like someone else might taste food at a buffet.

I keep a cautious distance from the few guards still around. If any one of them recognizes me, wandering around without my ever-present escort, I'm fucked.

Suddenly an awful thought hits me: *what if they took blond ponytail into town with them?*

I pause for a moment, then I hear something behind me. The sound of water slowly pouring onto the ground.

I turn and there's blond ponytail. About twenty meters away he stands with his back to me, taking a piss.

A guard watches him from nearby, seated outside the door flap of what must be the gringo's tent. The guard's face is unfamiliar. Probably a recent recruit.

He shakes his head at blond ponytail. "¿Por qué no vas a los baños?"

"Too far," the gringo complains, doing up his pants.

Lazy bastard. The nearest common toilets are all of a one-minute walk from here.

"And they smell like shit," he adds, passing by the guard and disappearing inside the tent. The guard makes a disgusted face and mutters, "Pinche gringo huevón."

I swallow, take a deep breath, and approach the guard, ready to make a run for it if he shows any sign of recognition. He sits up in his chair, eyes me carefully. His hands rest on the shotgun lying across his legs.

"¿Qué quieres?" he asks.

"Time for someone's prize," I answer.

He stares at me, confused. The guard doesn't speak English.

"Ahora le toca su premio," I say, nodding toward the tent. "Cortesía de don Flaco."

The guard looks suspicious. "¿Premio? No me dijeron nada de eso."

The tent's door flap folds inward and blond ponytail's head emerges. The skin of his face is like old saddle leather, wrinkled and cracked from decades under the desert sun. A pair of bright blue eyes peer out, suspicious and wary, shifting between me and the guard. "What's going on out here?" He squints at me. "I seen you before. You were there last night."

I remove the cap, run my fingers through my hair.

"You left the tent so fast you forgot your dessert."

He eyes me skeptically. The best bullshitters are like that: they always think they're being bullshitted too. "What was that between you and Guzmán?" he demands. "All that 'what about this one?' and 'he's fine' business?"

Shit. My mind races for an answer. I tilt my head and say, "He always asks his best girls if they want to first. He's a real gentleman that way, my sweet don Flaco." It's a real effort to keep the disgust out of my voice, to hide behind a coy, flirtatious mask.

He looks me up and down. "You don't look like no whore."

"The best never do," I answer. *Jesus, I'm really saying this.*

The guard moves his head back and forth between us as we speak, looking completely lost.

The gringo considers me for a moment, then smiles. The smell of his piss hangs in the air. "Always heard don Flaco was downright generous with his ass. Glad to see them ain't rumors."

He opens the door flap wider. "Puede pasar," he tells the guard.

The guard seems to understand at last. He nods and moves aside so I can get by. "Pasa."

I enter the tent. "I like a good quiet fuck, darling," the gringo says, his back to me as he removes his shirt and drops it on the cot. "So keep your mouth shut, you hear me?"

He turns around and looks irritated that I'm not undressing. "What're you waiting for? Get them pants off and get your ass on that cot."

I step toward to him. "You owe me a favor," I say flatly.

He chuckles, his moldy breath stinking of beans and coffee. "You reckon so, huh?" he oozes. "Well, I tell you what. You get them clothes off and we'll think on how I can pay you back. How's that sound?"

I remove the gun from my pants and level it at him.

His eyes go wide. "What the—"

Outside the tent, there's a short snapping sound like a piece of wood crackling on a campfire. The guard moans, and his shadow falls sideways off of the chair.

Rafa comes through the door flap. He shuffles in backwards, dragging the unconscious guard into the tent by the wrists. Strapped to one of Rafa's shoulders is the cattle prod he shocked the guard with. On the other he has the guard's shotgun.

Blond ponytail backs away from me, shows his palms.

"Sit down," I tell him, waving the gun at the cot. He sits.

Then to Rafa: "Check his pockets for keys."

Rafa kneels, reaches toward the guard sprawled out on the floor, pauses. "He's out cold," I assure him. "He can't hurt you."

He frets as he fishes around the guard's pocket. "Oh, what am I doing, what am I doing?" Then he finds something, removes a set of keys. He dangles them at me and grins. "Score."

"Okay, gag him and tie him up." I turn to blond ponytail. "Get your shirt on and don't say a fucking word."

Rafa takes out a rope and starts to hog-tie the sleeping guard. "Give me the collar," I tell him.

Rafa nods, removes the device from under his jacket, and passes it to me. Blond ponytail looks at the dog collar and shakes his head, his eyes large and terrified. "You're not putting that thing on me." He backs away, his eyes darting to the door flap like he's thinking about making a run for it.

I tuck the collar under my arm, step forward, and lift the pistol to his face. "Don't even think about it."

"Rafa," I say, keeping my eyes fixed on the gringo, "ayúdame con éste."

When he finishes tying up the guard, Rafa gets up and takes the collar from me. Then he goes around behind the gringo.

"Goddammit, you even gonna tell me what this is all about?" blond ponytail says, his voice cracking.

"Shhh," I hiss, "keep your mouth shut." A shard of amber daylight stretches across the canvas wall. "Rafa, hurry. We've got to go *now*."

Rafa's hands tremble as he fastens the thin metal collar around the gringo's neck. "Come on, come on, don't do this," the trader pleads. "I got me a big deal with Guzmán. I'll cut you in for a ten-point share. No? Okay, twenty, how about twenty?"

Rafa finishes and steps away. Blond ponytail instinctively reaches up to touch the collar.

"Ah-ah-ahhh," I say, waving my finger back and forth. "No touching." The gringo's hands freeze in mid-reach, his face a mask of horror.

Rafa hands me the collar's remote. "We're a bit rushed," I tell the trader, "so I'll give you the short version. You work your finger or anything else between that collar and your skin, and the nanowire inside will shrink to a hundredth of its diameter before you can blink, popping your head off like a champagne cork." I hold up the remote and wave it in front of his face. "If I key in my code, or if you get more than fifty meters away from me, same result."

I place the remote in my pants pocket. Blond ponytail stares at me, terrified.

"Nod if you understand," I say.

He nods slowly.

"Good. Now let's get out of here."

CHAPTER 6

We hurry—as much as we can without drawing attention—to the eastern edge of camp, where they park the vehicles. Rafa and I keep blond ponytail between us. The gringo looks pale and miserable, a condemned criminal being led to the gallows. Rafa doesn't look much better. The sun's already peeking above the horizon, painting the tent canvases with an orange glow. A few early risers, bent over their breakfast fires, notice us. My nerves twitch as they take second glances at the gringo, but no one says a word as they go about their business. Perhaps they're too groggy with sleep to make sense of our odd trio, or maybe they're too preoccupied with their morning duties to care. A third possibility twists my stomach: maybe they're simply waiting for us to pass by before they run to find a guard.

The gringo drags one of his legs, limping and kicking up dust. I wonder if it's a ploy to slow us down. I reach over and yank his arm forward, nearly pulling him over. "Move your ass," I growl through clenched teeth.

"Go get your gear," I tell Rafa, "and meet us at the lot." He nods and cuts through a gap between tents.

A couple minutes later, the gringo and I arrive at the

eastern edge of camp, where a long chain-link fence surrounds Guzmán's fleet of vehicles. Hundreds of trucks, cars, tractors, eighteen-wheelers, buses, lined up in neat rows, each with a number painted on the door. I reach into my pocket and remove the keys we took from the gringo's guard. The number forty-seven is etched into one of them. I scan the lot, find the matching vehicle.

There's a large gate at the far end, where a single guard is standing sentry.

Rafa joins us, out of breath and carrying a large bag over his shoulder. "Which car's ours?"

I point. "Over there."

"The forklift? Why would we take a forklift through the des—"

"Pendejo," I scold. "Not that one. The Humvee next to it. Forty-seven."

We make quick work of the guard, shocking him with the cattle prod before he can even get a word out. We take the key ring from his belt, open the padlocked gate, and enter the lot. We find a sedan that matches a key on his ring, open the trunk and stuff the guard in, hog-tied, gagged, and unconscious. Then we hustle over to the Humvee.

Rafa tosses his gear bag onto the front seat.

"Get in back," I tell him, "so you can keep an eye on him."

Rafa climbs into the back seat. "Get in," I order the gringo, tilting my head.

"Come on, can't we talk about this? I can cut you in for a piece of the action—"

"I don't give two shits about your made-up deals." I take out the remote and motion toward the door. "Now shut up and get in there." Blond ponytail licks his lips and steps up into the Humvee.

I hop into the driver's seat and start the engine. Full tank, good. I put the vehicle into gear and release the brake.

"Soledad," Rafa says, "your arm."

Jesus, I completely forgot.

I put the Humvee in park, roll up my sleeve, and place my arm on the seat with the tracker scar facing up. Rafa fishes a flashlight-looking gadget out of his bag. He presses it against my scar until a small red light turns green. The gringo watches.

Rafa turns the device sideways and moves it back and forth over my arm, scanning. "No beeps," he says. "You're good." The tracker's deactivated.

I touch the scar on my arm, the skin tender and sensitive. No bodyguard, no tracker, a full tank of gas and the wide open desert in front of me.

"What happened?" Rafa's staring at the dried flecks of blood on my hands and arms. "Are you hurt?"

"Nothing." I yank my arm away and slam the Humvee into gear. "I'm fine."

The vehicle lurches forward. I guide it through the gate's narrow opening and out of the lot. I glance around, see no one. I point the Humvee eastward and, for the first time in three years, I leave Guzmán's camp.

We rock back and forth as the Humvee rolls over the uneven terrain. I resist the urge to mash down on the pedal, driving instead at what I hope is an inconspicuous thirty kilometers per hour. Every few seconds I check the rearview mirror.

"You ever gonna tell me what this is all about?" The gringo's reflection stares at me in the mirror, more sullen now than afraid.

I don't answer.

"I got business with Guzmán. He ain't gonna be happy with anyone messin' with it."

"Sounds important," I say.

"It is." His voice resounds with the misplaced confidence of a natural-born bullshitter.

I steer the Humvee around an outcrop of rocks. "That natgas conversion business? How long do you think it would take them to figure out it was a scam? Believe it or not, you're better off here with us."

That shuts him up. I look past him in the mirror at camp, at the tents growing smaller.

"You're that reader, ain't ya?" the gringo hisses. "Guzmán's witch. The one they say can spot lies. That's you, ain't it?"

I don't say anything.

Rafa gasps. "How'd you know that?"

Fucking Rafa. Keeping secrets isn't his thing. I glare at him in the rearview.

The gringo trader shakes his head and grunts. "Hell, I thought you was all rumors and gossip."

"Listen," I say, "while that collar's around your neck, I'm God. That's who I am. I'm fucking Jehovah, Shiva, and Jesus Christ almighty rolled up into one. Power over your miserable life and death, you get me?"

Blond ponytail furrows his brow at me and scowls, the lines around his mouth deepening.

"If you want that thing off," I say, "all you have to do is help me find somebody. Simple as that."

The gringo narrows his eyes. "Find who?"

"A pair of Jeeps that left camp about this time yesterday, heading northeast."

"And what makes you think I can find them?"

"You're a freelancer, *ain't ya?*" I say, mocking him. And it's all I have to say. Everyone knows freelance traders are the best trackers in the Republic. When I read him the other night, the only things he *didn't* lie about were his tracking and hunting skills.

"Sol," Rafa says, his voice wobbly.

"What?"

"I think we have a problem." Rafa's turned around in the seat, looking back toward camp. I look in the rearview. A tiny figure stands at the edge of the car lot gate, facing our direction. Even from a distance, the silhouette is unmistakable.

Lela.

"Hang on to something," I tell Rafa, then I stomp on the gas.

*　　*　　*

"She's catching up with us!"

"Shut up, Rafa," I bark.

I push the Humvee harder. We jostle around the seats so much I can hardly steer.

The car Lela took from the lot is nothing special: some rusted out piece-of-crap sedan. I have the Humvee's oversized tires and V8 engine, but still she closes the gap between us. It's the better driver versus the better vehicle, and the better vehicle's losing.

I scan the terrain, desperate to find a flat patch where I can floor it and outrun her, but there's nothing. In every direction the landscape is rugged and uneven.

Camp's somewhere far behind us now. All I can see in the rearview is the dust cloud we're kicking up and a pair of headlights in the middle of it, growing larger and brighter by the minute.

And then a pop-pop-pop sound cracks the air.

"She's shooting at us," Rafa shouts, diving into the floorboard. Blond ponytail ducks down behind my seat.

I floor it, but the Humvee doesn't respond. The vehicle suddenly feels sluggish, as if it's stuck in mud.

Fuck. She shot out the tires.

In the rearview the headlights are gone. For an instant I think maybe she wrecked or busted an axle, but then something flashes in the corner of my eye. The sedan's alongside us. Lela glares at me from the driver's seat and lifts a gun, aiming it toward the Humvee's front tire.

I whip the wheel over, smashing into the sedan. There's a loud, violent crash of metal against metal followed by a scraping screech as the vehicles slide against each other. All I can see out of the window is the beat up roof of the sedan, so close I could reach down and touch it. I wrench the wheel further, feeling the monstrous weight of the Humvee crunch the smaller vehicle's rust-weakened metal. I can't see Lela, but I know she's there as more gunshots ring out. I hunch down and away from the window.

I peek above the dashboard just high enough to see where I'm driving. Then the firing stops and the steering wheel's resistance slackens. The sedan's no longer next to us. The Humvee rumbles forward, slowed but still running.

I check over both shoulders, careful to keep my head down. The sedan's gone. I look in the rearview. Nothing but dust.

Then red lights in the dashboard start blinking. The oil pressure needle drops, and the engine temperature shoots up.

"Why are you slowing down?" Rafa asks from the floorboard.

I don't answer, trying to will the dying Humvee forward, pumping the gas. "Move, you piece of shit." I check the rearview again. Nothing.

The vehicle stumbles over the ground another minute, then sputters to a stop. Steam hisses and escapes from under the hood.

For a moment no one moves or speaks. We're blinded, surrounded by a thick cloud of dust.

I stretch out across the front seat, snatch Rafa's bag from the floorboard, and pull out the Glock 9mm. As the dust settles, the sedan takes shape in my rearview. Lela stands next to it, holding a shotgun.

"Stay in the car," I tell them both, racking the slide on the pistol.

I get out and march toward Lela, holding the Glock at my side so she can see it. The wind picks up, swirling dust and sand around us.

"Párate." She cocks the shotgun as a warning, but doesn't point it at me. I stop a few meters away from her.

"I'm not going back."

She waves the gun barrel toward the desert. "Nothing for you out there."

"And what exactly is there for me back at camp? Tell me."

She knits her brow. "You safe at camp. Safe with don Flaco."

"Fuck safe." I swing the Glock around and point it at Lela. She shakes her head, then levels the shotgun at me.

For a long moment we stare at each other. The world around us seems to disappear. No desert, no windblown dust, only the two of us, our eyes locked. The pistol wavers in my hand. I can't pull the trigger.

Fine, then, Plan B. I place the gun against my temple. Lela's eyes go wide.

"No voy a regresar," I say. "Nunca." I can't go back. I won't.

I close my eyes and move my finger to the trigger. From inside the car Rafa cries out my name.

"Okay," Lela calls out, and there's a soft thud. I open my eyes and the shotgun's on the ground at her feet. She stands there, her face dark, immutable.

I lower the gun, careful to turn it away so she can't see the safety locked into place.

CHAPTER 7

"I don't care if it was a bluff," Rafa says, leaning over the Humvee's grille, his hands probing deep into the engine.

"Shhh," I hiss.

He lowers his voice, glares at me, tears still in his eyes. "I thought you were really going to do it."

"I'm sorry."

He turns away, focuses on his work. "Don't do that again."

"I won't. I promise."

He sighs, shakes his head. "Well, at least we've got a security escort now. Ouch!" He yanks his hand back, shaking it. "Still hot."

Lela's around back putting the spare tire on. Lucky for us she only shot out one. The click-click-click of the jack raises the vehicle in tiny increments.

Blond ponytail sits in the Humvee with crossed arms, brooding over what he must imagine was a missed opportunity to escape.

I take Lela's shotgun and place it in Rafa's gear bag, then I tell the gringo to move up into the front passenger seat. He grumbles something under his breath as he changes seats. The sun's well above the horizon and it's already hot. I wipe sweat from my forehead and take another look toward camp. Still no one following, but for how long?

I glance back at the crumpled mess of the sedan. Between that impossible-to-miss clue and our fresh tire tracks, our trail won't be too hard to follow.

Rafa clangs the Humvee's hood shut, then wipes his hands on his pants. "All done."

"Already?"

Rafa holds up a fat roll of silver tape and winks. "Nothing major. Bullets tore some hoses. A couple patches, top off the oil, and we're good."

The Humvee suddenly drops several inches, its suspension bouncing and squeaking like old bedsprings. Lela comes around the side of the vehicle and nods at me. She's finished changing the tire.

"You drive," I say, tossing her the key.

Rafa and I climb into the back. I toss his gear bag behind my seat, where I can reach it easily. The Glock pokes me in the back when I sit, so I move it to the pocket on my thigh. Lela gets in and starts the engine. Her head nearly touches the roof, and her massive hands and thick fingers make the steering wheel look like a child's toy. She leans forward and wipes off a layer of dusty sand covering the dashboard with her sleeve. Over her shoulder, I read the gauges. Oil pressure rises, temperature's back down, no red lights.

"Let's go," I say. She puts the Humvee into gear and we roll forward.

I have Lela drive in a wide circle toward the northeast. Based on where we are, due east of camp, we ought to run across Abner's trail within half an hour. If there's still enough of a trail left to run across.

We rumble along, rocking back and forth. The bumpy, rutted terrain limits our speed, but we manage to keep a steady, jarring pace, moving as fast as we can without smashing our heads into the roof. The air inside the

Humvee stifles, even with the windows down. The desert dirt—not quite sand and not quite dust, but something in between—attaches itself to everything. An ugly, sparse landscape stretches to the horizon all around us: leafless creosote, gray and craggy and looking more dead than alive; lonely, isolated patches of cacti.

The minutes pass slowly and no one speaks. I sit on my knees facing backwards, scanning the horizon, expecting cars or trucks or a telltale cloud of dust to appear any second, but there's nothing.

"We go back now," Lela says. "No trouble."

I sigh. "Just drive."

Next to me Rafa shifts in his seat. "Maybe we ought to think about going b—" is all he gets out before my glare cuts him off.

"No trouble," Lela repeats. "I make everything okay with don Flaco."

"You should listen to him, young lady," the gringo adds. "Turn around right now, and I won't have no hard feelings. I guarantee it."

"I should listen to *her*, you mean?" I snap. The gringo looks Lela up and down, confused. The keen, observant gaze of my tracker. Madre mía, help me.

"Shut up and keep your eyes out front," I tell him. "You don't spot that trail in the next ten minutes, you'll have more to worry about than some bullshit deal."

I turn around and sit facing forward. "Rafa, watch out back for cars."

"Sure," he says, then reaches out and squeezes my shoulder. I brush his hand away, but not before Lela notices in the rearview. She narrows her eyes at me in the same reproachful way Mama used to when she suspected me of shirking chores. *Unbelievable.* I send countless men and women to horrible deaths in the desert with a nod of my head, and she never even blinks. But fuck-baiting Rafa gets me the stink eye.

I glare back at her. "Watch where you're driving, would

you?" We trundle on.

Minutes later blond ponytail leans forward and points. "There it is." Lela stops the Humvee. We get out and examine the tracks. I kneel down and run my finger over the barest trace of tread marks pressed into the dirt. Definitely two sets of Jeep tires, though so faint and faded I don't know how the gringo saw them from the passenger seat. The trail points northeast.

"They're Dallas-bound," the gringo mutters.

I nod. "Can we catch up before they get there?"

"Ain't no *we* in this, young lady," he objects. "I done kept my half of the deal. Found your trail for you. Now take this damn thing off of me."

"When we find them," I insist. "Let's go." Blond ponytail grunts and limps back to the Humvee.

We press on, following the trail. Every so often the gringo mutters or points adjustments when Lela strays too far from the seemingly invisible tracks. Rafa keeps an eye out back. It's slow going. The Humvee trudges along the inconsistent terrain.

"How long to Dallas?" I ask.

"Twenty hours, give or take," the gringo answers.

My heart sinks. *Twenty hours.* With a day's head start, the only way we could catch them is if they stopped for the night. And you don't spend the night in the desert unless you're looking to get robbed and killed. But then again they're probably well-armed and carrying all kinds of Dallas tech: satphones, night-watchers, ground sensors, listening gear. Maybe a stopover in the desert wouldn't be such a risk with all that tech. Still, I feel Abner slipping away, taking whatever he knows Mama and Papi with him.

I try not to think of them. Between the kidnapped gringo, the reluctant driver, and the skittish boy next to me, I can't allow my attention to wander. One distracted moment and Lela could knock my lights out again and have us back in camp before I wake up.

We drive on. To the left of us, running parallel with our

path, lie the crumbled remains of highway I-20. In another era, it would have taken us to Dallas in a handful of hours, an easy ride over smooth concrete. Now it's mostly rubble, all cracked and broken with more missing than there, undrivable since long before I was born. The old highways are little more than navigational aids these days, reference markers for anyone desperate or foolhardy enough to attempt travel through the wasteland. Like the long-dead cell phone towers standing naked and rusting under a merciless sun, the highways are relics from another age, fossils of infrastructure from a time before Secession, before the Crisis. The sad events history books use capital letters for, mile markers measuring the journey from proud, defiant independence to humbled, isolated anarchy.

Two boring hours pass. The ground flattens out a bit, so I tell Lela to speed up. Blond ponytail protests, saying it makes it harder to follow the trail if we go too fast. Bitch, bitch, bitch. Rafa and I take turns watching out the back window. We're okay for now, but for how much longer is anyone's guess. By now they've surely pieced together what happened, and the Humvee's tires tracks are fresh and easy to follow. Still, we've got a big head start and a V8.

I don't envy the poor shit who had to tell Guzmán I've gone missing. I picture don Flaco raging, kicking over tables and berating security staff. The image of him throwing a fit brings a smile to my face.

The grin disappears a moment later when a drone attacks us.

*　　*　　*

"Get us out of here!" I shout, as Lela whips the wheel over, sending Rafa and me sprawling across the back seat.

Outside the Humvee, a row of rooster tails explode up from the ground where the bullets hit, missing the vehicle by inches and spraying us with dirt through the open window. The drone is somewhere high overhead. We can't see it or hear it, the sudden downpour of bullets the only evidence of its existence. The first volley tore through the roof behind our seat, punching several large holes but missing the four of us.

Get us out of here. A stupid thing to say. Like there's anywhere to go. Miles of nothing in every direction, not even a tree to hide behind. The Humvee's the barrel and we're the fish.

Lela zigzags the vehicle over dirt and scrub brush, accelerating, braking, then accelerating again, trying to make us a harder target. "Dios te salve, María," she prays aloud. "Llena eres de gracia…"

Next to her the gringo covers his head with one arm and grips the dashboard with the other.

Rafa sticks his head out the window and looks up. "What are you doing?" I scream, yanking him back inside.

"It's just a scout," he says. "Good."

Good?

Rafa dives into the back behind our seat and, somehow, amid the constant lurching of the Humvee, manages to unzip his gear bag.

"It's a scout for sure," he shouts. "High-end cameras and infrared, but guns and targeting systems are bare bones. And notoriously iffy. A Reaper XII, a *real* combat drone, would've taken us out in a second."

He digs through the bag. "Totally antiquated op system, not hard to—" The back window explodes, drowning out his voice, as another volley of bullets pounds the Humvee. Rafa scrambles back over the seat, holding a black box and nearly landing in my lap as the vehicle pitches sharply to the left. He pulls a long antenna from the top of the device and then taps the box's small screen with his finger.

"Not hard to jam up," he finishes. He taps away, then stops and nods his head. "There, that ought to do it."

A spray of bullets peppers the Humvee.

"What the heck?" Rafa cries, hitting the side of the device with his palm.

The vehicle slows down, seems to lose power. Up front the hood has several large holes. The motor's been hit.

"Puta madre," Lela yells. "Get out and run."

The Humvee jerks to a stop. I reach for the door handle, overcome with animal panic. I open the door halfway, then pause. *Run where?*

I look over at Rafa. He's frowning at the device, oblivious to what's going on around him.

"Rafa, get out," I yell.

Holding the device in both hands, he reaches out the window and moves it around, waving the antenna in circles.

"Rafa," I scream, expecting bullets to tear through the vehicle, and us, at any second. He doesn't seem to hear me. With the vehicle at a dead stop, we're an easy target now, even for a scout drone with crappy gun systems. Lela grabs me by the arm and yanks me out into the bright sunlight. We scramble away from the Humvee. I can't see blond ponytail. There's no cover anywhere.

I run, aware of nothing but the landscape in front of me. Blood pounds in my ears.

Somewhere behind me Rafa cries out. The drone must have gotten him. I flash back to our house in the Panhandle, overcome with the same sick helplessness I felt that morning, when Mama shoved me out the back door. I run faster.

Then Rafa screams again. I glance back and he's out of the Humvee, holding the device in one hand and pointing skyward with the other.

"Look, look!" he shouts, hopping up and down like an impatient child.

Before I can make sense of what he's doing, in the corner of my vision I see the drone falling like a rock out of the sky, then crashing a hundred meters away. The thudding impact sends dirt and plane parts flying.

I stumble to a stop, watching the dirt cloud settle. It takes me a moment to register what's happened, to find my breath again. I look back over to Rafa. He's leaning with one hand on the Humvee, smiling and giving me a thumbs up.

I lower myself to the ground, breathe deeply, and give my hammering heart a minute to slow down.

Lela stands next to me. The gringo's nearby, staring at the crashed drone.

"You hit?" she calls out.

"No," I answer. "You?"

She shakes her head, then lifts her Virgin of Guadalupe pendant and kisses it.

We gather at the Humvee. It's a mess of shredded metal and bullet holes. The front bumper is gone and the back one hangs precariously by a single bolted screw. Inside, pebble-sized shards of glass cover the seats and floorboards. Lela lifts the hood, assesses the engine, and frowns. Rafa pokes his head around her wide frame and grimaces.

"How bad?" I ask.

"Totalmente quebrado," Lela grunts. "We walking now."

Shit. I kick the tire in a rage, then kick it again, over and over. *Shit shit shit.*

A day ago I was almost close enough to reach out and touch Abner. Now he might as well be on Mars, long gone.

I turn and walk away from the vehicle. Ahead of me, smoke wafts up from the wreckage of the aircraft, then thins and disappears. I pause and stare at it for a long moment, thinking.

I walk back over to the Humvee and gesture toward the drone. "What's that thing doing out here anyway?" I ask Lela. She shrugs and takes a drink from her water bottle.

Rafa nods. "Yeah, right. We haven't seen a drone in

months."

More like a year, ever since Guzmán's war techs figured out how to fabricate an anti-drone chain gun. Matamoscas they called them, huge 50mm cannon-like weapons mounted on towers or atop vehicles. They proved to be a deadly accurate countermeasure to the Bullocks' drones, bringing down a couple hundred in a single month. After that, the drones stopped coming.

"Trader," I say to blond ponytail. "What's a drone doing around here?"

He's still staring at the crash site, his mouth hanging open. I repeat the question, louder, startling him. "Hell if I know," he mumbles, unconvincingly.

Lela and I exchange looks. We have no time to wade through his bullshit, so I let it go for now. Going back west toward camp isn't an option. There's probably already a hunting party out looking for us. And now that we know the Bullocks haven't stopped sending *all* their drones, walking around in the open doesn't feel like the safest place to be, either.

"How far is San Angelo from here?" I ask. "Forty clicks?"

Blond ponytail squints to the south, scans the horizon. "'Tween forty and fifty, I reckon."

"San Angelo?" Lela protests. I shoot her a hard look and her face twists as she swallows the rest of her complaint. San Angelo is Bullock territory.

"Rafa," I say. "Get your gear and our water out of the back. We're leaving."

Minutes later, the Humvee's broken shell and the smoldering aircraft are far behind us. We trudge across a flat, endless landscape of sun-scorched grasslands and bare trees the color of ash. Overhead the sun nears its midday peak, blazing and relentless. To our right, tabletop plateaus break the flat monotony of the horizon. Somewhere beyond them to the southwest lie the Glass Mountains, and beyond that Big Bend. A vast, rocky wasteland sitting atop billions and billions of cubic meters of natural gas, all of it under Guzmán's control.

We walk on. Rafa and blond ponytail are up front, followed by Lela, then me. Every couple minutes the gringo glances back, making sure he's well within the fifty-meter safe zone. Sometimes he looks at me, other times he gazes far behind me, as if expecting a search party to appear over the horizon at any moment.

Lela slows down, letting a bit of space build up between her and Rafa and the gringo.

"So in San Angelo, what?" she asks. It's her way of asking if I have a plan, if I've considered what's going to happen when we walk into a Bullock-held town.

"We find a squat," I say, but that's about as far as I've thought it out.

After the fall of Odessa, San Angelo became the westernmost Bullock-controlled town, sitting squarely in the path of Guzmán's land grab. By now a fair amount of its residents have abandoned their homes, fleeing the all-but-inevitable violence to come. There should be plenty of places where we can hunker down while I figure out what to do next.

"And what about this one?" She nods toward the gringo. A chill shoots down my spine as I realize it's not really meant to be a question. She uses the exact words Guzmán does after I've finished a read so I won't mistake her intention.

She wants the gringo dead.

CHAPTER 8

The gringo's a risk, Lela mutters so only I can hear. We can't take him into town. He'll say something to a Bullock soldier. He'll get us killed. And that limp of his is slowing us down. It'll take us another five hours to get to San Angelo. Without him we'd get there in four. And surely I noticed how he lied about the drone. Probably led us straight to its route on purpose. You of all people should know you can't trust gringos, she insists.

Every few minutes, blond ponytail glances back at us, squinting as he tries to make out what she's saying. Lela persists, serving up reason after reason why the gringo shouldn't live.

"Enough," I snarl, and she finally shuts up. Between the oven-heat and her pestering, my head's throbbing. I sip from my bottle, careful not to drink too much. It has to last until San Angelo. The water's warm like blood but it relieves the sticky dryness inside my mouth. When Lela turns away from me, I pour a small splash onto my hands, washing off the last bits of dried blood.

The last several hours keep running through my head, a movie I'm helpless to turn off. The horror on the guard's face as he writhes on the floor and gurgles through a mouthful of blood. Me tiptoeing around him, trying not to throw up, looking away from his face as I change clothes. And then fucking Rafa minutes later, the guard's blood still sticky and warm on my hands and arms.

Lost in thought, my pace slows. Lela must hear my footsteps lagging, because she turns and looks at me. I avoid her eyes, quicken my stride, and she turns back around.

I wonder how much she knows.

We walk on. An hour passes, then two more. No one speaks and the only sound in the world is the soft crush of Indian grass under our feet. Rafa stops, waits for me to catch up, then walks beside me.

"You doing all right?" he asks.

Lela looks over her shoulder and frowns.

"Fine," I answer. "Go on back up there with the gringo."

"I'd rather be here," he says.

"I need you up front to keep an eye out for San Angelo." I motion forward. "Go on."

Rafa's gaze falls to the ground. "Fine," he sighs, then he plods forward, his head down and shoulders slumped.

We keep moving, covered in dust under a sweltering sun, the air so hot I can feel my lungs heat up with each breath.

Soon a scattering of buildings rise over the southern horizon, growing larger as we approach. Then a few more, low-lying shapes clustered together. Ahead of us to the right, the crumbling remains of some long-forgotten dam stand guard over a wide plain of cracked, gray earth. It seems impossible that a lake once filled this empty, bone-dry expanse. Still, the sight of the old dam, overrun with deserts weeds and scrub brush, brings with it some relief. It's the landmark we've been looking for. We've arrived in San Angelo.

San Angelo is less a town than a sprawl of dilapidated homes, ancient and roofless and more collapsed than standing, surrounding a tiny downtown of concrete birdshit-covered ruins. Mesquite and juniper line the banks of a mud-colored river that snakes its way through town.

When I was fourteen, back before Abner came to live with us, we came here once, me and Mama and Papi. We were the honored guests of the local Bullock-appointed despot, a mean-faced woman named Schneider who chewed tobacco. Mama didn't bother to hide her disgust whenever the woman spit on the ground and wiped her mouth with her sleeve. *Naca*, Mama muttered to me under her breath, the insult she reserved for the unsophisticated rubes of the hinterland. *Totalmente naca*. They set us up on top floor of the tallest building in town, and we stayed a few weeks while Papi trained the locals on how to take volume measurements of the nearby natgas fields, of which there weren't many. San Angelo's located close to what Papi used to call the Big Empty, a large section in the middle of the Republic where there are no large gas fields. The Big Empty is surrounded by three major natgas territories. Below the western desert lies the Permian Basin, most of which is now controlled by the slave-buying, bastard-making hero of the huddled masses, don Flaco Guzmán. Then there's the Fort Worth Basin to the north, and the Gulf Basin to the southeast, both controlled by the Bullocks, which combined make up the largest share of the Republic's natgas fields.

We follow the riverbed toward town, passing through a ghost neighborhood where plumbing pipe, rusted paper-thin and brittle, and cement rubble foundations, rendered almost invisible by dense undergrowth, mark the only remaining traces of the people who once lived here. I need to find shelter, someplace I can get out from under this blast furnace sun and hunker down to figure out the next move. If there even is a next move.

A handful of low-rise buildings appear as we come out of a copse of mesquite trees. San Angelo's town center, maybe three or four clicks away.

The pop-pop-pop of gunfire breaks the silence with the suddenness of a rock shattering a window. The shots are loud and close, but it takes a moment for the danger to sink in. After hours under a relentless sun, my thinking's slow and muddy. Lela grabs my arm and pulls me into a thicket. Ahead of us, Rafa and blond ponytail hide belly-down in the underbrush.

A coyote bursts out of a cluster of trees, its tail tucked between its legs, and scrambles down the bank of the riverbed. A second later, a swarm of children emerge from the same spot, barefoot and shirtless and screaming, chasing after the animal. The tallest, a boy with filthy matted hair, holds a pistol in front of him with both hands as he runs. He pauses, aims, and fires off two more rounds. The shots send dirt flying near the coyote, but miss the target. The animal bolts into an old drainage sewer and disappears. The children jump and holler, reaching for the gun and shouting *my turn, my turn!* The tall boy holds the gun high, away from the others, and then follows the coyote into the sewer. The children run in after him, their shrieking voices echoing and then fading into the distance.

So clearly San Angelo isn't *totally* abandoned. Lela and I come out of the thicket, join Rafa and the gringo.

The closer we get to the center of town, the more likely we'll run into more locals. Here like everywhere else, the outlying sprawl of countless suburban homes has long since been deserted. Thousands upon thousands of rotten wood frames and roofless structures sit empty and unlivable, reclaimed by undergrowth, abandoned generations ago for the relative safety of the sturdy, thick-walled concrete structures of downtown. And since this is Bullock territory, the roomy top floor penthouses and large government offices are reserved for the families of local higher-ups, while everyone else crams into shared common areas. Cots and tents crowd the floors of cafeterias and auditoriums, hundreds or even thousands of people living under the same roof, breathing the same air. Disease is commonplace, filth and stench ever present. For most in the Republic, this cramped, huddled existence under the Bullocks is the normal way of life. It's a world removed from the safety and security of Dallas, but it's better than the alternative, the barbarous anarchy of the vast, unpoliced wastelands of the Republic.

"We have to find shelter somewhere around here," I tell Rafa. He and Lela nod. Blond ponytail's dust-covered face holds no expression other than total exhaustion. The long hike has taken its toll on him.

We move on, searching the immediate area and keeping our distance from the town's center. The wide canopies of live oaks provide some relief from the sun. Hearty, drought-tolerant giants planted untold eons ago by residents. When the downtown buildings finally fall apart and crumble into nothing and all the people are gone, they'll still be standing here, even bigger than they are today, spreading their shade over the coyotes, the only creature that's thrived since the Crisis. Papi once told me coyotes do well because they don't mind chaos. They'll scavenge, hunt, or steal as the situation requires. Like the oak trees, coyotes are survivors.

"Look," Rafa shouts, pointing to our left. I shush him and look over. Half a click away stands a four-story structure. One of the walls is missing, but the roof is mostly intact. A messy veneer of weeds and wild grass grows well beyond the second floor in places, hiding much of the building's ground floor. There's no sign of people.

I share a nod with Lela. The four of us move toward the house, watchful and cautious. I take out my gun and click off the safety.

We find the building empty, and there's no food or animal bones or shit smell, no evidence of anyone using it for shelter. Inside, finally out of the searing sunlight, we find an elevator shaft full of old bird nests and a stairwell still intact enough to make the upper floors accessible.

Plants push through fissures in the cement floor, growing waist-high in places.

Hidden, shady, and a safe distance from town, it's a good place to rest.

The gringo sits, groaning as he leans back against the wall. He closes his eyes and rasps, "Water," his voice thin and dry. Rafa pulls a bottle out of his bag and passes it to him.

"How many pellets do you have?" I ask Rafa.

He squats and fishes through his bag. "Maybe about five kilos."

"I want you to go into town and buy some food and water."

"What?" he protests. "Why me?"

"Because I need to stay here and keep an eye on these two."

He looks like he wants to argue back, but stops himself. "Fine." He takes several small bags of pellets and stuffs them into his pockets.

The next hour passes slowly as we sit against the wall and wait for Rafa's return. The gringo snores and Lela— maybe sleeping, maybe not—leans her head back with her eyes closed. I keep my hand around the Glock's handle inside my pocket. Next to me on the floor I notice a couple pellets that must have fallen from Rafa's bag. I pick one up and roll it between my fingers.

They look like rat poop, I used to tell Papi. He'd roll his eyes and insist how they were a wonder of gas technology. For your everyday citizens, natgas pellets were ordinary and commonplace, something they poured into a car's fuel tank or used as currency in the markets. But to scientists and gas techs, Papi insisted, pellets were nothing less than little miracles of modern engineering and chemistry.

I pocket the pellet. Why is Rafa taking so long? My mind crowds with all the different ways something could go wrong: a Bullock soldier recognizes Rafa as an out-of-towner; he gets beaten up and robbed of his pellets; he forgets how to find his way back.

I'm trying to come up with contingencies when Rafa walks through the doorless entryway, smiling proudly and carrying two large canvas bags.

"Buyer's market," he announces, tossing the bags to the floor. "After they heard about Odessa, half the town packed up and headed east."

There's an assortment of dried and cooked meats, bell peppers, tomatoes, coffee cups and a pot for brewing. We pack the meat and vegetables into still-warm tortillas, gulping down mouthfuls with the silent efficiency of starving animals. The food revives me, clears my head. The others seem to perk up as well. Even the gringo's wary blue eyes regain their liar's sharpness.

When I can't eat anymore, I trudge up the stairs to the top floor. The roof is rickety and filled with holes, but I'm able to clamber up top and take in our surroundings. It's getting late in the afternoon and the shadows are noticeably longer than when we arrived. Toward town there's little activity. I spot a few people milling around the larger structures, a couple cars moving through the streets. I turn and look northwest, scanning the brown, featureless plain we trekked across for hours. No telltale dust clouds on the horizon, no hunting parties on our trail.

So now what, Sol?

The answer doesn't come quickly, but it comes. I climb down off the roof, go down the stairs, and join the others.

I fix my eyes on blond ponytail, then pull out my stash of hierba. "We need to have a little talk."

*   *   *

Lela sits against the wall with her arms crossed, scowling at me as I wait for the hierba to take hold. Rafa keeps an eye on blond ponytail upstairs and waits for me to call him. Outside, the sun drops below the horizon and the trees' long shadows fade into twilight.

"We still can go back," Lela says.

I shake my head. "I don't think so." I motion to the doorway. "You can leave right now if you want. No one's stopping you."

She doesn't answer. I chew the bitter leaves in silence. Suddenly I notice the scent of Lela's body hanging in the air, pungent and sweaty, mingling with the gamey wisps of the squirrel meat we feasted on.

Lela stares at her shoes. "You know how I come to don Flaco?"

"What?"

"How don Flaco find me. I never tell you before."

I see things, hear things as the hierba begins to peak. Lela wants to tell me something, but the words won't come. Indecision and awkwardness contort her face.

All I know about Lela's life before joining Guzmán's cause is that she used to be a boxer. The only woman they let compete in the barefisted fight circuit. Strangers often approached her in camp, reminding her of the time they saw her knock someone's teeth out in Tijuana, or when she KO'd someone with an uppercut in Chihuahua. Over a hundred fights and not a single loss.

"Didn't he see you in the fights?" I ask.

"No," Lela says. "He never see me fight."

"What then?"

"Me rescató," she answers.

"Rescued you? From what?" It's impossible to imagine Lela, a streetwise human tank, in need of rescue.

Then she changes, seeming to sink inside herself. Her body tenses up and her face becomes childlike and anxious. It unnerves me, seeing her like this, feeling her.

"Sometimes when I finish a fight, they no want to pay me." She struggles to continue, forcing the words. "They say you not a woman. Too strong, too big. I not gonna pay you. I don't pay a liar." Her voice falters, cracks. "They tell me I have to show I'm a woman."

She doesn't have to say anything else. I can see her

shame, feel the secret pain she's kept hidden from me, from everyone. The dark ugliness that weighs on her soul.

Then something strange happens.

Images begin to flash through my mind, bright and vivid, jolting me like surprise crashes of thunder.

The sensations suddenly rushing through me are similar to what I felt that day I saw something else in Papi's face, something more than just truth or lies. But this feels a hundred times more powerful. A lightning strike to a carpet shock.

Lela's memories!

I'm *seeing* her memories, like I'm inside her head, feeling them as if they're my own.

This must be what Mama meant when she told me some readers could see more than lies. How some could *see the truth*.

My heart pounds wildly as pictures and sounds and sensations overwhelm my mind. From the chaos, a story begins to take shape.

Lela's nightmare started with a fat-bellied fight hustler, the one who refused to pay her until she proved she was a woman. She was starving, broke, and exhausted from a hard fight. She finally agreed, following him into a tiny dark room with a mattress on the floor that reeked of dog piss. Later he boasted about it and soon word got out and spread through the fight circuit. She'll bring a big crowd to the fight and after she'll spread those big strong legs for you too. Before long it became her sickening routine: man after disgusting man in town after town, drunk and crawling on top of her, her knuckles still raw and bloody from the fight, the dirty cigar taste of their tongues in her mouth, telling her how much she loved it, sometimes inviting friends to join in. She couldn't let herself get blacklisted from the fight circuit. She had to eat, had to survive, so she did it. It went on like that for years.

I can see them, smell them, up close and sweaty, their stale breath on my neck. My stomach roils and I gag. The men bring back my own horrible past, the freelancers who kidnapped me. I snap back to myself and Lela's watching me.

"When don Flaco find out," she continues, "he come with his people. They take me out of the fights. Bring me to camp. He tell me I don't have to fight no more." Her voice carries ten lifetimes of pain and loneliness.

She leans forward. "I know what you did back at camp. I find the guard in your tent."

I gasp and raise my hand to my mouth. *She knows.* I turn away.

"Don Flaco gonna be mad," she says softly. "About the guard, about taking this gringo. But he still take you back…"

She knows.

"…and I make sure nothing bad happen to you."

I shake my head.

"Mira mis ojos," she insists. "Do I lie or no?"

I squeeze my eyes shut. "I'm not going back."

A heavy silence falls over us. I take long, deep breaths. Soon my racing heart begins to slow and my mind settles.

I open my eyes. Outside it's nearly dark and crickets chirp. Lela stares at me. She's not lying about don Flaco. He's her savior, and she believes it to her marrow. And he is, I suppose. He's *her* savior, *her* truth. But not mine.

"He's not my family," I say. "And you're not my family, either." She's hurt but tries not to show it, and I try not to feel shitty for saying it. *She's not my family,* I repeat to myself.

Lela's eyes fall to the floor. She nods.

I walk over to the stairwell and call up to the second floor. "Rafa, I'm ready. Bring him down."

CHAPTER 9

"I'm going to ask you some questions," I say, "and you're going to answer."

The gringo sits on the floor, facing me and fidgeting. Lela and Rafa stand in the corners of the room, giving me space to concentrate.

"And if you lie," I continue, "I'll know. You understand?"

He nods. His nervous eyes bounce around the room, looking to my left, to my right, then to the floor. Anywhere but my eyes.

I swallow some water. "I want you to tell me what you know about the drone routes."

He says nothing, tightening his lips into a straight line. His face gives little away. A sunburned mask of stubbornness.

I remove the remote from my pocket. The gringo's eyes widen and he reaches up to touch the dog collar. His hand stops in mid-reach.

"The code's three numbers long." I tap two numbers with my thumb.

"Okay, okay." He shows me his palms.

"What was that drone doing out there?" I ask.

He sighs, seems to give in. "They're still running scouts out of Dallas, just not as much as they used to."

"How come no one in Guzmán's camp has seen any lately?"

"They keep up 'em high up, out of matamosca range."

"And what about Abner?"

"Who?"

"The Jeep we were tracking," I clarify. "Wouldn't it have seen them, too? Attack them like it attacked us?"

"Beacons," Rafa offers. "Bullock vehicles have beacons so the drones know they're friendly."

"Boy's right," the trader agrees.

I narrow my eyes at the gringo. "So you knew we'd get hit?"

He looks at his shoes. "Wasn't no way to be sure."

I glance over at Lela and she's giving me an I-told-you-so look. Traces of her past still cloud her face.

I turn back to blond ponytail. "Do you know their flight routes?"

He hesitates. "Some of them."

Bullshit. He knows more than he's leading on. A lot more.

But I sense there's something else. Something he's hiding, something he's worried I'll discover. A secret he values far more than what he knows or doesn't know about Bullock drones.

"I'll find out, you know," I say flatly.

"Find out what?"

"Whatever that thing is you don't want to tell me."

Again he gives me the tight-lipped grimace. "Don't know what you're talking about."

He's a hard read, giving me little to work with. Lela takes a couple threatening steps toward him and he cowers. The sudden worry distracts him, scrambling his thoughts and making it harder for him to hide from me. I start to see things, glimpses of thoughts. Nothing like the vivid, raw visions I saw with Lela, more like perceptions, echoes of ideas, phrases and sentences that don't use words. They flash like fireflies at the edge of my vision, but vanish as soon as I turn to look at them. Individually, they mean nothing, but together they speak to me, their patterns revealing the gringo's plans, intentions, and expectations.

The pieces begin to come together, start to make sense. The natgas conversion scheme was bait, a way of getting don Flaco alone for a face-to-face meeting, where the gringo could tell him about the *real* deal in private. The other deal, the one that's *not* a lie. The trade of a lifetime that'll make him so rich he can buy his way out of this godforsaken Republic. He sees himself lying on a beach somewhere, shirtless and facedown, a young brown-skinned woman with long black hair massaging his shoulders. No more stealing and hustling and scrambling. No more looking over his shoulder for someone he ripped off in the last town, chasing him down. He's one deal away from paradise. So close he can taste it.

"Take your pants off," I tell him.

The gringo sneers, shakes his head. "No way."

"Do it now," I insist.

"Hey," Rafa says, "what's going on?"

I look over at the puzzled faces of Rafa and Lela, then I point to the gringo's leg. "That limp's not an injury. He's carrying something."

The trader's facial muscles twitch with panic. "I ain't carrying nothing."

Lie.

I nod at Lela and she comes over, grabs him by the ponytail, and yanks him backwards to the floor. He kicks out and tries to resist, and Lela makes him pay for it, roughing him up with an elbow to the side of his head and a gut punch. He wisely stops struggling and she wriggles the pants down his hips. When she gets them around his knees, she stops and furrows her brow.

"¿Qué chingados es eso?"

There's a lemon-sized bulge stretching the skin of the gringo's right thigh. A pair of black trodes dangle out of a small, oozing wound near the bottom of it.

Rafa steps forward to study the lump. "He's got some kind of tech in there, buried in the thigh muscle."

"A bomb?" Lela asks. She stands and backs away from the gringo.

"No," Rafa says. "Bombs don't have trodes like that." He kneels next to the gringo, who's still groaning from Lela's blows, lying curled up with his hands cupped over his exposed cock and balls. Rafa tilts his head as he stares at the trader's leg and the small white letters running down one of the trodes. "Zephyr Intelligent Systems," he whispers.

Rafa springs to his feet, points to the gringo's leg. "You've got an *AI* in there?"

"¿Un qué?" Lela asks.

The gringo pulls his pants back up and scowls. I look at the spot on his thigh where the pants now cover the bulge.

"Very high-end tech," Rafa answers. "The Bullocks use AI systems to manage their infrastructure in Dallas. Power grid, bots, communications. AIs pretty much run everything."

But we aren't in Dallas. Outside of the Bullocks' protected enclave, the rest of the Republic is a sparsely populated wasteland, its technology scarce and outdated, cobbled together from pre-Crisis leftovers or contraband bootlegged in from the States. Outside of Dallas, an AI is about as useful as a glass hammer.

So what the hell is this freelance trader doing with one?

I lean forward. "What's the story with that thing?"

"Ain't no story," the gringo grumbles, pokerfaced. "Just wanna sell it. Thought maybe Guzmán might be in a buying state of mind."

"Why'd you hide it like that?"

"For safe-keeping."

Christ, this is going to take some time. My newfound

ability seems to have slipped away for the moment. But even if I could, I'm not sure I'd want to see inside the trader's head. Who knows what sick depravities I'd come across?

We go back and forth for a while. I ask, he evades. When I refine a question, thinking I have him trapped, he mumbles some one-word answer. It's infuriating. He doesn't lie, but neither does he reveal much. Typical tight-lipped traderspeak. Eventually I'm able to gather the following: he stole the AI in El Paso, swindling it away from some of his freelancer buddies; he had it implanted in his thigh to make it harder to detect; and he's convinced Guzmán will pay top dollar for it.

Which makes about zero sense. Guzmán has no robots, no drones, hardly uses tech at all. He actually vilifies technology, both as a tool of oppression and a sign of Bullock decadence. *We toil and starve here in the cruel desert sands while they hoard their wealth and lounge around pools of sparkling clear water, their robot slaves serving them martinis and cooking them feasts, their killer drones keeping them safe from high above.* I've heard that line about a hundred times, and it never fails to stir up the crowd. He used to say glasses of Bordeaux, until he realized no one knew what that was. Then he changed it to martinis.

I sigh and rub my temples. My head aches from playing cat and mouse with the gringo. There's a missing piece of his story somewhere, and he's damn good at keeping it hidden. I don't have much longer before the hierba wears off. Already I feel its effect lessening. In another half hour it'll be gone altogether.

Then something occurs to me, and I can't believe I didn't think of it before. *Pendeja.*

I focus on the gringo's face, watch him carefully. "Is this some kind of tech Guzmán can use *against* the Bullocks?"

The gringo licks his lips, and his eyes flicker like a dying light bulb.

Bull's-eye.

"That's it," Rafa blurts out, so loud he startles me. "A rogue," he says, then asks the gringo, "It's a rogue AI, isn't it?"

Blond ponytail looks down, avoids my gaze.

Now we're getting somewhere.

"Go upstairs," I tell Lela and Rafa. "I want to talk to him alone."

Lela shakes her head and crosses her arms. The gringo worried her before, when she thought he was nothing but a lying swindler. Now he's a lying swindler who led us into a drone strike, carrying around some black market tech worth who-knows-how-much. Suspicion and contempt light up her face like a neon sign.

She points to his leg. "We cut it out, take it with us."

Blond ponytail gasps, then turns to me, his eyes pleading and desperate. "I won't make no trouble, I promise. I won't make no kind of trouble."

Lela pulls a hunting knife out of her boot—her backup weapon I'd completely forgotten about—and steps toward the trader. He shows his palms and scrambles backwards, slamming his back against the wall. "No, don't. Please."

An image of the guard lying on the floor of my tent, bleeding out, drops into the front of my mind. The hierba intensifies the memory. I can smell his soiled pants and the coppery aroma of the blood pool spreading across the floor.

I shake my head, snort the stink out of my nose. "No, he's coming with us."

Lela looks at me, confusion clouding her face. "¿Cómo así?"

"He's coming with us."

She shakes her head. "Mala idea, niña." She gestures at the gringo with the knife. "This one no good. This one get us killed."

"Nothing of the sort," the gringo says, his voice quivering with fear. "Nothing of the sort."

Lela and I stare at each other. A crease forms between her eyebrows and her mouth bends into a disapproving frown. She lowers the knife, then grunts, turns, and stomps up the stairs.

Rafa looks uncertain, like he's not sure he should leave me alone with the gringo.

"Go on," I insist, nodding toward the stairs.

A moment passes, then his shoulders droop and he mutters, "Call out if you need help." He shuffles away, following Lela up the stairway.

It takes me a while to pull it out of him, but after a headache-inducing interview alone with the gringo, I see Lela was more right than wrong. The thing in the gringo's leg *is* a bomb. Sort of.

A rogue AI is like a crazy person. And not harmless crazy like Loco Lorenzo back at camp, who always has to tap his thumbs together five times before he speaks. This is psycho-killer crazy. Foaming-at-the-mouth, knife-wielding, insane person crazy.

Rogue AIs are underground tech, designed to take over, corrupt, and induce chaos into an AI-run system. Like the kind of system the Bullocks have in Dallas.

Now I get it. Buried in the gringo's thigh isn't merely some high-priced piece of tech, it's a weapon that could cripple the Bullocks' infrastructure in a matter of minutes. If it gets into their AIs' grid, everything in Dallas could go haywire: thousands of robots freezing in place, or maybe going crazy; drones falling from the sky; moving walkways jerking to a stop. The Bullocks' tidy, perfectly managed world, frozen with instant paralysis. The capital of the Republic, dark and dead.

And vulnerable.

Guzmán definitely would have paid a high price for something like that. But Guzmán's not the only game in town.

I rub my chin and give the gringo a stern look. Right before I speak, I realize it's the same gesture I've seen don

Flaco make countless times.

"I've got a proposition for you."

*   *   *

Rafa and I take shifts sleeping on the ground floor, while Lela keeps an eye on the gringo upstairs. Rafa makes a couple halfhearted attempts at conversation, but he can see I'm exhausted so he doesn't push it. It's a chilly night and I doze in fits sitting in a corner, the ancient cement walls worn and rough and cold through my clothes. My right hand rests on top of the bulge of the Glock in my pocket. In my left I hold the collar's remote control against my chest. When it's my turn to stay awake, my mind scatters in a thousand directions, asking a thousand questions.

There's only one place I'll find answers, and it's a long way from here. I try to get some rest, but sleep doesn't come easily and the night seems to stretch on forever. Finally morning shadows appear outside the doorway and the hazy outlines of tree branches take shape against the cold earth.

We get a fire going and Rafa makes coffee. The smell brings Lela and the gringo downstairs.

"Better get something to eat," I tell Lela. "We're leaving in a couple minutes."

"Para dónde?" Lela asks.

"None of your business," I say. "You're not coming with us."

"Wait," Rafa says, "we're not *all* going to—"

"Three of us are," I say, interrupting him.

"Why not Lela?" he asks.

I look at him and tilt my head. "So she can sucker punch me again and drag me back to Guzmán? No, thanks."

Lela moves her eyes between me and the gringo. "You going to Dallas, no?"

I glare at blond ponytail. He shows me his palms. "I didn't say nothing, I swear."

He probably didn't. Lela's smart. She knows I won't go back to don Flaco's camp, and we both know I can't stay here. San Angelo won't remain part of Bullock territory for long. From the rooftop it looked mostly abandoned and undefended, so odds are it's only a handful of days before Guzmán takes the town and starts fucking whatever's left of the local ass.

"So you a trader now?" she asks. Again I turn a sharp eye to the gringo.

"Not a goddamn word, my hand to God," he insists.

She's smart, but not that smart. She must have eavesdropped on us from the second floor. I gesture toward the gringo's leg. "Guzmán would pay a lot for that thing. The Bullocks would pay just as much to keep it out of his hands."

"Maybe more," the gringo says, rubbing his hands together.

Lela frowns at me. Displeased doesn't begin to describe the look she's giving me. The rogue AI—if it works as the gringo claims—is worth more to Guzmán than a thousand soldiers or a fleet of attack drones. It could tip the balance of power in her beloved don Flaco's favor. And here I am, ready and willing to hand it over to his enemies with a grin on my face. Until a few seconds ago, I was a headache of a runaway, a pain in Lela's ass. But I'm something else now. A traitorous whore, I suppose.

So be it.

Still, as she stands there glaring at me, there's some small part of me that wants to explain myself, to tell her it's the only way I see out of this mess, the only path that might lead me to Mama and Papi. If they're out there somewhere, still alive, they'll be in Bullock territory, and someone in Dallas will know where to find them.

But I don't say anything, too wary of Lela's reaction to speak. I stand away from her, half-expecting her to pounce on me in anger.

Instead, she grunts and shakes her head. "Too far. Too many drones. You never make it."

"We'll be careful."

She points her thumb at the trader. "You believe what this one tell you? You think you can trust this pinche gringo?"

"That's my business," I snap. "Now, get whatever food you want to take with you."

Lela considers me for a moment, then squats next to the fire and pours a cup of coffee. Steam rises around her face as she sips and stares into the fire. For a long time, no one speaks.

Then she looks up at me. "I go to Dallas with you."

I shake my head. "Sorry, but I've got my hands full. I can't watch him and duck your punches at the same time."

"No punches, no nothing." She touches her Virgin pendant. "I help you find them."

She gazes at me and nods once—her way of stamping her words as a promise. The effect of the hierba is long gone, but I know she's not lying. I swallow through the sudden tightness of my throat. I'm too stunned to speak, too overwhelmed to thank her.

I squat by the fire beside her, try to compose myself. I grab a piece of coyote jerky and bite off a mouthful. "First thing we need to do is get a car."

Lela sips her coffee. "No problem."

I lift my eyebrows. "No problem?"

A smile curls up one side of her mouth. She taps her chest and says, "I'm from Tijuana, remember?"

CHAPTER 10

Half an hour later we're driving out of town in a doorless antique Lincoln Continental with oversized suspension, enormous knobby tires, and a sheet metal body with more wrinkles and dents than the gringo's face. It's no Humvee, but it'll do. Rafa and I sit in back. Lela drives with blond ponytail next to her in the passenger seat.

"Ain't never seen nobody lift a vehicle that quick," the gringo says, his voice thick with a thief's admiration. "You got yourself a talent there."

Lela pays no attention to him. Behind us, San Angelo's small downtown grows smaller. The early morning sun is directly ahead, a swollen tangerine still low enough on the horizon that it doesn't hurt our eyes to look at it.

"How far east?" Lela asks.

"Till we hit I-45," the gringo answers. "Keep it going due east and we'll hit 45 around Fairfield or Corsicana."

Lela glances at me in the rearview and lifts her eyebrows.

I know, I know. It's a long way. Over four hundred clicks from here. And after that it's another hundred due north to Dallas. It's a huge detour, twice as far as a direct route. But that's the way we have to go if we want to keep a safe distance between us and the drone routes. If the gringo's intel can be trusted, that is.

Last night when I had him alone, I asked if he could get us to Dallas without being spotted by a drone.

The trader watched me for a moment, suspicious. "Dallas? What for?"

I told him that was my business, but if he got me within fifty miles of the capitol, I'd remove the collar and help him broker a deal with the Bullocks for the tech in his leg. First, though, he had to convince me he could get me there.

After I put that on the table, I could hardly shut him up. He spilled everything he knew about the Bullocks' fleet of drone aircraft and their flight paths, eager to convince me of his expertise. The trader chattered away, suddenly bright-eyed and animated, excited by the prospect of resurrecting his Big Deal. He could picture himself on that beach again, a cool drink in his hand and a warm pair of hands kneading his shoulders.

"Thing is," he said, "it weren't much of a fleet to begin with."

The Bullocks' robotic air force was made up of early-century drones, thousands left behind by the States during Secession. Flying artifacts that came in two flavors: scout drones with high-res cameras but minimal firepower and attack drones equipped with large-caliber guns or missiles. And thanks to Guzmán's matamoscas, there were a lot fewer of both types than there used to be. This much wasn't news, of course. Within don Flaco's camp, the Bullock threat from the air hadn't been a factor for some months. The war for the Republic had become a ground campaign, bloody and trudging.

The gringo went on to describe how freelance traders watch the skies—with telescopes and the occasional 'skygrabber' portable radar system smuggled in from the States—and share (or sold) information amongst themselves about the latest sightings and known flight paths. In their business of bartering and making trades throughout the wastelands, keeping up with the safest routes between cities is vital, and in recent months, they've only seen *a few* scouts flying at high altitudes.

"Define 'a few'," I probed.

"Less than half of what we used to see," he answered. "Maybe a third."

"And what about attack drones?"

"Only ones they've seen are within a few clicks of Dallas."

I considered his words, which lined up with what Guzmán's inner circle had suspected for some time. After losing scores of attack drones to don Flaco's matamoscas, the Bullocks would have been stupid not to pull them out of the battlefront. Old Chavez had even predicted as much, advising Guzmán the Dallasites would likely concentrate their airborne firepower to protect the capitol. From what the gringo was saying, it sounds like Chavez called it right.

"Look, even with a scaled-down fleet of scouts," I insisted, "it only takes one to spot us and we're done." I leaned forward. "And that means *you're* done, too."

He placed both hands on his chest in an overly sincere gesture. "You leave that up to me." Then he tapped his temple with his finger. "I got me a map right up here," he boasted, "and it'll get you to Dallas, guaranteed."

There wasn't a crack in his face or the slightest hint of a lie in his voice. It was probably the longest string of non-bullshit of his life.

Truth notwithstanding, I didn't like the idea of putting my life in his filthy trader's hands.

But what choice did I have?

*　　*　　*

The wind whips my hair around my face as we drive east through sparse, endless plains. The Lincoln glides over the ground, a surprisingly smooth ride. We're jostled far less than we were in the Humvee. The terrain's also easier to navigate, flat with fewer rocks and more wild grass. Lela opens up the motor and the landscape speeds by in a blur of beige and ash. Soon patches of green appear, mesquite shrubs and sumac, the tough woody plants that mark our transition from the western desert to the central plains.

Rafa lays his hand on top of mine. He leans toward me, his eyes earnest. "We'll find them. Don't worry."

I glance into the rearview and catch Lela looking back at us. Our eyes meet for a moment, then she blinks and looks away.

"Rafa," I say, "I need to tell you something."

"Okay."

I squirm and take a deep breath, not sure how to begin. Blond ponytail cranes his neck around, the nosy fuck.

I should have said something to Rafa last night, when we were alone. Should have said I'm sorry or what I did was wrong or I was desperate.

I look ahead, pondering the vast unknown that lies in front of us. No, I can't have this conversation. Not yet. It's a long way to Dallas, and I need all the help I can get.

"Nothing," I tell Rafa, forcing a smile. "Never mind, it's nothing."

We drive on, making good time, stopping only to pee. The day heats up and the air blowing through the open doors no longer refreshes. Sweat gathers under my arms, behind my knees, and the heat brings out the gamy odor of the goatskin seat covers. I hear the panicked bleating of our goats in the Panhandle as I run from the house, scrambling and slipping over the dew-covered switchgrass.

An hour passes, then two more. Trees begin to break up the monotony of the rolling plains. At first there's only a few here and there, live oaks and Ashe junipers standing alone like some lost or abandoned traveler, surrounded by miles of empty plains. Then more appear, clustered together in copses or lined up in crooked paths along creek banks. In front of me the gringo snores, his head resting against the seat, his stringy ponytail—more gray than blond, I notice now—hangs over into the back, nearly touching my legs as it sways back and forth with every turn of the steering wheel.

Another hour passes and the trader snorts awake. He turns to Lela. "What time is it?"

"Early afternoon," she answers. "Maybe one or two."

The gringo stretches. "Lordy, it's hot as all get out." He wipes sweat from his forehead, then he turns and gazes out the passenger side, toward the low-lying hills in the southern distance.

"Hill country," he mutters. Then he turns to Lela. "When you see Waco, go 'round to the south."

"*South?*" Lela she shakes her head. "¿Y los Fundies?"

Fundies. I shiver at the word.

"They ain't this far north," the gringo assures. "Not yet."

Lela grunts. "We don't go south," she insists. "I find a way through town."

"I'm with her," Rafa says. "I don't want to go anywhere near those lunatics. I hear they stone people and nail them up on crosses."

The gringo ignores Rafa. "Listen," he says, more to me than Lela, "Waco ain't like San Angelo. It's the first big town south of Dallas. Solid Bullock town. Blockades going in and coming out. Guards asking a million questions before they let you through. That ain't exactly what you're looking for, is it?"

"What about the north side?" I ask.

"If you want to get shot up again, that's fine," he answers, meaning that if we skirt around Waco's northern boundary, we'll be too close to a drone flight path.

We have to keep going east until we reach Interstate 45, where the gringo swears the drone coverage thins out enough for us to turn north and have a decent chance of making it to Dallas. But we have to get past Waco first, and each path eastward has its own hazards. Driving through Waco, a Bullock stronghold, invites the kind of scrutiny we don't want. Skirting around town to the north might attract a drone's attention. And to the south are thousands of well-armed zealots who don't like strangers.

"How close are the Fundies?" I ask blond ponytail.

"Last month they took Conroe," he answers.

South of Waco, north of Conroe. I try to picture don Flaco's map spread out across his table. It's a narrow corridor, not much room for error. But at least there aren't any drones overhead. And I can't see going through town. For all I know the drone got pictures of us before it went down, and now every checkpoint guard around the city knows my face.

"South," I say. "We'll go around to the south."

In the rearview Lela furrows her brow, scowls at me, then looks away.

*　　*　　*

I pick up a lot from the gossip of Guzmán's inner circle, from the whispers and mutterings that come through my headphones during a read. And the Fundamentalist Church of Divine Wrath is something they've talked about more and more lately, always with concern in their eyes and stress in their voices.

So I know a lot about the Fundies. More than most people know. Far more than I want to.

I know that they worry Guzmán and his top men, so much so that don Flaco has a constant flow of people going back and forth between his camp and Fundie territory, reporting back to him and keeping him up to date. I know that up until not long ago, they were little more than a bloodthirsty Christian cult, a handful of crackpots who lived in mud-and-brush homes in the remote swamps of Southeast Texas. But in the last couple years, under some new leader who seems to amass followers almost as fast as Guzmán, their faith has spread like a fast cancer across the region—or a cure, I suppose, depending on one's point of view. Now they control Houston and its outlying areas, from the coast at Galveston all the way north (as we've just discovered) to Conroe. The Bullocks, technically, still act as the local authority in Houston. Their technicians operate the natgas extraction and production facilities, and their security personnel maintain order. But with each passing month, according to Guzmán's spies, their grip on power seems to be slipping. Don Flaco says these days the Bullocks only hold Southeast Texas 'on paper,' and it's just a matter of time before the Fundies' religious fervor boils over into open rebellion.

They have a special hate for outsiders, anyone who's not a baptized, Bible-carrying, true-believing Fundie. Infidels, they call them. People like me and my three fellow passengers.

Still, of our three choices, the southern route feels like the least risky. We can see for miles in every direction, and with such a big motor we'd be hard prey to catch, even for the most determined predator.

Ahead of us, a gray cluster rises above the horizon and slowly takes the shape of midrise buildings. Waco's downtown.

"We gotta turn south now," says the gringo trader. "Can't get no closer or they'll send someone out for us."

Lela ignores him. We continue east toward town, the landscape blurring by, the buildings growing in size with each passing moment.

"Lela, *turn*," I holler.

She glares at me in the rearview. After a long moment, she slows the Lincoln, turns the wheel over, and we're heading south. I exhale hard, unaware I've been holding my breath.

We drive on. Half an hour later, the terrain becomes hilly and much greener, even lush in places. A thick carpet of switchgrass covers the ground and the trees cluster together by the hundreds to form large groves. There's no more dust in the air tickling the inside of my nose, only the living smell of leaves and grass and woody plants. We pass through dense, shady thickets of pecan trees and cottonwoods. Lela steers though the green maze, keeping us on a southward route.

"We oughta see Belton Lake soon," the gringo says. "When we hit the lake's south shore, you can turn us back east and it's a straight shot to 45. About fifty clicks, I reckon."

Minutes later we reach the top of a hill and the lake appears on our left, large and blue and stretching on for miles, its shores crowded with thick greenery. We stop for a moment so the gringo and Lela can pick out the best path around the lake's southern tip. I get out and look across the miles of water. A breeze blows little waves rippling across the surface, sparkling and shimmering in the sunlight. It's been a long time since I've seen this much water. Out west all the lake beds are bone-dry plains of cracked earth.

My mouth is sticky, my throat is dry, and I feel as if several layers of sand and dust cover my face and arms. If we weren't in a rush, I'd be running down the hill to jump in for a nice long soak.

Lela and Rafa exit the car. Lela cranes her neck and stretches, her upper arms bulging with muscles as big around as my thighs. Rafa comes over and stands next to me. Blond ponytail climbs up onto the car's trunk and gazes toward the south, his hands shielding his eyes from the sun.

"Good place to fill up our water," Lela notes, nodding at the lake.

"Yeah," I agree. Maybe we don't have time for a swim, but at least I'll be able to rinse my face off. I move to the trunk to fetch the water jugs.

Behind me Rafa blurts out "Sol," and then I freeze at

the sickening sound of shotgun racks sliding.

I turn and look. A dozen men and women emerge from the brush, each of them armed. Their arms, necks, and faces are covered in tattoos, and the largest man among them has JESUS SAVES branded into his forehead.

Shit. We should have gone north.

CHAPTER 11

They don't speak as they take our weapons and search the Lincoln. The one with the brand on his forehead, who seems to be in charge, takes away my Glock and the collar's remote. He pockets the gun and turns the remote over in his hand, furrowing his brow.

"What's this for?"

I nod toward the gringo. "The dog dollar."

"He your prisoner or something?"

I shrug. "Gets ornery sometimes. That keeps him in line."

Branded forehead looks over at the device around the gringo's neck and narrows his eyes. He hands the remote back to me. "Take it off," he orders.

The Fundies back away from blond ponytail as I key in the release code. "Go ahead," I tell the gringo, waving the remote so he can see the green light, "you can take it off."

The trader hesitates.

"Do it," branded forehead barks.

The gringo reaches up and with slow, careful movements works his thumbs under the collar. He stretches it out and works it up and over his face and forehead, exhaling in relief as it clears the top of his skull.

One of the Fundie women takes it from him, holding it gingerly between her thumb and forefinger, then tosses it into the brush.

"Satan tech," she says and spits on the ground. The others repeat the words and make the same gesture.

"What are they going to do with us?" Rafa asks, his voice trembling.

Nothing, I hope, at least for now. They look like a scouting party, maybe based out of Conroe. And a good scout doesn't shoot a suspicious group of travelers. A good scout collects what he finds and brings it back.

But at the moment they're staring at us with hateful eyes, looking more like crazies thirsty for blood than good scouts.

We stand there, lined up side by side, our hands clasped on top of our heads. Branded forehead walks back and forth, looking us over, trying to decide what to make of us. He stops at Lela, leans forward and narrows his eyes, noticing the Virgin pendant around her neck.

"Mary-worshipper," a woman behind him says as she looks over his shoulder at the pendant. "Idolater." The other Fundies spit and grumble in agreement. He reaches for the pendant. Lela grabs him by the wrist before he can touch it.

Oh, shit.

"No la toques," she growls. Don't touch it.

I glance at Rafa. He grimaces and shakes his head. Blond ponytail's eyes are wide and his mouth hangs open.

The Fundies behind branded forehead rush forward, guns raised to shoulders, fingers on triggers. My heart jumps into my throat.

Branded forehead raises his free hand behind him and waves them off. They stop, back up a couple steps, and lower their guns. He stares at Lela and smiles.

"I saw you fight," he says. "Out west a couple years back." He nods slowly. "I know who you are. And I know who you're with now."

Lela lets go of him and he turns to his crew. "Load 'em up."

"I ain't with 'em," blond ponytail insists. "Them three's together, but I ain't got nothing to do with 'em." A shirtless Fundie with a huge crucifixion tattoo on his back jabs him hard between the shoulder blades with the butt of his shotgun, sending the old trader sprawling face-first to the ground. Then they tie our hands behind our backs and pile us into separate pickup trucks hidden in the nearby brush.

"Get on up there," one of them growls at me from behind, urging me forward with an impatient push in the back. I climb up into the rear seat of an old Ford. A few meters away, I get a glimpse of Rafa in the back of a rusted pickup, his face twisted with fear. Branded forehead gets into the driver's side of the Lincoln, starts the motor, and waves his arm, gesturing for the others to follow him. Half a dozen more trucks emerge from the brush, painted in dark green and brown camouflage, large-caliber guns bolted onto their roofs and gunner's chairs mounted into the truck beds. The Fundies holler and celebrate their catch, firing into the air as they follow the Lincoln down the hill.

My driver, a woman with long black braids and harsh features, won't tell me where we're going. "Find out when ya get there, won't ya?" she answers, then snorts like I have no business asking in the first place. Her forearm has a tattoo of Jesus impaling Satan with a fiery sword. I crane my neck around and see a boy of about eleven wearing old-style aviator goggles and standing in the truck bed. His hands grip the handles of the mounted gun and his head swivels from side to side, keen eyes watching the countryside for danger.

The trucks follow the Lincoln through the forest, cutting a path around the southern tip of the lake, then we turn southeast. My guess is they're taking us to Conroe.

We drive on. An hour passes and then it's late

afternoon and the sun warms the back of my neck. My driver follows close behind the Lincoln.

The caravan moves along at a hurried pace. Every couple minutes, my driver checks the sun's position in the rearview. This is open country, and even a well-armed group like this one wouldn't want to be caught here after dark.

Another hour passes. Behind my back, the skin around my wrists is raw and sensitive from the scratchy rope. It's dusk now and ahead of us the Lincoln's lights come on. My driver follows suit, and around us the headlights of the other trucks blink to life. The darkening outlines of the trees begin to change. The wide, rounded canopies of live oaks and mesquite give way to towering forests of thin pines that stand taller than buildings, squeezed together in tight bunches. The foliage becomes more dense and the caravan has to slow and pick its way through. The truck's large, knobby tires crunch through the thick undergrowth of twigs, ground cover, and fallen pine needles.

The boy behind me in the bed slaps the roof hard and I start, mistaking the sound for a gunshot. "I see 'em," he shouts, slapping the roof again. "Two clicks straight ahead." The woman waves to him outside the driver's window and then mutters, "Thank you, Jesus. Thank you, Lord, for watching over your believers." The first words she's uttered in hours.

Minutes later our caravan pauses at the top of a ridge overlooking a huge clearing crowded with hundreds of tents. Beyond them lies the broad expanse of Lake Conroe, its glassy surface an enormous mirror, reflecting the orange and purple clouds of the sunset sky. Dozens of torches atop tall poles illuminate the camp, and four guard towers made of metal scaffolding stand at opposite corners. Children run and play, adults huddle around campfires and cook dinner. It's like a smaller version of the place I just escaped from.

A spotlight from the closest tower swings in our

direction. I squint as it finds us, bathing the cars and nearby trees in blinding white light. The trucks honk their horns and branded forehead waves his arm out the Lincoln's window. The lights swings away. The Lincoln moves forward, creeping down the ridge, followed by the trucks.

We've arrived at the Fundie camp.

*   *   *

Guns everywhere. That's the first thing I notice when they jostle me out of the truck. Everyone in camp seems to be armed. A mother passes by with an infant clutched to one shoulder, a semiauto rifle strapped to the other. Children who can't be older than eight carry rifles taller than they are, their faces grim and weary like tiny versions of Guzmán's battle-withered soldiers.

The caravan drivers bring over Rafa, Lela, and blond ponytail. We stand with our arms bound behind our backs, looking at each other. Dozens of camp residents pass by, all of them walking in the same direction. Their destination seems to be a wide wooden scaffolding at the edge of camp near the lakeshore. A stage, empty except for a podium, illuminated by one of the searchlights. In front of the stage, a crowd of hundreds sits on the ground, expanding outward with each moment as more arrive.

Fundies glare at us as they pass by.

"Infidels," a woman with face tattoos sneers.

"Heathen devils," cries a man carrying a backpack full of RPGs. He spits at our feet, and a grimy-faced child following him does the same.

My driver asks branded forehead, "Where we taking them?"

"Keep an eye on them for a bit," he says. "Be right back." Then he turns and jogs off toward the stage.

My driver's face bunches up as if she's just been asked to shovel horseshit out of a barn. She turns and lifts her head, pointing her chin at some point behind us.

"Get on over there," she orders, then she pokes me hard in the ribs with the rifle. I clench my teeth as pain shoots through my torso.

They move us over to a small rise away from the crowd, where they sit us down shoulder to shoulder. To my left, Rafa and the trader stare at the ground in front of them. To my right, Lela watches the crowd, her face silent and expressionless.

"Barely made it back in time," says the Fundie standing behind me.

"God's will," my driver says.

"God's will," another one repeats.

We have a clear view of the crowd and the stage. There's a hum of expectation in the air, a tangible excitement in the crowd's restless murmuring. The evening sky is black and moonless, and the only light comes from the torch poles and the white intensity of the spotlight illuminating the stage.

"Send them up," someone shouts, followed by cheers and shrieks of joy.

Young boys shimmy up each of the torch poles, as if racing to see who can reach the top first. Over their shoulders they carry buckets filled with dirt, which spills over the sides as they scramble upwards. The Fundies clap and root them on. The first boy who reaches the top takes his bucket and dumps dirt over the flame, dousing it. The others do the same.

The camp is suddenly dark except for the haloed podium. The cheering dies down to a chatty buzz.

Behind me a voice squeaks, "Water, brothers and sisters?" I look back and there's a girl, maybe about nine, holding a bucket of water with a ladle. Around her wrists and ankles are rusted metal cuffs, connected by chains. A slave.

The Fundies don't speak to her. My driver snatches the ladle from her hand, takes a long slurping drink, sloshing water on our heads, then passes the ladle to the man next to her. After they've all had their fill, my driver tells the slave girl, "Wet their whistle. But don't you dare touch that ladle to their heathen mouths, you hear me?"

The girl comes around in front of us. "Heads up," she says. "Mouths open."

I watch her as she starts with blond ponytail and works her way toward me, pouring a ladle's worth of water into each mouth. There's something about her. Something familiar, though I'm sure I've never seen her before.

She steps in front of me, her chains clattering. She's pale and underfed. Her wrists are raw and blistered from the metal shackles.

She knits her brow at me and tilts her head. A kind of recognition.

"What's your name?" I ask her.

She looks at me, suspicious, and doesn't answer. Then a boot shoves me in the back, sending me sprawling facedown into the dirt.

"Ain't none of your business what her name is," my driver hisses. "Go on now," she barks at the girl, who scampers away and disappears behind a row of tents.

One of the Fundies yanks me up by the arm and puts me back into a sitting position. I spit dirt from my mouth and my back smarts.

On the stage, the spotlight blinks out and we're plunged into total blackness. The crowd gasps.

For a moment, I consider making a run for the woods, but then I feel a rifle barrel press against my back. "Don't you think about going nowhere," my driver says.

The spotlight flashes on again, and a man has appeared behind the podium. The crowd springs to its feet in unison and erupts into a deafening roar. A thousand arms wave in frantic adoration. The man on the stage is large, his middle stretching wider than the podium, and he wears a white suit with a matching wide-brimmed hat. He stands serene and unmoving, his hands holding each side of the podium, waiting for the crowd noise to die down.

Behind me Fundies start speaking in tongues, jabbering nonsense that sounds like the delirious babble of a crazy person.

"Puta madre," Lela murmurs, just loud enough so I can hear. "¿Sabes quién es?"

I nod. I know who it is.

There's only one person who could put the whole camp into a mad frenzy like this.

Reverend Zachariah Wright, the founder and sole leader of the Fundie faith, raises his hand and the crowd falls instantly silent.

If we were fucked before, we're double-fucked now.

CHAPTER 12

"Brothers and sisters in Christ," the pastor begins, "I want to tell you the tale of the Republic."

Wright's tone is slow, measured, and warm, a grandfather telling a bedtime story.

"It's a tale of pride and greed and failure, one you may have heard before, but it's worth retelling, for we all have a part to play in this tale." He gestures for the audience to sit down. "Please take a seat, brothers and sisters, and be so kind as to lend me your attention for a few precious moments."

The audience sits. I've never heard so many people make so little noise. It's eerie, unsettling. As Wright pauses and waits for the crowd to settle in, the only sounds in the night air are chirps of crickets from the forest and throaty croaks from frogs around the lake.

"Long ago, many years before any of us were here, long before our grandparents were born, a catastrophe befell our world. The followers of Mohamed rose up and burned the fields of oil, the black gold upon which the wealth of nations depended. And without it, the world withered and suffered like a man with no food to eat.

"But the Lord our God looked kindly upon the States,

blessing it with an abundance of energy, with endless fields of fuel for machines and factories and homes. Our manna came not from Heaven, brothers and sisters, but from the rich earth beneath our feet. Praise the Lord."

"Praise the Lord," the crowd repeats.

Natural gas as underground manna. Now there's a version I never read in the history books.

"And the markets rewarded this bounty," the reverend continues. "The value of our gas soared to the heavens, higher than the eagle's flight, higher than the sun at noon." Wright's arms stretch skyward. "And the gas traders prospered, selling our blessed energy far and wide to all the nations of the world."

The reverend pauses as he lowers his arms. "But there were those who were seduced," he says, his voice dropping low, "by such easy wealth, those who were cursed with the sins of gluttony and greed. No matter how much they had, they longed for more. More, more, more. More houses, more cars, more possessions. Even as their wealth surpassed the riches of Solomon, they still longed for more. And when money and treasures could not fill the emptiness of their souls, they conspired to become lords of their own land."

Someone cries out, "Infidels," followed by grumbles and hisses from the audience. The reverend shows his palms and the noise subsides.

"'Why must we render unto Caesar?' these gas barons asked. 'Why should we not control our own destiny? Why should we not have our own nation to govern as our sovereign will guides us?'"

In other words, now that oil's out of the picture, and we're sitting on a mountain of natgas money, why not give Washington, D.C. the old middle finger and start our own country like we've always wanted to?

"And the wicked men persuaded the people of our great land with lies and empty promises of a paradise where all would prosper. And the goodhearted people trusted them and believed them, foolishly placing their faith in these false prophets. And when the ties with the States were severed, the people cheered and celebrated their glorious Secession. And so the Republic of Texas was born."

But the party didn't last long. The best parties never do.

"Then God looked down from Heaven at the people He had blessed with such bounty, and seeing what they had created, He wept. He wept at the naked avarice of His people, at the grievousness of their sins. And the Lord laid His hands upon the markets, bringing His divine judgment upon this land, its leaders, and those who followed them."

Laid His hands upon the markets. Another interesting interpretation. In our histories back home in the Panhandle, scholars disagreed on what caused the global crash of natural gas prices. Some said it was a glut of supply, some said it was market speculation gone haywire, others blamed conspiracies of shadow governments and secret organizations.

Add divine intervention to the list, I suppose.

But whatever the cause, after that pretty much the whole world's economy collapsed, ushering in a period known as the Great Carbon Crisis. The Crisis, for short. And the newly formed Republic of Texas, with its overreliance on natural gas, went bust within months.

Wright moves his history forward, weaving God and Satan and Bible verses into the brutal post-Secession relations between the U.S. and the Republic. The mass migration of starving, penniless Texans during the Crisis finds its analogy in the story of Adam and Eve. The sad march northward in search of food and work becomes a modern day expulsion from paradise.

I have to bite the inside of my cheek to keep from smirking. *Texas as Eden?* The reverend's clearly never been to El Paso.

Reverend Wright leaves out much of the politics, skipping over how the sudden flood of millions of immigrants pushed the tense relations between the States and the Republic to the breaking point. He also doesn't mention how U.S. politicians responded to the "Texan refugee problem" by passing the Emergency Frontier Containment Act, sealing up the States' southern border with a barrier wall and hundreds of airborne drones on constant vigil. And he leaves out the part about the impact of the U.S.'s trade embargo, how it crushed any hope of the Republic's financial recovery, even as natgas prices began to creep slowly back upward.

No, he mentions none of these things, because it doesn't serve his purpose to cast the Americans as the villains in his story. That role's reserved for the Bullock clan, the evildoers who built an empire on the ashes of a dead state. Guzmán's speeches, the longer ones he saves for holidays, follow the same general narrative, only without all the Jesus and hellfire.

Wright goes on. "And during this great Crisis, a time of great suffering and need, God smiled upon the good people of Texas, shining the light of his favor upon those who would not leave our precious land." As he says this, Wright removes something from his jacket pocket and raises it high above his head. Between his thumb and forefinger he holds a natgas pellet. The audience groans in unison, as if he's just reached into his pants and pulled out a turd.

"And how did they use this gift of providence, these Bullocks?" he booms. "Did they take this seed and harvest its bounty to raise their brothers and sisters out of poverty?"

A few in the crowd shout, "No!"

"Did they feed the starving?"

The audience and the guards behind me cry out in unison. "NO!"

"Did they clothe the naked?"

"NO!"

"No, brothers and sisters, they did not. Like the money

changers in Herod's Temple, Bullock greed knew no bounds. They traded with heathen nations, hoarded their wealth, and built themselves a shining city with glass and metal towers reaching to the heavens. They hardened their hearts and turned their backs on God. They learned nothing from the great Crisis, selfishly abusing the Lord's bounty to enrich themselves and their friends. These self-anointed few prospered while we, the multitudes, lived in agony, watching our children die of hunger, waiting for the day of our salvation."

Wright's account of the Bullocks' rise to power weaves the divine into every detail. It's a study in utter horseshit, a far cry from the histories I read back home or the books Guzmán lent me from his collection. But the one truth common to all these versions is the how the tech behind natgas pellets changed everything.

Before there were pellets, natural gas storage and transportation was costly and dangerous. You either stored it under high pressure in containers, which had an unfortunate tendency to explode, or you froze it at super-cold temperatures until it liquefied, a tedious, expensive process. But then some genius Bullock gas engineer came up with something new.

This engineer took an old pre-Crisis process for making carbon pellets—basically little chemical sponges that stored dense amounts of natgas—re-engineered it, and improved it tenfold. All of a sudden the Bullocks could store more natural gas in a bucketful of pellets, safely and at room temperature, than they could have previously across a dozen heavy storage facilities. Those little rat turd cylinders didn't look like much, but they gave the Bullock clan (whose avarice knew no bounds, brothers and sisters!) an historic commercial opportunity. And they didn't waste any time cashing in, loading up huge tanker ships and sailing them out of the Gulf of Mexico, selling countless tons of pellets to gas-poor nations in South America and the Caribbean. Even with depressed global natgas prices and a trade embargo with the States, they accumulated a vast fortune in a few years. And with the help of robots and AIs smuggled in from the U.S. and shipped in from China, the Bullock clan built a sleek modern capital in Dallas for themselves and their loyalists. A jewel of a city sitting atop the garbage pile of a failed state. A diamond on a dung heap.

The reverend goes on, his voice rising with each dramatic peak, then floating downward, soft as a feather back to earth. Crescendo followed by falling action, like the Beethoven symphonies Mama used to listen to, slowly building in waves toward a climactic movement. The spellbound Fundies watch him in awe, and he plays them like some giant instrument, arousing screams of righteous indignation from them in one moment, reducing them to tears in the next. Watching him work the crowd so effortlessly, I begin to understand how he's built up such a massive following in so short a time.

"The Dallasites blaspheme and fornicate and worship their mountains of money as false idols while their soulless machines clean for them, cook for them, do everything for them. They live a life of wanton pleasure, but their time is coming to an end, their judgment is near." Wright looks up to the sky and spreads his arms wide.

"Brothers and sisters, the Lord has spoken to me. In a voice clear and beautiful and holy, He has revealed His sacred plan to His humble servant. He has blessed me with His vision."

The audience fidgets and whispers in anticipation as the reverend takes a long pause, gazing skyward, his arms outstretched, palms up.

"WE ARE THE CHOSEN ONES," he shouts, "AND WE SHALL DELIVER HIS VENGEANCE!"

A roar erupts from the crowd. Everyone leaps to their feet and frantically waves their arms back and forth. Behind me, our watchers explode into tongues.

Reverend Zachariah Wright stands and watches the

delirium in front of him. Even from a distance I can see a satisfied grin stretching across his face.

Branded forehead appears near the edge of the crowd, then scrambles up the rise toward us. He has to shout to be heard over the raucous din of screeching hallelujahs. "Bring 'em round to the reverend's tent. He wants to see 'em."

I swallow hard and look over at Lela. For the first time since I've known her, I see real fear in her eyes.

*　　*　　*

The four of us sit on the floor of a large square tent, waiting, our hands still awkwardly tied behind our backs. A pair of shirtless, hulking Fundie guards stand nearby, their torsos covered with tattoos of Bible verses arranged in neat lines, making their chests look like muscled book pages. They hold semiauto rifles and watch us with cold stares. The tent's hardwood floor is spotless and polished, and a large, ornate desk sits on the other side of the tent. Cherubs carved into legs of dark mahogany blow on trumpets.

It's warm and humid and outside there's the familiar din of camp: children squealing as they play and mothers calling after them, telling them not to wander off.

No one speaks until Rafa says, "What do you think they're going to do with—"

He's cut off by a knee in the back from one of the guards. Rafa hunches forward, coughing and gasping as Reverend Wright enters the tent followed by branded forehead.

Wrights knits his brow at Rafa and removes his hat, revealing a pink, hairless pate. He tosses the hat on the desk. Without his spotlight, stage, and adoring throng, he seems smaller somehow.

Wright turns to branded forehead. "Which one?"

Branded forehead points to the gringo. "That one,

Reverend."

Wright motions to the trader. "Take him."

A guard comes over and yanks blond ponytail to his feet. He removes a hunting knife from his belt and saws through the trader's bonds. His hands freed, the gringo rubs his wrists, then nods at the reverend. "Thank you, sir," he gushes. The guard then leads him out of the tent.

Shit. A tightening deep in my stomach tells me we've just been fucked over. Who knows what the slimy bastard told his driver on the way here, what kind of deal he might have cut to save his ass?

I glance over at Lela. She stares, expressionless, at the floor in front of her outstretched legs.

"Give it to me," the reverend says, and branded forehead passes him a small burlap bag. Wright tosses it on the floor in front of me.

My stash of hierba. *Double shit.*

"So the rumors are true," Wright says. "You're Guzmán's witch, the one they say can spot lies?"

I gaze at the bag, numb, unable to find words to answer.

Wright's boots thud against the floor as he approaches. He leans over me. "I got people watching his camp, young lady, just like he's got people watching mine."

I look up at him. Small green eyes sunken behind puffy bags of skin stare back at me. A reptile's eyes. The things I've heard about him and his zealots pop into my thoughts. Enemies burned alive, dozens at a time in huge pyres. Nonbelievers tortured, their skin peeled off in strips until they repent. They call them Fundie "conversions."

The reverend shakes his head. "And here I thought it was a made-up story. Some curveball that old desert snake was throwing to confound the Bullocks."

His reptile eyes narrow into slits. "You're a long way from your patrón, aren't you, jovencita?"

When I don't answer, he scoots the bag toward me with his boot. "I'd like to see this talent of yours for myself."

I shake my head. Wright frowns and nods at one of the guards, who then starts toward me. Lela scoots between us, blocking his way. "No la toques," she hisses.

No, Lela, don't.

The guard shoves her in the chest with the heel of his boot, sending her sprawling backwards. She lands facedown and tries to wriggle back up. The other guard stomps on her between her shoulders and flattens her back down. He pushes his shotgun's barrel against the base of her skull.

"Stop it, stop," I shout. "All right, I'll show you."

Wright nods again and the guards grab Lela by the shoulders and lift her into a sitting position.

"I have to eat something first," I say. "It works better that way."

They untie my hands and lift me into a folding chair facing the desk. Wright tells them to bring food, and a minute later the slave who brought us water earlier enters the tent with a large loaf of bread tucked under one arm. She tears off a chunk and hands it to me, keeping her eyes turned down, her tattered clothes little more than rags, chains jangling from her wrists.

I tilt my head toward Rafa and Lela. "My friends need some, too."

"They can eat later," Wright snaps.

The girl places the water bucket on the floor, steals a curious glance at me, then turns and hurries out.

I break off a piece of bread and eat, staring at the door flap for some moments after she leaves, again feeling the same odd sensation. Like I've met her before, but haven't. Like I know her, but don't.

One of the guards hands the bag of hierba to me. After a couple gulps of water, I take a handful and begin to chew it, wincing at the sharp, bitter taste I've never managed to get used to.

I feel everyone's eyes on me. "How long does it take?"

the reverend asks.

"About half an hour."

"All right, then." The reverend rubs his hands together. "I'd like to show you something first."

The reverend and I exit the tent, escorted by two new guards carrying semiauto rifles. I look back, worried for Rafa and Lela. The reverend notices the look on my face and chuckles.

"Don't worry, young lady. They'll be there when we get back."

We walk through camp. The flickering torchlight reveals families settling down for the night, dousing cooking fires and wiping off dinner plates. Dogs yelp and whine for leftover scraps. Groups of old men huddle around barrel fires, murmuring to one another and warming their hands against the evening chill.

We have to pause often for handshakes and chats with doe-eyed followers. Wright handles most of them with quick, polite hellos or god-bless-yous. He lingers only for the women, the fawning ones with fuck-me eyes and an idiot's easy laughter, who stand close enough to (oops!) rub their tits against him. I think of Guzmán, how he would have already had two handfuls of ass by now, scanning the area for the nearest empty tent.

The reverend's in his element. He has a comfortable, seemingly effortless charm, as clever with people as the trader is with the truth. The locals stop whatever they're doing to greet him and compliment him on his sermon. Then when they notice me, the stranger who arrived with bound hands and a rifle at her back, their flattery stops and their bright faces fade into suspicion and wariness.

Eventually we make our way to the edge of camp, where things become much more shabby and rundown. The tents here are old and threadbare, their frayed edges fluttering in the breeze.

Ahead of us, a long line of people snakes around a row of tents. As we approach, heads turn to look at us. Tired faces, sunken eyes, bony hands and fingers curled around empty metal soup bowls. Malnourished children gaze up at us, little skeletons with hollow cheeks and expressionless faces.

The smell of food hits me. Some kind of stew, maybe squirrel.

"Thank you, Reverend," a woman blathers, then covers her face with her hand and sobs. At her legs two toddlers look up, bewildered.

"Be well, sister," he says, laying his hand on her shoulder.

Others offer Wright their thanks, though their faces don't smile and their broken bodies move with a painful slowness. Like the first woman, many break down in tears.

It's a food line. Bare feet shuffle forward in the dirt, slowly approaching a large cast iron kettle, where two women stand on either side and ladle steaming servings into proffered bowls. Past the kettle, hundreds of ragged people sit in a small clearing, eating in total silence, each a study in concentration, focused on the careful business of eating without losing a drop.

Refugees.

"Every day they arrive from every corner of the Republic," the reverend tells me, "each one with a story of suffering that'd break your heart, young lady."

The smell of the stew sharpens and expands. I notice traces of cumin and onions that weren't there a moment before. The hierba's starting to open my senses, sharpen my perception.

Wright turns and looks at me, motioning toward the crowd in the clearing. "This is the legacy of the Bullocks' reign. This is the misery they've brought upon us."

I blink, noticing the details of his face, suddenly aware of all the little creases in the skin and, underneath them, the muscles that contract and relax, shaping his expressions, revealing his inner self. A kind of curtain draws open, exposing the details of the room inside.

"Poor souls," he says, turning his gaze again to the crowd. "So many poor, lost souls."

His face, his voice, his body language betray a pure, unselfish concern, utterly and unmistakably sincere.

I stare at the man, at the folds of worry running across his forehead. Is it possible his image as a bloodthirsty cult leader is more rumor than fact? Or maybe it's a deliberate invention, like Guzmán's bullshit projection of a modern-day revolutionary, concocted to win over followers and strike fear into the hearts of his enemies.

Maybe this fat preacher's no more of a monster than Guzmán. Or the Bullocks, for that matter.

The benefit of my doubt doesn't last more than a moment. Behind me there's a clanking noise, and then the slave girl walks past, bearing four buckets that hang from a pole bent across her shoulders. Water for the refugees. Her feet walk a crooked path like a drunk as she battles to keep her balance against her heavy, sloshing burden. Half a dozen more children in chains, boys and girls, none of them older than ten, follow her with more buckets of water.

I nod toward them. "And what about *those* lost souls?"

Wright frowns. "The keys to the kingdom are not for everyone, my dear. The sins of their fathers were great, and they must share the burden of punishment."

"They're *children*." *You fucking bastard*. I don't say the last part, but he must see the disgust in my expression.

"This is our way," he says. "The Lord's way. It's not your place to sit in judgment." Scorn twists his face and I feel anger bubbling under the surface, hot and volatile. He doesn't like to be challenged, least of all by a *young lady*.

He stares at me. There's a chaos behind his eyes: wild thoughts, dark and dreadful. Horrible monsters hidden by shadows.

I swallow, recalling the fear on Lela's face. I turn away, not wanting to see more, and the slave girl is standing in front of me.

"Water, ma'am?"

I kneel down. "Please." She hands me the ladle and watches me as I drink. "What's your name?"

She takes a cautious glance at Wright, then answers, "Steffa."

The hierba's peaking. Now I can see what I couldn't before. Now the familiarity makes sense.

Little Steffa's a reader like me.

CHAPTER 13

Wright grabs my arm and tells me my half hour's up. He pulls me back in the direction we came from. I glance back at Steffa. She stands and watches us, her buckets on the ground beside her manacled feet.

A reader. *Another* reader. Mama told me there could be others out there, though she wouldn't have bet on it. *We're practitioners of a lost art*, Mama used to say, then she'd smile in a kind of sad way and tap my forehead.

The woman who trained Mama in true seeing died long before I was born. Marineth was a teacher in Mama's school in Dallas. She saw Mama's gift—I suppose the same way I saw it in Steffa—and took it upon herself to teach Mama how to use hierba, how to develop her reading skills. She told Mama the gift was unique to women, and in rare cases like me and Mama, it was passed from mother to daughter. There wasn't much history to learn. There was no secret society, no underground sisterhood, no ancient instruction manual passed from teacher to pupil. If there ever had been one, it had long since been lost.

Mama's lessons were kept secret from her family and from the other teachers at school. Marineth warned her people would fear her power to see what they couldn't, and some might even want to hurt her.

When we return to the tent, there's one guard still there, but Rafa and Lela are gone. "Sit." Wright gestures to the chair in front of the desk.

"Where are my friends?" I ask. The guard grabs my arm and jostles me into the chair.

Wright sits and folds his hands on the desktop. "Your friends are fine."

Not lying. They're okay for now.

"I still don't know your name, young lady," he says.

"Soledad."

"Soledad." He smiles. "It suits you." He puts one of his hands behind his back. "All right, Soledad, tell me how many fingers I'm holding up."

"It doesn't work like that," I tell him, resisting the urge to roll my eyes.

"Ah, yes, of course. Let me put it another way. I'm holding out two fingers behind my back. Yes or no?"

"No."

"Four, then."

I shake my head.

"You're right. It's neither two nor four. It's three."

"Yes."

He tilts his head and narrows his eyes, trying to figure out what to make of me. We do it again, then another time. After five rounds he's still not convinced. I can read it on his face. He thinks I'm getting lucky or maybe it's some kind of carnival trick. I try to keep my cool, but with each stupid repetition I feel my patience ebbing away. Back at Guzmán's camp, I was revered, feared, even hated. But I was never doubted, never looked at like some scammer with a trick deck of cards.

It never fails. The biggest bullshitters always think they're getting bullshitted too.

By the tenth round, I can't take it any longer. He puts his hand behind his back, and before he can speak I say,

"You don't have any fingers held up this time. You stopped trying to calculate the odds of me guessing the answers three rounds ago because the math got too hard, and you have a headache because you skipped dinner before your sermon."

The reverend's mouth drops open. His eyes go wide and the brows, once furrowed in doubt, now lift in amazement. He nods, and every trace of disbelief fades from his face. I silently curse myself for being so stupid, for revealing so much.

Wright leans back in his chair and whistles. "Well, now, that's quite a gift you have. Indeed, quite a gift." He nods toward the guard. "My men thought for sure that trader was making it all up. You know how those freelancers are. Can't trust a thing they say." He strains to keep his face impassive and calm, but behind his eyes I sense a sudden, anxious scattering. Alarm bells ringing.

He tells the guard to wait outside. The guard hesitates a moment, but obeys.

"Why are you running away from Guzmán?" Wright asks.

I don't answer.

"I'm sure you have your reasons. I can't imagine anyone wanting to keep such company. He is a wicked man whose sins are far too many to count."

Lie. His voice holds no conviction, no sincerity. His hatred for Guzmán is nothing more than words.

"They have refugees at his camp? Refugees like you saw here?"

I nod.

"Yes, of course they do." He purses his lips. "These are the times we live in, child. Starvation, lawlessness, moral corruption. Neighbor turned against neighbor, fighting for survival."

Wright waves his hand at some point beyond the tent, beyond the camp. "They refuse to share their hoarded wealth, the Dallasites, though they have more than enough to feed and clothe their fellow Texans a thousand times over. What sort of evil has grabbed hold of their hearts that lets them live in such luxury, safe and carefree in their protected city while their brothers and sisters starve in this blighted land?"

He leans forward. "But their time is coming to an end. We're on a sacred mission, the Lord's people, and he's sent you here to help us."

I blink. "Help you?"

"Of course. The Lord knows that desert snake desires to rule this land, but He won't let that happen. That's why He set you free, why our people found you. His hand has guided your journey, young Soledad. He *wants* you to help us in our holy war against the Dallasites, can't you see that?"

Lies, all lies. He doesn't believe a word of it, but he's so confident, so assured from years of preaching, from thousands of cheering converts, that for a moment he forgets who he's talking to and what I can see.

And what I see is a con man. A hustler selling a cure-all to the desperate. A peddler of snake oil.

I also see fear. He's afraid of me, of my power. I've sensed the same thing a thousand times from Guzmán's men and from strangers in camp. But however much I worry Wright, his curiosity outweighs it. He sees a use for me and already his mind is working out plans and possibilities, how he might take advantage of this new tool he's unexpectedly stumbled across in the forest.

That's what I am to these men. To Guzmán, to Wright, to those nameless freelancers who took me away. To all of them. I'm a payday or a tool to be leveraged. A secret weapon to use against their enemies.

I see Steffa out there somewhere, struggling to walk with her heavy water buckets, her feet chafed and raw from the rusted metal, her lifeless eyes.

Fuck these men and their power trips. I won't help another slaver.

"You're lying," I say.

Wright's face tightens up as if he's just been splashed with cold water. "Pardon me?" he sputters. "Lying about what?"

"About all of it. Everything."

His expression drops, like a poker player who suddenly realizes he doesn't have the winning hand.

"You think I can't see it?" I sneer. "That dark panic that never goes away, that thing in the back of your mind you hide from everyone? That fear of death?" I grab the edge of the desk and lean forward. "How do you do it? How do you tell them there's some nice man waiting for them up in the clouds, who'll take them into his loving arms after all this mortal suffering and misery? How can you do it when you don't even believe it yourself?"

Wright takes a long, shaky breath. I brace myself for his eruption, for the furious explosion building up behind his eyes. But it doesn't come. Instead, he swallows down his emotion, maintaining a surprising amount of control for someone who'd love nothing more than to reach across the desk and strangle me. Then without a word he gets up and leaves the tent.

For some minutes I sit there, staring at the top of the desk, wondering how badly I've fucked things up. Then outside there's a commotion, an excited clamor of voices. It's only a few at first, but it spreads quickly, growing into a chatty buzz that seems to come from everywhere. Shadows pass by the tent like dark ghosts, all rushing in the same direction. I can't make out any words, but voices squeak and strain with something close to hysteria. After a few more minutes the din fades and camp is quiet and still again.

A guard enters and yanks me out of the chair, hustling me outside. Reverend Wright stands a short distance away, waiting for us. The guard urges me forward, and we follow Wright. The reverend stomps through the dirt, disregarding the outstretched hands of his followers, ignoring their hellos, leaving a wave of awkwardness and confusion in his wake. The guard squeezes my upper arm, and I stumble forward until we arrive at a clearing near the lakeside.

A dozen or so torches on top of tall poles form a large circle, illuminating a crowd standing around its perimeter. No one speaks as the assembly parts to make way for Wright. There's a grim expectation floating in the air, thick and palpable, and the expressions of the crowd remind me of Guzmán's men when they're waiting for my judgment after a read.

I swallow hard. Someone's going to die.

The guard holds me at the front edge of the crowd, where branded forehead joins us and grabs my other arm. To my right, two guards hold Rafa. His face is bloody and one eye is swollen shut. Tracks of tears run down his cheeks. He sees me and shakes his head. What I see in his face makes my stomach sick.

Where is she?

Wright reaches the center of the circle, removes his hat, and clears his throat. Next to his boots is Lela's head. She's buried in the dirt up to her neck, breathing heavily, her face as bruised and beaten as Rafa's. Around the edge of the crowd I notice piles of rocks, stacked neatly. The woman who drove me here stands next to one, holding a fist-sized stone in each hand, her face beaming with bloodlust, waiting for Wright to give the word.

Oh, God.

"Then the Lord spoke to Moses," Wright begins, "and said, 'Bring the one who has cursed outside the camp, and let all who heard him lay their hands on his head; then let all the congregation stone him.' Leviticus twenty-four."

A murmur of approval ripples through the crowd. Lela's labored breath blows clouds of dirt in front of her face.

"LELA," I scream, trying to squirm free of the guards' grip. Then to Wright: "I'll help you. Don't do this, please."

Wright ignores me. Branded forehead elbows my ribs to shut me up, sending the air rushing from my lungs.

"She has denied the one true way," Wright booms, spreading his arms wide, "and refuses to repent."

I gasp, doubled over. I try to scream but the only thing that comes from my mouth is a sputtering noise and a spray of spit.

My breath comes back and I yell, "I'll help you, you hear me? I'll do what you want." Branded forehead hits me again, this time in my belly, and I drop to my knees. He looks down at me and shakes his head. There's concern behind his eyes. He's afraid for me.

He leans down and whispers. "You keep yelling like that, he's gonna put you out there too."

I look at Lela, my sight blurry with tears. *I'm sorry, I'm so sorry.*

Wright goes on, elaborating Lela's sins of idolatry and Mary-worship, pacing around the circle like a circus ringleader. He struggles to keep his face grim, his voice somber. He's enjoying himself, savoring each moment, the murderous bastard.

He turns and fixes his eyes on me. Without words, he tells me this is what waits for me. And for Rafa too. He wants me to watch, to see how I'll end up if I don't help him.

There's no bargain I can make. Nothing I can do to save her.

"May God have mercy on your soul," he says, then he bows his head. After a moment he mouths *amen* and puts his hat on. The crowd parts for him as he walks forward, and then he's gone, leaving the mob to their work.

The crowd surges to life. Greedy hands snatch stones from the piles. I look over at Rafa and he's sobbing, his head hanging.

"Heathen," someone shouts, and from the corner of my eye I see a large rock flying through the air. It lands close and sprays Lela's face with dirt as it thumps into the earth and rolls harmlessly away. In the next moment the crowd roars and the air is suddenly filled with hurled stones. I turn away and hear a sickening thud of flesh. The din of angry shouts and shrieks grows louder, more frenzied. My legs go numb and I collapse to the ground.

Branded forehead picks me up to my knees and puts his mouth near my ear. "Look at her," he says, raising his voice against the wild cries.

Another thud, followed by cheers.

"Look at her," he repeats.

"I can't."

He kneels and grabs my shoulders. "Listen to me." His voice is urgent, pleading. "What do you want her to see in her last moments? These monsters or your face? What do you think *she* wants to see?"

Oh, God.

With his help I stand, my legs shaking, and I look at her. Her scalp is ripped open in several places and blood pours down the side of her head. One side of her face is already purple and swollen.

"LELA!" I shout. She hears me and cranes her neck until our eyes meet. "I'm sorry," I yell, but I don't know if she hears me over the deafening roar.

Her lips are swollen and bloody. Everything slows down and I feel as if I'm with her now, out there buried in the dirt, barbarous screaming faces all around me. I can see her thoughts, feel them like I'm inside her head.

There's no fear for herself, no panic at her looming end. Her thoughts focus only on me. *On me.* She worries what's going to happen when she's not around.

Who will take care of her girl now? Who's going to keep her safe?

There's a loud crack, then the world blinks away and her mind goes black.

She's gone. My Lela's gone.

CHAPTER 14

After the stoning, they dragged me to this tent and tossed me inside. I don't know how long I've been sitting here, my legs outstretched, staring at the Virgin pendant in my hand. Branded forehead slipped it into my pocket when no one was looking, his eyes full of shame and pity. I run my finger over the folds in Mary's dress, worn smooth by countless good luck touches.

She's gone. I felt it when the big stone knocked her out, felt it when she stopped breathing and slipped into darkness. I still can't believe it, even though the only image in my head is that of her lifeless face, grotesque and swollen, her mouth hanging open. I can't believe she's gone.

Lela. Big, strong Lela. In three years she hardly left my side. Always there, never more than a few steps away. A world without her doesn't seem possible. My guardian shadow, watching over me with worried eyes. No, it was more than worry. In those last few moments I saw the whole of her, the entirety of her soul. All the childhood pain and suffering, the miserable nightmare of her life before Guzmán. What strength she had, what toughness. And love. There was so much love, but so few she dared to give it to. Only two: me and Guzmán. And only one of us had done anything to deserve it.

And she knew about me. Somehow she knew what happened after the freelancers took me away. I never told her what happened, what they did to me. But she knew.

Oh, Lela! Why didn't you knock me out again when you had the chance? You should have dragged my selfish, stubborn ass back to camp. Why didn't you? And why didn't I listen to you? I should have flipped off the safety when I had the gun to my head, pulled the trigger and spared her from this madness, from this fool's errand.

And that's exactly what I've been: a fool, hanging on to the fantasy of Mama and Papi living a miserable existence without me, praying for my return.

I wish I'd never seen Abner.

Lela, I'm so sorry.

"Get in there," someone says from outside the tent, and then Rafa bursts through the door flap, shoved from behind. He stumbles toward me and I catch him by his shoulders. His hands are still tied behind his back.

"You okay?" I help him sit.

He nods. "Yeah." His face is red and splotched from crying. It's hard for me to look at him. The hierba's fading, but enough of the effect lingers for me to feel his anguish, a horrible new wound that will never fully heal. Rafa's seen death before, but never like this. Guzmán killed plenty, but always reluctantly, and never without a reason. Death was never celebrated in don Flaco's camp, never made into a cheering public spectacle.

"Savages," he mutters, staring at the floor. "Mindless savages."

There's nothing I can say, no words that will help him. There's something different in his face, in his manner. Something more than sadness for Lela. It's like a part of him, some soft boyish part of him is gone, ripped away by Lela's death and replaced with a heaviness. A light's been doused, never to shine again.

"I'm sorry, Rafa."

He looks up at me. "For what?"

"Everything. For everything."

He shakes his head. "Don't be. We didn't have to come. We wanted to help."

I wonder. I think back to how ruthlessly I seduced him, how insistent I was.

He looks up at me, as if he knows what I'm thinking. "I could have said no."

Lie. I look away from him, shame washing over me.

Shouts from outside the tent, some distance away. I hear surprise, fear in the voices. "What's going on out there?"

Rafa shrugs. "I don't know. There was something happening out in the woods."

"Like what?"

"Don't know," Rafa says. "They brought me here before I could see anything."

More shouts, closer this time. Shadows dart back and forth across the tent walls. I catch a few words and phrases.

"What's happening?" a woman cries.

"Get down!" a man shouts. "GET DOWN!"

A popping crack of automatic gunfire sends Rafa and me diving to our bellies onto the dirt. Shrieks and cries of panic erupt all around us.

"Stay down," I yell. Outside, the camp explodes into a chaos of gunfire and screaming. More shots burst out, louder and closer than before. Returning fire.

"What's happening?" Rafa shouts.

"I don't know." My heart races, thoughts scramble.

We lie there for a minute, listening to the growing panic all around us. Then a pair of boots appears next to my face. I look up and branded forehead stands over us holding a hunting knife.

He kneels and cuts Rafa's bonds, then pulls us to our feet.

"It's a raid," he hollers.

"A raid? But who would—"

"We don't know, but you have to get out of here." He takes my hand and places something into it. A car key.

"There's a Humvee parked on the ridge where we came into camp. You remember?" I stare at the key, stunned. He repeats, louder, "Do you remember?"

I nod, and then he grabs both of us by the arm and pulls us out of the tent.

We step out into total mayhem. People run screaming in every direction, tripping over each other, scrambling on all fours to keep out the line of fire.

Branded forehead points. "It's that way. Go straight that way and you'll see it."

More gunfire. "I have to go," he shouts. He's loading shells into his gun. "Get of here now while you still can."

"Thank you," I yell. More shots ring out and I duck in reflex.

He nods. "Your friend...I'm sorry about your friend." He slides the rack on his shotgun and says, "God bless." Then he leaves us, taking off at a run toward the forest.

Another burst of gunfire rips through the air. A woman in front of us drops to the ground, a ghastly exit wound oozing from what's left of the back of her head; the baby she was holding goes tumbling across the dirt. A man picks up the baby and runs, clutching the child to his chest.

"Rafa," I shout, shoving the key into his hand, "go to the truck. I'll be right there."

"What? Where are you going?"

"The girl with the water. I'm going to get her."

Rafa shakes his head. "There's no time, Sol. We have to go now." He grabs my arms and pulls. I yank it free.

"Two minutes. Just give me two minutes." I'm already running toward the sound of the gunfire, knifing my way through screaming pandemonium. I look back over my shoulder and Rafa's staring at me, his face contorted with indecision. He frowns, turns, and runs in the direction of the Humvee.

Seconds later I'm at the clearing where I saw the refugees. I look around but I don't see her. The kettle of stew and the table it sat on are knocked over. The clearing's nearly empty except for a small group of people huddled together in a ditch, their faces frozen into expressions of terror. One of them, an old man, spots me and stands on wobbly legs. He reaches out to me and opens his mouth to say something. A short burst of gunfire crackles from the tree line behind him, and he crumbles to the ground. In the next moment, muzzle flashes light up the forest around the clearing. I hit the dirt and take cover behind the large kettle. Bullets thud and twang as they hit and bounce off the thick cast iron. I keep my belly tight to the ground.

Green tracers whistle past my head, clang against the kettle. I'm pinned down. I crane my neck around and look behind me for a way out, and I see her.

Steffa.

She's standing behind a torch post, her face poking out just enough to see me. Her eyes are wide with fear. A shot strikes the post above her head, sends splinters flying. For a moment she's gone and I think she's been hit, but then she peeks around the other side of the post. I wave for her to get down and her face disappears again.

A wide stretch of open space separates us. She's too far away. I'd be lucky to make it three steps before getting hit. Dirt flies up all around me in rooster tails. Bullets whiz over my head. I hunker down, my body flinching with each bell clang when a bullet strikes the kettle.

From the tree line someone shouts, "Fire in the hole!" I bury my face in the dirt, squeeze my eyes shut, clapping my hands over my ears. An explosion sends a shock wave through my body and a bright flash of white penetrates my eyelids. My ears buzz with a high-pitched ring and large chunks of earth rain down on my back. I lift my head and open my eyes. All around me there's a cloud of fine dirt floating in the air, kicked up by the grenade. My breath comes in shaky gasps. I move my legs, arms, checking myself for injuries. Except for a throbbing head and ringing ears, I'm not hurt.

And then I notice the kettle's gone. The blast from the grenade sent it flying. I look around and spot it, far behind me, somehow still intact and on its side, rocking back and forth.

The cloud of dirt hiding me from view is already disappearing. In a couple seconds I'll be an easy target.

"SOL!"

I turn and see the Humvee, halfway between me and the torch pole. Rafa's behind the wheel, leaning over the front seat and holding the passenger door open. "Come on," he shouts. "Run!"

I spring to my feet and sprint to the vehicle. A shot from somewhere behind me pops like a firecracker. Then another one, then more. The Humvee's front blinker explodes into tiny fragments.

Instead of diving onto the passenger seat, I run around the front of the vehicle and past it.

"What are you doing?" Rafa shouts.

I scramble to a stop behind the torch post, where the girl's lying flat to the ground. I scoop her up in my arms and carry her to the Humvee, her legs dangling back and forth as I run. I yank open the back door and toss her onto the floorboard, throwing myself on top of her. Bullets ping and ricochet around us. Rafa stomps on the gas, sending me and the girl tumbling.

Rafa steers the Humvee into the forest, away from the chaos of gunshots and explosions. Minutes pass and the light from the camp's torches fades, their flickering orange replaced by the pale glow of a full moon. The sounds of the skirmish fade behind us, until there's only the crunch of pine needles under the tires.

"Are you hurt?" Rafa asks. "Shot?"

"No, I'm okay."

Underneath me Steffa whimpers. I move up to the seat and notice she's no longer shackled.

"What happened to your chains?"

"They shot my watcher," she says. "I took her key when she fell down."

She winces as I pick her up and place her on the seat next to me. There's something wrong. "Are you hurt?"

She looks down. The left leg of her pants is stained dark red above the knee. On the floorboard, there's a pool of blood where she was lying.

"Oh my God." I reach for her leg and she pulls away. "Please, I have to take a look."

"What's wrong?" Rafa asks, glancing back at us.

I hook my fingers into a small rip in her pant leg. "Stay still, okay?" Steffa nods and I carefully tear open the fabric so I can see the wound.

Christ.

"What is it?" Rafa insists.

"She's hit."

"How bad?"

I start to answer, then pause as I notice Steffa's eyes wide in fear, staring at her leg. "You're going to be okay," I tell her.

The girl yelps as I lay her injured leg across the seat. "Rafa, slow down some so I can get a better look." He eases off the gas and turns on the dome light.

I rip off a wide length of fabric from her pants, tearing off the end with my teeth. Her thigh is dimpled with several small wounds from shotgun pellets, each oozing with blood that runs in rivulets down the sides of her leg.

"You're going to be okay," I insist.

I tie the cloth tight above the wounds and she grimaces. I tear off another piece and ball it up. "This won't feel good," I warn her, "but we have to stop the bleeding." I press the wad of cloth against her thigh and she cries out.

"Steffa, look at me. Are you hurt anywhere else?

Anywhere besides your leg?"

Her face contorts in pain, tears streak down her cheeks. She grits her teeth and shakes her head. "No. Just my leg."

"What do we do?" Rafa asks. The Humvee rumbles quietly through the forest. I glance out the back window. The torch lights from camp, now tiny like candle flames, glow faintly in the distance.

Think, Sol.

I peer over the seat at the dashboard. Tank's nearly full. I turn around and check the back, finding a dozen bags of pellets. At least running out of gas won't be a problem.

Steffa moans and squirms in pain. "I know it hurts," I say, hoping she doesn't hear the desperation in my voice. "Try to keep your leg still."

She needs medical tech. I lean toward Rafa. "Are we heading east?"

Rafa glances down at the dashboard. "Yes."

"Okay. We should hit I-45 soon. When we do, turn north."

"North?" Rafa asks, his voice cracking in doubt. "As in north to Dallas?"

I swallow. "Yes. We have to get to Dallas."

CHAPTER 15

"Are you finished yet?" Rafa calls out from inside the Humvee.

"Almost," I answer. "How's she doing?" I'm on my hands and knees on the Humvee's roof, scrawling the last letter into the paint with a rock. I hang my head over the side and look into the back seat.

Rafa sits next to Steffa, who's dozing with her leg wrapped up. She's weak and exhausted, but at least the bleeding's stopped. Rafa looks worried, forces a smile when he sees me. "She's resting."

I go back to the roof and finish scratching out the Z. When I'm done, I toss the stone back to the ground and rub my sore, blistered hands. I stand up to inspect my work.

Beneath my boots it reads SOL PAZ in large, squared letters. There wasn't enough room for my whole first name. This'll have to do.

I jump down off the roof and climb into the back seat. "All right, let's go."

Rafa goes back up front and starts the motor, and the Humvee rolls forward. To our right, the sun's coming up, thin clouds of orange and purple lie across the horizon. To our left, the broken remains of I-45 guide us northward toward Dallas. We haven't seen any drone lights in the night sky, haven't heard any telltale propeller buzzing. They might be watching us from way up high, of course, but at least they're not attacking.

"You really think that'll work?" Rafa asks.

"I don't know." Steffa's face is pale, her forehead beaded with sweat. I dab it dry with a scrap of her pant leg.

To the west of us, on the other side of the highway, there's an outcropping of low-lying buildings.

I lean forward and lay my hand on Rafa's shoulder. "Listen, that's Corsicana over there. I'll drop you off and drive the rest of the way. Take the pellets in the back and hire a driver to take you back to camp. You can tell Guzmán I forced you to come with a gun to your head."

Rafa keeps his eyes forward, maneuvering the vehicle around large clumps of bushes and trees. "I told you before. I could have said no."

"You *did* say no, at first."

Rafa nods. "I would have gotten around to yes. Even if we hadn't...you know."

We drive on. Steffa shivers in the chilly morning air. I take a blanket from the back and tuck it snugly around her, careful not to touch her injured leg. Around us, the landscape slowly takes shape in the hazy morning light. The towering pines of the south, packed together in tight bunches, are gone. Large, solitary oaks with thick trunks and wide canopies take their place. Overnight, thunderstorms passed through the area, saturating the soil. We slog through a flat, muddy plain covered by a thin layer of green switchgrass.

"What do you think that was back there?" Rafa asks. He's talking about the shooting at the Fundie camp.

"I don't know." I remember what blond ponytail told us, about Lake Conroe marking the northern boundary of Fundie control. "Maybe a local clan trying to take the lake back. Maybe the Bullocks found out Wright was going to be there and they sent commandos to take him out. Did you see any of them?"

Rafa shakes his head. "All I saw were muzzle flashes from the tree line."

I nod. "Same here."

My hand moves up and touches the Virgin pendant hanging from my neck. It feels strange not having Lela close by, hovering over me with her crossed arms and frown. As we drove in the darkness, I nodded off a few times, and every time I snapped awake I'd turn to the seat next to me, expecting her to be there.

Steffa stirs and opens her eyes. "Are we there yet?" Her voice is scratchy and weak, barely above a whisper.

"Less than an hour now. Try to rest."

She frowns. "They say the Dallasites are evil."

"Who says that?"

"The reverend." She seems to consider this point for a moment. "But I think he lies a lot."

I smile at her, recalling similar thoughts that passed through my nine-year-old mind, before Mama told me about the gift. The strange feeling I'd often have that there was some other language people spoke, a language without words. A language truer than words.

She looks at me, blinks slowly. "Do you like Dallas?"

"I haven't been there in a long time." I touch her cheek. Her skin feels cold and clammy. "Rafa, can you go any faster?"

He looks at me in the rearview. "If we bust an axle out here, we're screwed. I don't want to push it too—"

His eyes widen at something behind me.

"Shitfuck." He stomps on the gas, sending me sprawling. Steffa whimpers, clutches at her thigh as the acceleration rolls her against the seat back. I pull myself up to my knees and look out the back window.

Holy Christ.

About a two clicks back are a couple dozen cars and trucks, chasing after us.

"Who are they?" Rafa cries.

"I don't know."

Steffa props herself up on her elbows. She grips my arm, her face blooming with panic. "Are they coming after me? Are they coming to take me back?"

"They won't catch us," I tell her, trying to keep my voice steady. "We've got a good car."

"I don't want to go back," she cries.

The Humvee lurches sideways and she yelps in pain. Out the back window the wide line of vehicles bears down on us. They look a bit larger now.

I climb into the rear and search the storage compartments. No weapons.

"Do you have a gun?" I call out.

"No." He pounds the steering wheel with his palm. "Dammit."

"There wasn't time," I say, inwardly cursing myself for not grabbing a weapon off a dead Fundie back at the camp. With all the chaos of people getting shot and bullets flying everywhere, all we could think about was getting out of there.

"I saw a scope somewhere back there," Rafa says.

I rock back and forth, feeling the back tires beneath me slide, lose traction, then catch again, jolting me forward.

"Jesus, it's really getting sloppy," Rafa says, more to himself than me.

I find the scope in a small side pocket and raise the small end to my eye. I can make out individual trucks and cars behind us, but in the early morning light they're little more than hazy silhouettes. I thumb through the magnification settings, but the vehicles are still too far out for me to make out the drivers.

"Fundies?" Rafa asks, as the Humvee slips sideways again. He accelerates, sending a spray of muddy water up from the back tires.

"I don't know." I lower the scope and move my eyes around the landscape. The flat terrain stretches unchanged in every direction to the horizon. There's no cover anywhere, nowhere we can hide.

The chase party grows larger, closer. I climb back over the seat, look down at Steffa. Her face has gone from pale to ashen; her mouth is pressed into a tight line, like she's struggling to keep from crying out. I brush cold, damp hair away from her forehead.

"Look!" Rafa cries.

I look up and squint at the horizon where he's pointing. Far away to the north of us, a dim outline of tall, rectangular structures appears. It's been so long since I've seen buildings—real buildings, not the squat, crumbling relics of most towns—that it takes me a moment to register what I'm seeing.

Dallas.

"How close are we?" I ask. The Humvee loses traction in a mud slick and Rafa whips the wheel over, struggling to keep control. He straightens out the vehicle again and nervously checks behind us in the rearview.

"Not close enough," he mutters.

I turn around and gasp. The chase party's already covered much of the distance between us. They're close enough now to fire on us, but they don't.

"Freelancers," Rafa says. "Gotta be freelancers. That's why they're not shooting. They want to rob us."

I look through the scope and notice one of the vehicles—a Humvee toward the center that's a bit closer to us than the rest—has its flashers on. The roof hatch is open and there's a figure visible from the waist up, holding a gun toward the sky. I can't hear the shots over the revving of the engine and the sloshing of the tires, but I see white bursts of muzzle flashes as the man fires the weapon into the air. I thumb the magnification to the highest setting, but with all the jostling I lose the shooter. A moment later I find the Humvee again, then I hold the scope steady and move it slowly upward. Now I see his features clearly, down to the unmistakable wide mustache.

Guzmán. Holy fucking shit. It's don Flaco, chasing us.

I lower the scope. "He found us," I mutter.

"What did you say?" Rafa cries.

"Guzmán. I can see him back there."

"WHAT?" he exclaims. My stomach presses against the top of the seat as Rafa pushes the Humvee faster. We slip and fishtail through the mud-soaked terrain.

Rafa looks into the rearview. "How did he find us?"

"I don't know."

Then it hits me. The attack at the Fundie camp. It wasn't some local clan fighting to take back control of the lake. The shooters from the tree line were Guzmán's soldiers, coming to take me back. Then when all they found was Lela's body, it didn't take a genius to guess I'd make a run for Bullock territory. And with the rain-soaked terrain our trail wouldn't have been too hard to follow. The Humvee's been leaving a trail of tire tracks for hours, pressed clean and neat into the wet grass. A child could have tracked us down.

"Shit," Rafa blurts out, then a sudden jerk yanks my body forward, slamming my shoulder into the back of Rafa's seat.

Rafa turns back to me. "You okay?"

I rub my shoulder. "What happened?" Then I realize we're not moving. "Why are we stopped?" A surge of panic twists my stomach.

"We ran into a bog." Rafa turns the key over again and again, jumping up and down in the seat as he frantically pumps the gas. The engine won't turn over.

Outside, water reaches halfway up the side of the Humvee. Small rivulets seep inside the doors, trickle downward.

I look into the back seat and find Steffa on the floorboard, still wrapped up in her blanket. Her eyelids are halfway closed. Spit collects in the sides of her mouth. When I say her name she responds with a sluggish groan.

My shoulder throbs with pain as I move her up onto

the seat. She looks frighteningly frail and weak. Pasty white face, eyes listless and dull. The blood loss, the jostling, the stress of our escape. It's taken so much out of her.

Rafa gives up trying to start the Humvee, hits the steering wheel with his fist. "Engine's flooded. We're stuck."

For a moments it's quiet, nothing but the tinkling of water leaking into the cab, the shaky sound of our own breath. In a few seconds we'll hear the chase party's engines.

I don't want to look out back, don't want to see how close they're getting. I fix my eyes on Steffa, trying to will some of my energy into her. *Don't die on me.*

I touch the Virgin pendant, feel the smooth timeworn folds of the Virgin's dress.

"Sol," Rafa says, his voice rising with anxiety.

I look out the front window, blinking in disbelief. They're rushing straight at us, about thirty meters off the ground. Wide, bulky frames, guns and missiles hanging from their undercarriages, cutting an unmistakable silhouette against the blue sky.

Attack drones.

I count ten, a dozen, growing larger each second. Even if there were someplace to hide, there's no time to get out and run, nothing we can do. I pick up Steffa, hold her close to me, the low-pitched hum of the engines growing louder. I want to tell her I'm sorry, but the words won't come. I reach forward, squeeze Rafa's shoulder. He places his hand on top of mine.

I close my eyes, waiting for the sound of bullets piercing through the roof, for the white flash and searing heat of a missile strike. A moment passes, then another. Nothing. The drones' buzzing engines grow into a deafening roar as they get closer, louder and louder until it sounds like they're on top of us. My teeth chatter and the Humvee vibrates around us.

No thudding bullets, no explosions. The engine sound

lessens, then seems to shift. Now it's coming from behind us.

I crack open my eye, look out the back window. There's a flash of white, then a bright orange ball of fire envelops several cars in the chase party. Large chunks of earth explode up and out, and a moment later the shock wave hits us with a booming thud.

Rafa and I hit the floorboards. Steffa groans and murmurs incoherently.

Another missile hits, the concussion rocking the Humvee, ringing my ears. I climb up and peek over the back seat. Behind us there's total mayhem. Guzmán's chase party scatters like ants from a disturbed mound. A few of the larger vehicles, the ones with matamoscas mounted on top, are already returning fire. The sound of automatic gunfire crackles the air. The vehicles fan out across the muddy plain, slipping and sliding southward in a mad, chaotic retreat.

Rafa and I exchange a confused glance, then watch as the cars grow smaller and the gunfire fades.

"They passed us over on purpose," Rafa mutters to himself. Then he looks upward and a smile creeps across his face. "My God," he exhales, "the roof. They must have seen your name on the roof. They were *protecting* us."

I let out a long breath, feel my heart hammering against the inside of my chest.

"I can't believe it," he laughs, shaking his head. Relief washes over his face. "It worked."

I lay my forehead against the top of the seat, recovering my breath.

Somewhere in the distance a siren wails. Rafa and I turn our attention northward toward the sound. We see the lights first, blue and red, oscillating in the distance. Then we see vehicles, six Humvees speeding toward us, lined up single file in close formation. The first and last ones have large guns attached to their roofs. The ones in between have strobe lights on top instead of guns, flashing blue and red like emergency vehicles.

The sirens grow louder as the convoy approaches, then stops about ten meters away. Darkened windows hide whoever's inside. The flashing lights stop, sirens go quiet.

Up close the large-caliber weapons on the rooftops look more like small cannons than guns. Servos whine as they swing toward us in unison.

I swallow, then slowly lay Steffa on the seat. "Show your hands," I tell Rafa as I reach out the open window with both hands. "We don't want to get shot."

Rafa nods, then stretches his arms toward the Humvees, showing his palms.

The door of the second vehicle opens. A tall, well-dressed woman in a business suit and sunglasses that cover half her face exits the Humvee and strides toward us. Her auburn hair is long and wavy and streaked with gray. She stops at the edge of the water hole we're stuck in, removes her sunglasses.

It can't be...

A flood of emotions suddenly well up and overpower me. Tears instantly fill my eyes, blurring my vision as I leap out of the window into the waist-high muddy water. My entire body erupts into a scream.

"MAMA!"

CHAPTER 16

"She'll be fine," Mama says, referring to Steffa. "We'll take good care of her. And your friend, too."

I nuzzle closer to her, my arms locked around her waist. It's like a dream, a glorious dream, being here with her, safe and warm.

"Pretty clever," she says, "scrawling your name onto the roof like that."

The back of the Humvee is clean and quiet. The soft leather seats and chilled air feathering my cheeks feel luxurious beyond description. Our driver maneuvers through the mud and wet grass at a steady, unhurried pace as Dallas grows larger in the front window. Behind us in the next vehicle, a medic tends to Steffa. I wanted Rafa to come with us, but he shook his head, smiled, and waved me off. "You two have some catching up to do," he said, climbing into the next vehicle. "I'll keep an eye on our little water carrier."

I'm still trembling. I try to let the reality of what's happening sink in, settle over me.

"Your father's on a survey trip near the Oklahoma border," Mama tells me. "We sent a message to his satphone. He's probably rushing back already."

Papi! It hardly seems possible: my parents are alive, and by some miracle I made it back to them.

No, I think, *not by some miracle*. I touch the pendant hanging from my neck, feel some of the joy leak out of me.

"What happened that day, Mama? How did you and Papi make it out?"

I feel her body go rigid. She doesn't answer. I let go of her and straighten up in the seat so I can see her face. Her expression is cold, distant. She turns toward the window, stares out at the moving landscape.

You idiot. I've triggered a horrible memory from that day, maybe one worse than my own. "I'm sorry."

She squeezes my hand. "It's all right." She swallows. "They shot us. Left us for dead."

"But how are you okay?"

She looks at me. Her face is more wrinkled than I remember. The little lines around her eyes and mouth are deeper, clearer.

"Your father had an emergency beacon. It was small, hidden in our closet."

"He never told me about that."

"For your own protection. I didn't know about it, either. Bullock soldiers choppered in after he set it off. They brought medics, blood bags. They saved us." She puts her hand to her mouth. "But those monsters had already taken you away. The Bullocks sent out drones to find you. They looked for weeks and weeks." Her eyes fill with tears. "We thought you were gone."

I wrap my arms around her, bury my face in her hair. The aroma of her shampoo floods my nose with lavender. The smell of home.

"We never should have left Dallas," she says. "Outside the city they're all murderers and barbarians."

"It was protected territory," I answer, trying to soothe her. "We thought we'd be okay."

"*Protected territory*. Yes, your father insisted it was." She shakes her head, her voice strains with agitation. "I never should have let him drag us out there."

"It's okay. I'm here now. I made it back."

She presses her cheek against the top of my head. "You're right. That's all that matters."

The Dallas skyline grows larger, details of the buildings come into focus. Long, vertical stretches of colored glass, twinkling in the sunlight. Elevators traveling up and down.

Mama presses a button on the door handle, closes the privacy screen between us and the driver.

"There have been rumors," Mama says, keeping her voice low, "about someone who helped Guzmán, someone who could pick a good deal from a bad deal *every time*. They say that's how he got so rich so fast." She lifts an eyebrow. "Was that you?"

I nod.

Mama lifts an eyebrow. "I should have known. I should have guessed it might be you." She kisses the top of my head.

"Do you think Abner guessed it was me? Is that why he came to Guzmán's camp?"

Mama straightens up, looks at my face and frowns. "Abner came to you? When? Where?"

"A few days ago in Odessa. I saw him as he was leaving, but he didn't see me. At first I thought maybe you sent him to find me."

Mama's brow furrows as she considers this. "I didn't know he went to Odessa. Abner's a trade commish now."

"A what?"

"A trade commissioner. He travels all over the Republic, checking up on conversion plants, negotiating deals with freelancers. He's gone more than he's here, so I hear. Our paths don't cross much these days."

"Do you think maybe he was there *on business*?" As I say it, I wonder what kind of business it could have been. A payoff of some sort? The Bullocks were famously practical. They'd have no problem offering their enemy a bribe. And Guzmán was greedy. He'd have no problem accepting one. Maybe that was it. Maybe his visit had nothing to do with me.

"I don't know," Mama says, shifting in her seat. "But if we had known you were there, Rudder would have sent drones and soldiers to get you, not a trade commish."

"Rudder Bullock?" I ask reflexively.

Mama nods. "He's still Executive Minister. It's a lifetime appointment, remember?"

She'd called him Rudder, not Minister Bullock. "Do you know him?"

"Your father and I both know him. A lot has changed in the last three years."

"Like what?"

Mama smiles, but not in a happy way. "There's plenty of time for all that. Let's get you home, fed, and cleaned up first. And then I'll catch you up. How's that sound?"

"Good."

Mama lowers the privacy screen and I gasp. A massive monolith looms large in front of us, as tall as a ten-story building. It's been years since I've been this close to one of the tower compounds. There are three dozen in all, standing a kilometer apart from one another, forming a defensive ring around the city. Each houses a complement of Republican Marines and has a stockpile of large-caliber weapons, grenade launchers, shoulder rockets, and who knows what other hell. The tower compounds are a formidable barrier some ten kilometers beyond the city's edge, a defensive perimeter that's never been breached. I recall a dim memory of Papi pointing the towers out to me from the observation deck of a building in downtown Dallas. I pressed my nose against the glass, thinking they looked like faraway posts in an unfinished fence. Guzmán kept a map of them in his stacks of papers and pondered over them endlessly, discussing possible tactics with his military leaders, debating the best way to fight past them.

Our driver waves out the window, a gesture returned

by a small figure high up in the tower. We pass a checkpoint, then slowly roll forward through a maze of sandbags and concrete carstoppers until we arrive at the front gate, where a stone-faced guard waves us through. Our driver rides the brake as we creep past a long row of barracks. A few soldiers mill about, their rifles hanging from shoulder straps, boots covered in mud from the recent storms. They watch us as we pass by, their faces painted with the ominous, unblinking stares of professional soldiers. Moments later we reach the rear gate. I squint against the gleaming reflection of razor wire atop the chain-link fence. After a moment, the fence gate swings open and we roll forward out of the compound.

"Now we're *really* in protected territory, hijita preciosa," Mama says, squeezing me closer. Then she sniffs the top of my head. "Mmmm. You could definitely do with a shower, young lady."

Hijita preciosa. Precious little daughter. Tears stream down my face, drip from my cheeks. I want to tell her everything, every horrible thing that's happened. How I've sent so many to die in the desert. What the freelancers did to me. The awful things I did to get here. How Lela helped me. I want to tell her everything, but I can't stop crying.

"It's okay," she murmurs. "It's all right. You're home now. You're home."

*   *   *

Puffy-eyed and sniffling, I manage to compose myself by the time we reach the edge of the city. The rocking, sloshing drive through mud and waterlogged grass transitions into a smooth ride over paved streets. Mama lowers the privacy screen so I can get a better look at the city. A telltale beep comes from the dashboard as the vehicle switches over to autonav. The driver lets go of the wheel, turns his head toward us. "Welcome to Dallas."

It's all so clean!

Spotless sidewalks run across the fronts of gleaming skyscrapers of glass and polished granite. Gently rolling hills of grass fill the spaces between buildings, lush and emerald green, crisscrossed by walking trails filled with well-dressed pedestrians. A few cars glide along the streets. New cars with no dents that sparkle in the sunlight.

"How long has it been since you were here?" Mama asks. "Six years? Seven?"

"Nine," I answer. We lived in Dallas until I was eleven. After that we became nomads, hopping from city to city for Papi's survey work, until we finally settled in our house on the plains.

All around us, robots far outnumber pedestrians. Ten to one, maybe more. I lower my window to get a better look at them. *Such variety.* Robots of all shapes and sizes. Little rolling ones no bigger than a soccer ball. Walking ones that look like tall, thin people with transparent skin and carbon fiber skeletons. Boxy ones that beep and snort and trudge along the sidewalk.

"So many bots," I marvel.

"And they're always coming up with new ones." Mama tilts her head. "I imagine you haven't seen many robots lately, have you?"

I haven't. Guzmán territory was robot-free. "Bots are for lazy, decadent gringos in Dallas," I say, mocking Guzmán. "I've heard the speech so many times I could give it myself."

Mama grunts. "Barbarians. Filthy, backwards barbarians."

I sit back against the soft leather. "You look so different now."

She lifts her eyebrows. "Better? Worse?"

"Different. Your clothes, your hair. You look like a big shot now."

She laughs, looks down at her outfit. "Big shot, huh? Well, I guess you remember me as a prairie cook with a stained apron and frazzled hair. I never really thought of myself that way, you know. Even while we lived there." She shakes her head. "That frontier living. Your father loved it, but it wasn't for me."

Your father. Not Papi, not Martín. I don't remember her ever referring to him as *your father.*

"All these Humvees," I say. "Are they yours?"

"Ay, hijita. I'm not *that* much of a big shot. They belong to the Ministry of Justice. That's where I work."

"You work at the Min of J? Like with lawyers and judges?"

Mama presses a button on the door handle. My window rises, shuts, and the privacy screen closes again.

She leans toward me and winks. "Can you think of any better place for a reader to work than the Min of J?"

Mama seems so different. Bolder, more confident. "But do they know?" I murmur, glancing at the privacy screen. "The people you work with?"

"A few. Those who need to, they know. Anyone who matters knows."

I remember Mama's stories of her teacher's warnings. "But what about keeping it secret?"

Mama's lips pucker like she's tasted something sour. "Right, old Marineth's warning." She sighs. "My teacher was a good woman and I loved her, but she was wrong about keeping our power all to ourselves. Completely wrong. What we have makes us different, and yes, even feared. But that doesn't mean we shouldn't use it to make a better life for ourselves."

"So you don't mind...being used?"

Mama shakes her head. "This isn't some filthy rebel camp where I'm forced to read people. This is *my* choice. And my gift has earned me money, respect, and the protection of powerful friends. Do you think I'd have any of that if I hid myself away and kept my mouth shut like my teacher wanted me to?"

The Humvee slows, stops. Mama lowers the privacy screen. There's a large crowd a couple blocks ahead of us, gathered around a platform in the near distance that reminds me of Reverend Wright's stage. A man in a suit stands at a podium and addresses the mass of people.

"Sorry, ma'am," the driver says. "It's another one of those rallies. We'll be around it in a minute."

I crane my neck to get a better look. "What's going on?"

"These are tense times, hijita. People are worried. Guzmán's out there, taking town after town, stealing our gas, all those illiterate wastelanders flocking to him, buying into that modern-day revolutionary story of his."

I lower my window to listen. The speaker's voice booms through a sound system, echoes off buildings.

"Those are OUR conversion plants, and it's OUR money that built them." Applause and shouts from the crowd. Next to the podium a rectangular screen emerges from the stage, rising to twice the height of the speaker. Guzmán's face fades in, scowling, his eyes crazy and bloodshot. Boos and hisses fill the air. It's such an exaggerated, cartoon version of don Flaco, I nearly laugh.

"For ourselves and the lives of our children," the speaker shouts, "this criminal must be stopped."

The Humvee turns a corner and we leave the crowd behind us.

"Who was that?"

Mama taps a button, raising my window and shutting it. Outside the muffled blare of the speech continues. "Simpson or Swindon or something like that," Mama says. "Runs the Marines' recruiting agency. Talented public speaker. Really brings them in."

I turn and look out the back window. Hundreds of fists are raised, and through the glass I hear angry shouts. Don Flaco's oversized face looms over their heads, staring out at me. I wonder if he's still alive, if he managed to survive the drone attack on his convoy. The idea of him dead, strangely, doesn't bring joy, doesn't give me the sweet sense of retribution I'd hoped it would. The Humvee turns a corner and don Flaco disappears from view.

My hand reaches up and touches the Virgin pendant around my neck.

CHAPTER 17

"She's beaten up and bruised pretty good." The doctor at St. Luke's Hospital turns my hands over, examines my wrists, which are still raw and chafed from when the Fundies bound them together. "But otherwise she's all right."

I sit on an examination table, dangling my legs over the edge and wearing a scratchy white gown.

The doctor turns to Mama. "Pretty well fed for wastelander."

Wastelander. He keeps calling me that, the Dallasite pejorative for anyone who lives outside the city. When he walked into the room and saw me, his face went sour like he'd just bitten into a bad piece of fruit. As he looked me over, he talked to Mama instead of me, like I was a dog or something. But compared the nurse who came in earlier and sneered at me while she slapped on a double layer of rubber gloves, the doc was downright friendly.

Outside the city limits, everyone in the Republic hates Dallasites. I suppose I'd forgotten how mutual the feeling is. Mama endures the doctor's *wastelander* comments with a forced smile, but doesn't correct him or come to my defense.

Welcome fucking home, Soledad Paz.

"Where's Steffa?" I ask.

The doctor knits his brow.

"The girl we came in with," Mama clarifies. "The one with the injured leg."

"Ah," the doctor answers. "She's one floor up," he tells Mama (not me). "We checked her in. They're prepping her for surgery."

Rafa steps into the doorway, looking silly in his own white gown. "How you doing?"

The doctor sees Rafa, makes the bad-fruit face again. "Lord, it's a regular refugee camp in here." He turns to Mama. "She's fine," he tells her. "Just needs some rest. Now, if you'll excuse me." Rafa moves aside to let him pass.

"Doctor," I call. He turns to look at me, but doesn't answer. "Do me a favor, will you? Tell that cunt of a nurse with the rubber gloves that I'm *from* here. I was born in this very hospital."

Mama gasps. "Sol!"

The doctor shakes his head, mutters something under his breath, and leaves.

Rafa steps into the room, his mouth stretched into a wide grin. "Back to your old self, I see."

"Sol," Mama scolds, "do you know who that was? Doctor Phillipe-Bullock. He's a first cousin of the Bullocks. *A first cousin.* You can't talk that way to people like him."

A voice behind Rafa says, "My little girl can say whatever she wants to whoever she wants."

"PAPI!" I leap off the table and throw myself onto him, wrapping my arms around his neck, burying my face in his chest. I feel my feet leave the floor as he straightens up, his strong arms lifting me.

We sob and blubber at each other. "Un milagro," he cries, his voice fluttering. "Es un milagro." A miracle. Yes, that's what it feels like. His shirt, now wet with my tears, smells of sweat and pollen, triggering memories of our life in the Panhandle. *Papi's outside smell.*

For a long time neither one of us lets go, gripping each other tight. I don't want the moment to end.

"Martín," Mama finally interrupts, "give the girl some space to breath. You're going to crush the poor thing."

Papi sets me back on the table. He wipes his eyes, sniffs. His olive skin has deeper creases across the forehead, and the sun freckles under his eyes look darker, but otherwise he's the same as I remember him. His clothes haven't changed a bit: beat up jeans, hiking boots, and a wrinkled shirt with threadbare elbows, the kind Mama used to beg him to throw out. *Your sloppy papi*, she used to say, clucking her tongue at the state of his clothes whenever he arrived home from a survey.

He squeezes my hands. "I can't believe it. I can't believe it." His lower lip and chin quiver as he speaks.

"Papi," I say, motioning to Rafa, "this is Rafa. He helped me. I couldn't have made it here without him."

He reaches out, shakes Rafa's hand, squeezes his shoulder. "Muchísimas gracias, Rafa."

Rafa nods, looks at his feet. "Sure," he mumbles. "It's nice to meet you."

"He's a tech wizard, Papi. You two are peas in a pod."

Papi's face brightens. "Is that so?"

Rafa shrugs, smiles awkwardly.

A robot opens the door and rolls into the room. It's long and rectangular, with lots of storage compartments and two pairs of grasping arms.

"Supply refill," it announces, "please excuse me." Papi steps out of the way and it moves over to a cabinet and starts refilling drawers with cotton balls, tongue depressors, little white baggies. Rafa watches it work, fascinated, until it finishes and leaves.

Papi shifts his weight from one foot to the other. He looks nervous and unsure of himself, like he wants to say something, but doesn't know how to start.

"So how'd the survey go?" I ask. Papi lifts his eyebrows, seems relieved to be rescued from his own thoughts.

"Easy peasy," he answers. "Gas fields around these parts, I know them like the back of my hand."

"How's the volume looking?" I use the phrase I've heard him utter countless times.

He looks at Mama for a moment, then lowers his voice. "The gas fields around here aren't what they used to be."

My eyes widen. "Really? Is it bad?"

Papi nods. "We counted three depleted wells up near Gainesville." *Depleted wells.* There are no two graver words for anyone who works the natgas fields.

"Martín, please," Mama interjects. "The last thing the poor girl needs is more to worry about."

The door opens, and Mama's face brightens. "Our special guest is here," she sings.

I'm hoping it's an orderly bringing Steffa in for a visit, but instead a man comes through the doorway. Sixtyish, white-haired and wearing a stylish suit, he moves into the room with the brisk confidence of someone in authority. "So you're the young lady I've been hearing about," he declares. "Soledad Paz, it's wonderful to finally meet you."

"Sol," Mama says, "this is Executive Minister Bullock."

Before I can say anything, he's grabbing me by the shoulders and kissing my cheek. "Welcome home, Soledad. Corissa's so happy to have you back."

"Thank you, Minister Bullock," I manage to respond, still flustered by the fact the EM's *here*, to see *me*. And then his words echo in my head. *Corissa's* so happy. Not *your mother's* so happy.

He turns to Papi. "Martín," he nods.

"Minister." Papi's voice is flat, expression wooden. They don't shake hands.

There's a tension in the room, a discomfort on all their faces. Mama introduces Rafa, her voice lilting with a nervous flutter. Without the hierba I can't see any deeper, but I'm not sure I want to. A sick feeling twists my stomach as Bullock speaks to Rafa, uses Mama's first name again. *Corissa.*

I force my thoughts in another direction. "Minister, what happened to the group chasing us?"

Bullock waves his hand. "Don't you worry about them. They're gone. We took care of those scavengers."

"You got them all?"

His smile fades a bit. "The ones we didn't get scattered like cockroaches. I'm sure they're hiding back under their rocks by now."

There's a hint of embarrassment in his voice. Maybe they didn't get Guzmán after all. Maybe he's still out there somewhere.

The door opens and a blond-haired man pokes his head into the room. "Excuse me, Minister. It's time."

"I'm afraid I have to go now." Bullock flashes me a politician's smile that reminds me of Reverend Wright. "I hope to see you again soon, Soledad. I can't tell you how happy I am you got away from those freelancers and found your way home."

I stare at him, digesting his words as he excuses himself and leaves the room.

Escaped those freelancers?

"Mama, why does he think—" She silences me with a look and a small shake of her head.

My thoughts scatter. There's too much to take in, too many questions crowding my brain. But one thing rises to the surface, displacing all others.

"I want to see Steffa."

* * *

The nurse on duty limits Steffa's visitors to two at a time. Papi and Rafa wait outside the door as Mama and I enter and find her asleep. Tubes and wires run from her arms to machines next to the bed. There's a quiet electronic beep keeping time with her heartbeat. Her injured leg is wrapped up in what looks like a thigh-high sock filled with blue gel.

"It's a bio-sleeve," the nurse says. "It's getting her tissues ready for surgery."

The girl looks so small in the big hospital bed.

"The doctor says she might lose the leg," Mama says.

I whirl around, furious. "Hush!" I hiss. "What if she hears you?"

Mama looks crossly at me.

I sigh. "Sorry, Mama. I'm just...overwhelmed."

She nods. "It's okay. You've been through a lot."

"Can I ask you something?"

"Sure."

"Why did Minister Bullock think I've been with freelancers all this time? Doesn't he know about Guzmán?"

Mama starts shaking her head before I finish the sentence. She turns and pulls the door shut. "Not here, hijita. We'll talk at home."

Steffa stirs, opens her eyes. She blinks at me. Her medicated gaze is glassy and unfocused.

"Hola, Ssssol," she croaks.

My eyes widen. "¿Hablas español? No sabía eso."

"Claaaaro," she says, blinking slowly. She lifts her arms, starts counting fingers. "Uno, dos, four, six, nueve. I know all the nummers since I was little."

I cover my mouth with my hand to keep from laughing.

Steffa looks past me to Mama, squints at her.

"Hello, little one," Mama says softly.

"Who are you?"

I place my hand on Mama's shoulder. "She's—"

Steffa's eyes flutter and she falls back to sleep. I sigh. "She's exhausted. We should let her get some rest."

I turn to leave and notice Mama staring at Steffa. Her brow's furrowed in concentration, like she's trying to work

something out.
   Like she sees something in Steffa's face.

CHAPTER 18

Mama's penthouse apartment feels like the home of a stranger. A rich stranger. There are vaulted ceilings with thick wooden beams, stylish, expensive-looking furniture, large canvases of artwork covering the walls. It's the kind of place a Bullock inner circler would live in. I feel out of place, as if I've opened the wrong door and walked into a party I wasn't invited to.

Mama shows me to the bathroom, and I take my time getting cleaned up. I can't remember the last time I showered. I could stand here for hours, luxuriating under the warm drizzle. It's only when Mama calls through the door, joking with me about melting and going down the drain, that I at last shut off the water. I dry off, get dressed in the shirt and pants Mama gave me—they fit snug and look like exercise clothes—and wipe the steam from the mirror with a hand towel.

I stare at myself, my *clean* self, turning my head back and forth, almost not recognizing the person looking back at me. The tiles beneath my bare feet are cool and smooth. The sand and grit of the western desert feel a million miles away.

I search the drawers, but I don't find a hair brush.

Then I check the cabinets under the sink—nothing. I open the medicine cabinet and gasp, recognizing a small wooden box from our house in the Panhandle. On its lid is a carving of a horse, and I run my finger over it, wondering if Mama still keeps her stash of hierba inside.

I place the box on the counter in front of me. I hesitate a moment, then open it. Six small plastic bags stuffed with hierba.

"Dinner's ready," Mama says through the door, startling me.

"Coming." I take one of the bags and hide it in my pants pocket, although I'm not sure why. Then I return the box to its place.

The dining table is next to a wall of paned glass. Twenty stories below us, the nighttime city sparkles and twinkles in a rainbow's variety of incandescence. In the near distance the glimmering lights stop abruptly, marking the edge of the city. Beyond it, there's nothing but a darkness.

I wanted Rafa to join us for dinner, but Mama insisted on having some time alone with me. When we arrived at the building we dropped him off on the fifth floor, where one of Minister Bullocks' staffers—a skinny man with a fake smile and tanned skin so smooth it looked lacquered—had set up an apartment for Rafa. I told him I'd stop by in the morning, that we'd go see Steffa when she got out of surgery.

Mama comes out of the kitchen, a plate of steaming pasta in each hand. "Angel hair with butter and garlic still your favorite?" She places them on the table.

Two plates, two place settings.

I can't hold back the question any longer. "You and Papi aren't together anymore, are you?"

Mama pours wine into our glasses without answering. She sets down the bottle, pulls the chair out for me.

"No, hijita," she says, sighing, "we're not."

All the signs were there. The strange tension between

them at the hospital, the way she kept saying *your father.* When we lived on the plains it was always *your papi.* On the drive over from the hospital I'd debated with myself, hoping I was reading too much into things. Without the hierba you can never be sure. Sometimes the mind sees things that aren't there, makes connections that don't exist, jumps to the wrong conclusions. But when I stepped into the apartment, all my doubts dropped away like a curtain falling to the floor, revealing the truth standing bare behind it. At a glance I knew this was *her* space, and hers alone. There was no place for Papi here.

I stare at the plates. "Where is he? Is he coming?"

"He's at his place," she answers. "It's not far from here. I asked him if we could spend tonight alone so I could tell you. You'll see him tomorrow."

I stand there, numb.

"Please, Sol, sit down."

I sit. "When?"

"About a year after you left." She shakes her head, corrects herself. "A year after they took you."

"What happened?"

Mama takes her fork, pokes at her noodles. "We grew apart, wanted different things."

"Different things like what?"

"It's hard to explain, hijita." She sips her wine. "When you're young and in love, you see the person you want to see, I suppose. Then you get older and you start to see who they really are. You start to understand who you really are, too."

I don't say anything.

"Please," she gently insists, "eat something. You must be starving."

I try to silence the child inside me ready to wail. I want to be adult about this. People grow apart, get divorced. It happens. I shouldn't pout about it like a spoiled brat. I made it here, alive. Mama and Papi are alive, doing well. *That's* what matters. And that ought to be enough. Yes, it's more than enough. Don't be a fool, Sol.

I twirl the pasta around my fork, put it in my mouth. She made it the way I like it, with a bit of oregano. I take another bite.

"This is so good."

Mama smiles. "You eat as much as you want, hijita. You could stand to put on a kilo or two."

I slurp up a noodle. "Right. You don't get fat on beans and squirrel stew, that's for sure."

"Yuck." She wrinkles her nose.

I'm halfway through my second helping when my mind wanders to the question I'd asked Mama earlier. "Why did Minister Bullock think I've been with freelancers all this time?"

Mama's wineglass stops halfway to her mouth. She sets it down. "Because that's what I told him."

I blink. *"That's what you told him?"*

"Yes, and that's the story we're going to have to stick to. Your friend Rafa too."

"But why?"

Mama puts her elbows on the table, clasps her hands together. "Sol, things have gotten pretty bad around here. Every month the Bullocks lose more gas territory to Guzmán, and the basins they still control are starting to run dry. The whole city's on edge."

I think back to the crowd on the street when we first arrived, to the jeers and vicious cries that erupted when Guzmán's image appeared.

"No, it's more than that," she amends. "It's become hysteria at this point. If they had any idea you were with him for a day, much less *three years*, they'd lock you up in a room and question you nonstop. And even if we managed to convince them you're not a threat or a spy, you'd always have a cloud of suspicion hanging over you."

I consider her words. "I guess I didn't think of it that way."

She puts her hand on mine. "Do you want to tell me

about it?"

"Now?" I'm not sure I'm up for it.

"We can wait until you're ready."

"No," I say, reconsidering. "It's okay." I'm sure Mama wants to know what happened with me as much as I wanted to know about her and Papi.

I pick up my half-empty wineglass and finish it in one gulp.

"Okay," I say, taking a deep breath. "When they sold me to Guzmán, at first he didn't use me that much. He'd have me watch the faces of the other players during card games, give him signals if I saw someone bluffing. He told me later that was his way of testing me, to see if I could really spot lies. For months he thought it was some kind of carnival magician's trick, but when I proved what I could do over and over again, eventually I convinced him. After that, he started having me read people from a hiding place. He'd give his men questions to ask, things they could work into a conversation, so I could tell him whether some trader with a big deal was full of crap, or whether some spy from Dallas had real info about drone routes or if he was making it up."

I go on, recounting for her the endless parade of scam artists, wannabe deal-makers, and information brokers. Maybe one out of ten was legit, and Guzmán shrewdly leveraged the handful of good deals to make himself rich. And those guilty of false claims or wild exaggerations got their "thanks, but no thanks" in the form of a stroll in the desert that ended with two bullets to the brain.

"So that's how he built his army," Mama observes. "With all that money."

I nod. "Indirectly, yes. The more money he had, the more refugees he could house and feed and bring under his protection. You keep people safe, keep their families safe, and they'll trust you. They'll buy whatever you're selling, and they'll fight for you. I've seen it."

Then she asks me how I escaped. I tell her again about

seeing Abner, how his visit to camp started it all. I don't tell her everything, though. I leave out the embarrassing details about Rafa, the grisly truth about what I did with the guard. And I don't mention blond ponytail at all. I don't want to remind myself how stupid I was to bring him along, how his scheming ass sold us out to the Fundies and what that led to. I keep the story simple, summarized. Rafa helped me deactivate my tracker, and together we stole a truck and hightailed it to Dallas. I tell her about Reverend Wright's people surprising us and taking us to his camp, how we took Steffa with us and escaped in the chaos of the raid.

I can't bring myself to mention Lela, can't bear to think of her. I'm suddenly conscious of her pendant hanging heavy around my neck. Maybe someday I'll tell Mama the whole ugly story, everything about Rafa, blond ponytail, Lela, but not today. I can't go through it all again.

Mama stares at the tabletop, sips her wine. She seems lost in thought. Even without the hierba, she can probably see I'm holding things back, but she doesn't press me. "It's so strange. And funny, in a way. You out west all this time, helping Guzmán, whispering the truth into his ear. And me here, doing the exact same thing for Rudder."

Exact same thing? "What are you talking about, Mama?"

"We've been doing the same job." She smiles at me, winks. "The only difference is I've been getting paid for it."

*　　*　　*

Later, I lie in bed and stare at the ceiling. Nothing feels right. The bed's too comfortable, the sheets are too clean, the air's too free of dust. I picture Steffa in that big hospital bed, alone and scared, wondering where I am. I should have stayed at the hospital. I shouldn't have left her there alone. If it had been me, Lela wouldn't have left. She would have stood there all night next to the bed, arms crossed, watching over me with that stone-faced frown of hers.

I try to think of something else. I go back over what Mama told me about her job. She has some made-up title at the Ministry of Justice, a generous salary, and an office with her name on the door, but all she really does is read people for Minister Bullock. I was amazed when she described her work, how similar it sounded to what I'd been doing for Guzmán. Mama observed subjects from behind one-way glass, watching for telltale body movements and facial twitches that were invisible to anyone else's eyes, listening for flat notes in the music of a speaker's voice that no one else could hear. Then afterwards she'd debrief Bullock, just as I did with don Flaco. And the Bullocks were no less lenient with liars than Guzmán. Mama said they *took care of them*, lowering her voice carefully so I wouldn't mistake what she meant.

Mama said with all the territory losses, Minister Bullock had grown more and more irritable as his family's hold on the Republic became less secure. He'd fired half his direct staff for not doing enough to stop Guzmán, and as things got worse, he began to see conspiracies to undermine him everywhere, even from his blood relatives.

If pure chance hadn't placed Mama in the room with Bullock when he got the call about the convoy approaching the city, he wouldn't have thought twice about having us taken out along with the chase group, no matter what name was scrawled on top of our truck. But Mama was there in Bullock's office, and she saw the drone's video feed, saw my name on the Humvee's roof. And somehow she managed to talk him out of making us a target. She even convinced him to let her go and fetch me herself. Mama was like that: an unstoppable, relentless storm when she needed to be. She wouldn't let you breathe until you saw things her way.

"The *last* thing we need is Rudder knowing you were involved with that desert snake," she said during dinner, shaking her head and taking a long sip of wine.

"But what about Rafa?" I asked.

"We can tell him everything in the morning. You're both officially under my supervision, which means no one can talk to you without getting my okay first. Building security has instructions not to let him leave tonight, and first thing in the morning they'll bring him up here for breakfast."

"You sure we should wait?" Rafa had a bad habit of blurting out the wrong things at the wrong time.

She waved her hand, unconcerned. "Let the boy get a good night's sleep. Believe me, Rudder's office has far bigger problems to worry about right now than a teenage refugee. If that little girl says something, though…"

"Steffa?" I said. "She doesn't know anything to tell. She first saw us at the Fundie camp, has no idea where we came from. And on the way up here she was barely conscious most of the time."

"Good," Mama sighed. "I'll rest easier tonight knowing that."

When we finished our pecan pie dessert, she came back around to Steffa. What did I know about her? Were her parents alive? Would they come looking for her?

I wondered if Mama had seen something in the girl's face. Steffa had been sedated and we were only in the room a minute, so how much *could* she have seen?

Still, there was something strange about Mama's questions. Something I couldn't quite put my finger on, something odd. But then everything here felt odd. I'd been gone for so long.

I look over to the nightstand, at the sleeping pill and glass of water Mama left for me. I sit up, swallow the pill, and settle back under the sheets. *Clean* sheets that smell of flowers. Finally my body relaxes and a delicious blackness overtakes me.

*   *   *

When I walk into the kitchen the next morning wearing Mama's spare robe, Rafa's already seated at the breakfast table.

He points at me with a fork. "So that's your morning hair, huh? It's not that different from your regular hair."

I wrinkle my nose at him. "Chistosito."

Outside the wall window, the sun's already well above the horizon. Beyond the city's edge, the endless empty expanse of grasslands is broken only by the ring of tower compounds in the near distance. From here the towers look like wooden planks stuck in the mud by some giant.

Mama comes out of the kitchen holding a pan in one hand, a spatula in the other. The smell of fried eggs and fresh tortillas makes my mouth water.

"Sleeping Beauty awakens," she says, sliding a couple eggs onto a plate.

Rafa bites off half a rolled tortilla, then speaks as he chews. "Caray, your mom can *cook*."

I sit and nod at his dark pants and narrow-collared shirt. "Where'd you get the clothes?" He's so cleaned up he could pass for a local.

"Wardrobe courtesy of the Ministry of Justice," Mama says in a TV announcer's voice as she sits down and fluffs her napkin.

There's a bowl of fruit on the table; my mouth waters at the sight of it. Fresh fruit in Guzmán's camp was a rarity. I grab an orange and slice it up. It's a real, honest-to-goodness orange, perfect and unblemished. I bite into a wedge and my eyes roll back into my head as juice fills my mouth. "Oh, God. I have no words."

Mama chuckles. "Rafa and I were having a nice chat."

"Yep," Rafa says. "She got me up to speed. I'm now officially a softhearted freelancer who helped you escape the evil clutches of your captors."

Mama goes over the details of our cover story. Instead of being Guzmán's slave for the last three years, I've been with a couple dozen freelancers led by a man named Morales. We moved around a lot, traded with local clans, and stayed far away from the big territory battles. Morales, apparently, had no stomach for violence.

"And most important," Mama insists, shaking her finger at both of us, "don't say *anything* to *anyone* about Sol's abilities. You understand?"

I nod, then look at Rafa. "Not a word, okay? All I want to do is go back to a normal life." No more true seeing, no more hierba.

"Sure," Rafa agrees. "I understand."

Mama sips her coffee, looks Rafa over. "Soledad tells me you can fix just about anything."

Rafa smiles, shrugs.

"Well, there's plenty of work for a budding engineer in Dallas."

"And Mama's got connections," I add.

She nods. "Sol's mama *does* have connections."

Rafa fidgets. "No, really, Señora Paz, you don't have to—"

"Hendricks," Mama corrects. "My last name is Hendricks now."

Corissa *Hendricks*, not Corissa Paz. I deflate a bit. Mama and I don't have the same last name any longer.

"And I don't mind putting in a good word for the young man who helped bring my Sol back to me." Mama leans toward Rafa. "In fact, I insist on it."

After she finishes her coffee, Mama leaves the room for a moment. When she returns, she places a flat rectangular device in front of me, and another in front of Rafa.

"Here you go," she beams. "They're all yours."

Rafa's eyes light up. "Satphones? No WAY." He picks it up, taps it with his finger, and the front side lights up in brilliant blue and pink. His smiling face glows with reflected light. "In camp all we had were walkie-talkies and radios."

Wasteland tech.

"You still need to voice-train them," Mama points out, "but I already put my profile in there so you can call me."

"Thanks, Mama."

"Yeah, thanks so much, Señora Pa—uh, Hendricks." Rafa gets up from the table, paces back and forth, following the phone's prompts, repeating words and phrases so the device can learn his voice. A happy boy with a new toy.

"I called over to the hospital," Mama tells me. "They're operating on little Steffa in about an hour."

A pang of guilt moves through me. I should have been there this morning when she woke up.

"Did they say anything about her leg?" I ask.

"Yes. There's no infection, nothing to worry about. She's going to be fine."

I sigh, feel my neck muscles relax. Without thinking, I reach up and touch the Virgin pendant.

"I meant to ask you about that," Mama says, nodding toward the necklace. "Where'd you get it?"

I remove my hand from the pendant, fiddle with my fork. "I don't remember. One of those traveling bazaars, I think. They used to come through Guzmán's camp all the time." The lie comes out like a reflex, surprising me. *Why don't you just tell her?*

Mama wipes her mouth with a napkin, places it on the table. "After we stop by the hospital, I have to go to work."

"Work?" I whine. "Really?"

"I know, I know." Mama shrugs. "But I can't get out of it. Something's come up and they want me to interview someone." She takes a furtive look at Rafa. He's paying no attention to us, still absorbed with the phone. It's a wonder he hasn't walked into a wall yet.

"They said I could bring you, so I doubt we're talking about world-shaking espionage." She reaches into her jacket pocket and pulls out a plastic bag of hierba, then she

winks at me.
"You want to watch your Mama do her job?"

CHAPTER 19

"Where am I?" Steffa blinks slowly. Her glazed eyes wander around the room, then fix themselves on me.

"What happened?" she asks, her voice a croaking whisper.

I move to place my hand on top of hers, but she flinches before I can touch her. "Everything went fine. Your leg's going to be good as new."

Mama and Rafa are behind me, looking over my shoulders. A nurse stands on the opposite side of the bed, studying Steffa's vitals on a small wall screen.

"I'm sleepy." Steffa closes her eyes, falls asleep.

"We're going to keep her sedated for a few hours," the nurse says. "We'll run a post-op scan once the swelling comes down a bit, just to make sure everything looks good, then we'll wake her up all the way."

Minutes later, we're walking through the hospital lobby toward the exit.

"Am I going to have to live with that worried face all day?" Mama asks, her heels clicking on the marble floor. "She's fine, the nurse said so. And I'll have you back here right after the interview, all right? She'll be in la-la land the whole time. Won't even know we're gone."

"You're right," I admit, though a large part of me wants to stay, even if she doesn't know I'm here.

"And your friend will be here with her."

"Rafa."

"I know his name, hijita."

I motion toward the lobby restroom. "I'll be right back."

Alone inside, I take out the bag of hierba from Mama's apartment, open it, and put the leaves in my mouth. I watch myself chew in the mirror as a child's naughty smile spreads across my face. It's strange how only a couple days ago I wouldn't have cared if I ever saw hierba again, but now I can't wait to show Mama what I can do, how much I've learned. Maybe she'll even let me help her with her job. The idea of hurting Guzmán by helping the Bullocks definitely has its appeal.

I come out of the restroom and join Mama, keeping the leaves tightly balled up in the side of my mouth so she doesn't notice.

We leave the hospital, exit doors sliding shut behind us. A block away to our left, there's a crowd gathered on the sidewalk, spilling out onto the street. Robots weave their way between the bodies as everyone gazes upwards at an enormous display spanning the side of a building. Rudder Bullock's face appears. His politician's smile is gone. He looks haggard, like he hasn't slept since I saw him yesterday.

The Humvee stops in front of us and the back doors slide open.

I pause. "Where's the driver?"

Mama laughs. "Goodness, you *have* been gone a long time."

I shake my head. "Right, sorry." I've been off the grid for so long I'd forgotten nearly all vehicles travel the Dallas streets on autonav, their movements coordinated by the AIs for maximum efficiency and minimal traffic delays. The only Dallasites who drive manually are police and anyone who has the bad luck to have to travel outside the city into the un-gridded technological desert of the hinterlands.

I climb into the seat and Mama follows. I shift the ball of hierba to the other side of my mouth, away from Mama's view. As the doors close, I catch the words *no cause for alarm* from the video feed.

Mama settles in next to me. "Rafa seems like a nice boy. Are you and he…?"

Blood rushes to my face. "No, Mama."

She nods like she doesn't believe me. "I see."

"Really, Mama, it's not like that at all."

I look out the back window at the crowd. "What's going on back there?"

Mama waves it off. "Some security situation. We have them all the time." She looks back as we pull away. "It's not even a status yellow, I wouldn't worry about it."

"But all those people. Why would they stop and watch if there's nothing to worry about?"

Mama puts her satphone to her ear. "I told you, hijita, people are on edge, and a big part of Rudder's role as EM is reassuring the public, making them feel safe." She speaks into the phone. "We're on our way…Five minutes…Right…Bye."

"How many people at your work…*know* about you?" I ask.

"Not many," she answers. "Rudder and a few of his direct staff." She reaches over and tucks a strand of hair behind my ear. "They're very nice. I'm sure you'll like them."

Mama smiles at me, but it fades quickly. The hierba hasn't taken hold yet, but the same odd feeling from last night strikes me, as if she's holding something back.

"Mama, is there something you want to tell me or ask me about?"

She straightens up, surprised. "What do you mean?"

I shrug. "Well, for one, you haven't asked me anything

about Guzmán's plans." I tap my temple with my finger. "I've got lots of intel up here. How many soldiers he has, what towns he wants to take next, how he operates, all that stuff. Don't you think the Bullocks would like to know all that?"

She lifts her eyebrows. "I'm sure they would. But how would you propose to convey this information without giving away where you've been for the past three years?"

Good point.

"But don't *you* want to know? In case you can use it for your job?"

"I do, hijita. I want to know everything." She tilts her head to one side. "But won't it bring up a lot of bad memories, going through all that?"

I nod. She puts her hand on my knee, squeezes. "There's plenty of time for all that."

* * *

Mama's observation room is much nicer than my cramped corner of Guzmán's dining tent. It's got sofas, a fridge full of drinks and snacks, a music player.

Not bad at all. I take another sip of soda and lean my head against the soft, cool leather of my chair. The sweet, syrupy taste doesn't quite wash away all the bitterness leftover from the hierba I spit into the trash when Mama wasn't looking.

I shift in my chair, trying to get comfortable in the new clothes Mama had delivered this morning. The pantsuit feels stiff and itchy, so different from the comfortable rags of Guzmán's camp.

Mama sits across from me, chewing her hierba and reading something on her phone. She looks up at me. "Jason's on his way."

"Jason who?"

"Bullock-Melville. He's Rudder's security chief. He'll brief us on the subject. And he's *family*—Rudder's son-in-

180

law—so best behavior, please."

The wall to our right has a large rectangular pane of one-way glass. On the other side there's a small room, empty except for a single chair. Mama says after they brief us, they'll bring the subject in and sit him down, and Mama will question him from behind the glass.

"What if they see you later, like on the street or someplace, and they recognize your voice?"

Mama shakes her head. "Couldn't happen. Audio from this side gets scrambled and re-toned. What the subject hears sounds like a man with a deep voice."

Mama moves her hand along a small red bevel that runs across the bottom edge of the glass. "You see this border here? When it's red, he can't hear us. When it's green, he can." She swipes her finger along the bevel and it changes to green. Then she reverses the swipe and it goes back to red.

The door opens and Mama stands. A handsome thirtyish man with wavy black hair and dressed in a business suit enters the room. He shakes Mama's hand and greets her politely, but he seems rushed, preoccupied.

Mama introduces me. "Wonderful to meet you. He smiles, extends his hand. "Jason Bullock-Melville."

"She's cleared to be here," Mama says, sounding a bit defensive. "Your staff gave me the okay."

"Yes, they told me. It's fine." He lifts his eyebrows at me. "Your mother's got an extraordinary talent, but I suppose you know that. She's been a godsend for the family. For all of Dallas, really."

He turns to Mama. "I'm sorry, but I can't stay. There's a situation outside the city." His voice inflects when he says *situation*. "I have to get back to the command center."

Mama looks concerned. "We saw Minister Bullock on public address. What's happening?"

"We don't really know yet. They're still collecting intel."

"Should we cancel the reading?"

Bullock-Melville shakes his head. "No, no, go ahead without me. Should be pretty straightforward, we only need a backgrounder. Who he is, where he came from, how he acquired it." A beep comes from inside his jacket. "All right, all right, I'm coming," he huffs. He taps his pocket and the beeping stops.

He nods at me. "Nice to meet you, sorry to rush off like this." He moves to the door, opens it.

"Wait," Mama pipes up, "how he acquired what?"

"Right, sorry," Bullock-Melville says, pausing in the doorway. "Underground tech from the States. Between you and me, I think it's a scam. I don't see someone like that getting hold of high-end tech." He shrugs. "But better safe than sorry. After you get his story, we'll take it out and test it."

"Take it out?" Mama asks.

"He's got the tech hidden in his leg, surgically implanted."

My stomach twists itself into a tight ball.

Bullock-Melville's pocket beeps again. "Sorry, I have to go. I'll talk with you soon." Then he leaves and shuts the door behind him.

Through the glass, the door opens in the other room, and there he is.

Blond motherfucking ponytail.

CHAPTER 20

Bad pennies always have a way of turning up. It's an expression I sometimes came across in old storybooks in our library back home.

That's what blond ponytail is: a bad penny.

"Lord," Mama says, "look at this one." Her face wrinkles up like the stink of a cow turd just hit her.

I stand there, dumbfounded by his sudden appearance, staring at the cagey old bastard. *Of course he's here, you idiot. Where else would he turn up, except right here so he could fuck up your life again?*

I open my mouth to tell Mama about him, but a thought stops me and I look around the room.

"Mama," I say, then I lean in and whisper. "Do they record these sessions?"

She furrows her brow at the worried look on my face. "Yes. I archive every reading, but I haven't turned it on yet."

I cup my hands over my mouth and around her ear. As quietly as I can, I ask, "Could someone be listening to us right now?"

"No," she says, pulling away, puzzled by my sudden secrecy. "I run the show in here. No one's listening or watching. What's gotten into you, hijita?"

I step back, tilt my head toward the gringo. "I know him."

"You know him?" she echoes, and then it takes a moment for what I've said to sink in. Mama looks at the gringo. He sits facing us, fidgeting and tapping his foot, anxious to start his pitch. Then she turns to me, confusion clouding her face. "*You know him?*"

I take a deep breath. "He was with us, when we left Guzmán's camp. I needed a tracker to find Abner." Mama's eyes widen as I tell her the rest: how I forced him to come; how I found out about the rogue AI in his leg; how he fucked us over and ditched us at the Fundie camp.

When I finish, she puts her palms to her forehead. "My God, Sol. Why didn't you tell me any of that last night?"

I feel stupid, clumsy. "I didn't know he'd show up here. I didn't think it mattered."

"Didn't think it mattered?"

I glance over at the old crook, a surge of anger welling up inside me. I want to break through the glass and wrap my hands around his scrawny neck. *I should have listened to you, Lela. I should have let you take care of him.*

"My God, what have you done?" Mama shakes her head. "What have you done to me?" She tries to compose herself, then reaches toward the glass. She swipes her finger and the red-colored bevel turns green.

"Please wait," she says, struggling to keep her voice even, "we'll be with you in a minute. Thank you."

The disembodied voice startles blond ponytail. He looks around the room, then settles his gaze on the glass in front of him and nods. "Fine."

Mama swipes her finger in the opposite direction and the bevel becomes red again. She crosses her arms, glares at me. "What a mess you've brought me."

She scolds me like a child who's dropped a glass of lemonade on the kitchen floor. "If he's said anything to anyone about you, we're sunk. You realize that, don't you?"

"He hasn't."

She doesn't seem to hear me. "If he says one thing that connects you to Guzmán, or anything about your abilities, they'll think you're a spy. And they'll think *I'm* helping you."

"Even if he has," I argue, "why would they believe him? It's his word against yours. Wouldn't they trust you?"

Mama looks at me like she can't believe she birthed such an idiot. "Trust? How can you be a reader and even use that word?" She shakes her head. "Trust is for children and fools. How could you not have learned that by now?"

I look at the floor. Neither of us speak.

An odor distracts me, a strong aroma of lavender and vanilla that wasn't there a moment before. Mama's shampoo.

My knees buckle as the hierba hits me hard. I grab the back of the chair to steady myself. My perception explodes outward, like a quiet night sky suddenly bursting with fireworks. The room around me takes on a new universe of details. The geometric shapes in the carpeted floor, the familiar smell of Mama's body under the shampoo, the deep cracks in the face of old trader beyond the glass. I watch him, feel him, jittery and bursting with greedy expectation.

"Your hierba's strong," I sputter without thinking, without realizing what I'm admitting to.

Mama blinks at me. "My WHAT?"

Crap. As if I weren't in enough trouble. "I found the box in the bathroom. I wanted to surprise you, show you what I can do."

She grabs my face between her palms and leans in, checks my eyes like an unhappy doctor. Then she grunts in disgust when she sees my pupils are dilated.

I'm already feeling the full effect. Rage lights up Mama's face, twists her mouth and tightens her neck muscles. And underneath it all there's panic.

"He hasn't said anything," I insist.

Mama eyes narrow. "There's no way to know what he's told them already."

"If they knew something, they wouldn't have left him alone with us." It's a basic rule of interrogation. You *always* separate conspirators so you can tease out inconsistencies in their stories or manipulate them against each other. If the Bullocks had known there was a connection between me and the gringo, neither of us would be where we are now. And if they suspected Mama of plotting with me, the last thing they'd do is leave us alone to interview the old trader.

She looks away from me, studies the gringo. "Maybe." I sense her thoughts scattering, fear expanding. She doesn't know what to do.

"Let me interview him," I suggest.

"You can't be serious."

"I am. Let me do it."

"So you can put me in more hot water?" Her words stab at me. "Gracias, no, hijita. I think you've brought me quite enough from the wasteland to deal with."

"Listen," I plead, "I can fix it. I know what to ask him. I know how he'll answer."

She studies my face for a long moment. Underneath all the panic and anger, I sense the smallest fragment of curiosity.

I lock my eyes on hers. The hierba she chewed is taking effect. Her pupils are large black saucers encircled by a thin halo of blue iris.

"Trust me, Mama, I can burn him."

*   *   *

It takes me some time to convince her, but Mama finally, reluctantly agrees. Dread gnaws at my stomach, a sense that she's making contingency plans, anticipating my failure. It's understandable, given the circumstances. In her shoes I'm not sure how much I'd trust me either. Still, her lack of faith unnerves me, makes it difficult to concentrate on what I have to do.

Trust is for children and fools. I push her words out of my head and focus on the gringo.

I tell her I'm ready, and Mama swipes the bevel from red to green. "Go ahead," she says. I try to ignore the suspicion burning in her eyes, the wariness reverberating in her voice.

I take a deep breath, tell myself not to fuck up.

"Please state your name," I say to the gringo.

Blond ponytail straightens up in his chair. "Brin."

I let out a small breath of relief. He doesn't recognize my voice through the scrambler.

Brin. I can't think of him as Brin, as a human being with a name. For me he's blond ponytail, a being more reptile than human, like one of those desert lizards that'll eat their own young if there's no other food around.

I already know his story inside out, so it's not hard to pull pieces of it from him that exclude me, Rafa, and Guzmán. All I do is avoid asking him about the last three days. And just as when I read him before, he's cautious and measured in his replies, answering only what I ask, careful to offer no other information. I focus on how he acquired the rogue AI, what it does, and how much he wants for it. A story begins to take shape, one where I have no role.

The interview goes on. As I question him, I try to keep my awareness in check, holding myself back so I don't see too much. The last thing I want is another peek into his fantasies of ultra-wealth and private beaches and young women fawning over him. The fantasies that cost me Lela.

Question after question, the gringo pours out his little black heart, describing how dangerous the rogue AI is, how the Bullock techs can reverse engineer it and beef up the Dallas grid's countermeasures, how thankful they should be he's brought it to them. He's relaxed, confident, even cocky at times.

"This here tech took the Pentagon offline for two days," he boasts. "*The Pentagon.*"

As he gets more comfortable, he begins to exaggerate and distort. This is what I was counting on. He's a natural liar, blond ponytail. He can't help himself. Asking him to tell the truth for more than an hour is like asking anyone else to hold their piss for a whole day.

He's too smart to tell a big, glaring lie, but not so clever that he doesn't pile up a damning amount of small ones. I catch the occasional crack in his lizard's smile. It's a small reaction, the barest quiver at the edge of his mouth, but I see it. And so does Mama. Out of the corner of my eye, she nods as she notices the giveaway. "Mmm-hmm," she mutters.

That's it, I think. *Keep digging your grave.*

After about a dozen lies and twice that many half-truths and deceptions, I figure he's said plenty. If this were don Flaco's camp, the gringo would have already been lying facedown in the desert, making a meal for coyotes and buzzards.

I swipe the bevel back to red and turn to Mama. "Is that enough?"

Mama's eyes are fixed on the trader. She nods once. She's still brooding, but less than before. Beneath her frown, I feel her coming around. She's impressed with me, surprised even.

"Run him through everything again," she says. "I want to be sure before we start archiving."

She has me walk him through the interview a second time, repeating all the same questions. Blond ponytail's patient, his answers the same as the first time around, almost to the word. Even the embellishments and lies. He has his story and he's sticking to it.

Perfect.

"All right," Mama sighs. "That's good. Now one last time for posterity."

She places her palm on the wall next to the glass. A white circles appears around her hand. Now everything's being archived.

I start the interview a third time. The gringo fidgets and knits his brow, his impatience growing, but like a disciplined actor he keeps to the script. He senses his big payday getting closer, and he doesn't want to blow it.

When we finish, Mama leans forward. "Thank you," she tells the trader. "Someone will be along shortly to escort you out." She swipes the bevel to red, cutting the connection, then palms the wall again to stop the archiving. She lowers her head and exhales.

I watch her, waiting for her to say something.

"You did good," she admits. "We're not out of the woods yet, but I've got plenty on file now."

"What will they do?"

"They'll take him over to St. Luke's, remove that tech from his leg, run tests on it. But they won't pay him, not after I tell them he's nothing but a blackmailing hustler."

"Are you sure?"

"If I tell them he's a security risk, they'll take care of him, no questions asked. They don't take any chances these days."

Not lying. It's the same kind of trust Guzmán had with me. All Don Flaco needed was a nod, and off to the desert they'd go.

I swallow, turn to the gringo. For a long minute I watch him, smug and happy and oblivious to his fate. My hand reaches up, caresses the Virgin pendant with my finger.

Lela says hello, motherfucker.

Mama takes out her phone. "Jason…Corissa…The trader, high risk…He conned someone out of it…I've got it all archived…Right…Yes…He's ready to go." She disconnects.

In the other room the door opens, and a uniformed man motions for blond ponytail to follow him. The gringo stands, nods toward us—a thank-you gesture, of all things—and then exits the room.

"What a disgusting creature," Mama hisses. She gets up, goes over to the fridge. "I'm starving. You want a sandwich?"

I stare at the trader's empty chair. "How will they do it?"

"Do what?" Over my shoulder, I hear her rummaging through the fridge.

"Take care of him?"

Mama sets a plate with a sandwich on my lap before sitting heavily on the sofa and sighing. "I don't know."

I look at her. She bites her sandwich, chews. "*So* good," she marvels, rolling her eyes. "Genoa salami smuggled in from the States. Worth every credit."

"I'm not hungry." Something feels wrong. Something besides the gringo.

"Don't know what you're missing," Mama says, taking another bite.

She swallows, then smiles at me. "You're good. *Really* good. You knew what to ask, when to ask it. You kept him off balance, checked his facts from different angles. Led him right down the path you wanted him to follow. He was a slick one, and you handled him easily." Mama reaches over, pats my knee. "I'm impressed, hijita."

Her face glows with relief, but underneath there's something else, raging and turbulent like an underground river. Something she's trying to hide from me.

Fear.

She's afraid...of me. *Why would Mama be afraid of me?* I don't want to believe it, but it's there, clear and unmistakable.

"Mama, what are you scared of?"

She jerks her head up from the sandwich. "Scared? You think you see fear in my face?" She laughs. A false laugh, forced.

I stand and step to the side, looking at her from

another angle. "I can see it, Mama."

"Sit down, hijita. What you're seeing is worry. Until that trader's taken care of, we should both be worried."

"It's not about him. It's me. You're afraid of *me*."

She stands. "That's ridiculous. Now why would I be afraid of my own daughter?"

"Are you?"

"Of course not."

Lying.

"Mama. Why are you lying?"

She doesn't answer. She tries to bury it, clearing her face of all expression.

"You can tell me," I plead. "What is it?"

As she turns away, I feel her thoughts scatter like a flock of birds frightened by a hunter's gunshot. "There's nothing to tell, hijita. You're just not used to hierba this strong. You're seeing something that isn't there."

Lying.

I move around her so I can see her face. "Look at me," I demand, grabbing her by the shoulders. Her eyes go wide like a scared child's. She freezes.

I breathe deep and concentrate, feeling my awareness expand and wrap around her mind. Images of people and places begin to flicker through my perception. A woman glares at Mama at a cocktail party. Mama smirks at her, amused at the woman's hatred. Then again during intermission at the opera house, the same woman only in a different dress this time scowls at Mama. Next to the woman stands a silver-haired man in a tuxedo—somehow I know he's the husband—his hand touching the small of her back. *Rudder Bullock.*

I snap back into myself, a sick feeling overcoming me. I let go of her shoulders.

Mama stands with her mouth hanging open, her face pale.

"What happened?" she gasps. "What did you just do?"

"You're his mistress?" I burst out. "Rudder Bullock's

mistress?"

She places her hand over her mouth. "How did you do that?"

"That's why you and Papi aren't together." I recall the awkwardness between them at the hospital. Between all three of them. "All that 'growing apart' crap you told me was nonsense, wasn't it?"

The shock on Mama's face fades into something darker, meaner. The muscles around her mouth harden into a frown. "I don't have to explain myself to my own child. I told you it's complicated."

"*Complicated?*"

Something inside her breaks, like a dam bursting. "Your father would have kept us out there in that godforsaken wilderness *forever!* I put up with that life for years, living out there with the bugs and dirt and stinking animals. You think he cared? You think he gave a damn about what I wanted? And after all I did for him!" This last is pregnant with some hidden, ugly meaning.

My body shudders. "And Rudder Bullock cares? Is that it?"

Scorn fills her face. "You wouldn't understand."

I put my palms to my forehead. "Jesus, Mama. I've been living in *Ernesto Guzmán's* camp for three years. You think I haven't seen sex traded for status, for wealth?"

Mama glares at me. *Who is this woman?*

I shake my head, not wanting to believe it. "How could you?"

"Don't get holier-than-thou with me," she snaps. "When I left your father I had *nothing.* Not a credit to my name. I did what I had to do, and you would have done the same."

"Bullshit."

A mean smirk stretches across her face. "Oh, so you think you're above that kind of thing, do you? You think I haven't noticed how that Rafa kid follows you around like a puppy dog? Are you going stand there and tell me you didn't fuck-bait that boy into helping you out?"

I shake my head. "No, it's not the same."

"How is it not the same?" Mama insists.

"It's just not."

"I see." She taps her ear. "Did you hear that tiny little tremor in your voice? No? Maybe you didn't want to hear it. Maybe you ignored it."

I don't say anything.

"You can lie to yourself," she says, "but not to me."

I study Mama's face, my own within it. We have the same round eyes, same thin nose and sharp cheekbones.

I feel sick. I want to look away from her, to stop seeing what I'm seeing. But I can't. There's something else there, something worse. The skin around her eyes quivers, a tiny vein in her temple throbs. She's hiding more than her affair with Bullock, much more.

I *have* to know.

Again I push my awareness into her mind, feeling her body stiffen against the intrusion. An animal fear radiates from her like heat from a campfire. She feels threatened, cornered.

Her mind begins to unfold, revealing itself. Snippets from a recent memory, fresh and strong, appear like a vision. It's Mama naked in bed, watching a drone feed on a wall screen. The feed shows a large group of cars speeding over a marshy field. They're so small they look like toys, slipping and sliding through mud and standing water. After a moment I recognize what I'm seeing. It's Guzmán's chase group from yesterday.

The shaky overhead shot pans forward, comes to a stop on a car stuck in a bog. A Humvee.

My Humvee.

"Is that the one they're chasing?" a man's voice asks. I see the profile of Rudder Bullock, sitting on the edge of the bed next to Mama, pulling his pants on. He watches the feed with intense interest.

"Affirmative, sir," a disembodied voice answers.

Bullock stands, steps closer to the screen. "Can you zoom in closer?"

"Yes, sir. One moment."

The feed quivers and jumps as the Humvee grows larger. The words on the roof become legible.

Mama pulls the covers up to her chin. *No*, she thinks, *it can't be.*

"My God," Bullock gasps to Mama, "do you see what it says?"

Mama's hands begin to tremble. Her stomach lurches with dread.

"It's a trick," she snaps. "It has to be."

Bullock turns to Mama. "But what if it's not? You always said she was smart, capable. Maybe she wasn't killed after all."

Mama shakes her head. "It's not her. It can't be."

"We have to find out."

She clears her throat, tries to hide the anxiety in her voice. "It's a trick, Rudder. It has to be."

He looks at Mama, confounded at her reaction. "Don't you want to know? Even if there's a sliver of a chance? It's your daughter, for Christ's sake."

Mama tries to control herself. "Of course," she says. "Of course I want to know. But..."

He turns again to the screen, speaks to it. "Hit the chase group, but leave this one alone. And get a ground team ready. We're going to bring them in."

"Affirmative, Minister Bullock."

Mama's mind blooms into blaring panic. *What if it's her? What do I do if it's really her?*

Bullock turns to Mama. "Get dressed. If she actually *is* in that car, you should be the one welcoming her home."

The memory fades and disappears, replaced with an image of Mama's hand opening a car door, her leg stepping out into a rain-soaked field. She's trying to keep herself together, holding on to the hope that the name on the roof is a ploy, a ruse of some sort. Then she recognizes my face and her mind explodes into a frenzy of confusion and fear.

Not joy, not relief.

Then another memory flashes. It's minutes later and we're on our way back to Dallas in the Humvee. She has her arm around me, pretending to be overjoyed at my return while her mind scrambles to come up with a way out. What to do, how to get control of the situation, how to get rid of me without arousing suspicion or putting herself at risk. Her stomach's balled up with anxiety, her desperation growing as the skyline looms large in the front windshield. She tries not to recoil at my smell as I nuzzle closer to her.

Then a door seems to slam shut, and the side of my face erupts in a stinging, burning pain. It takes me a moment to understand what's happened, to figure out Mama's just slapped me hard across the face.

"Get the hell out of my head," she sneers.

My cheek tingles. The taste of blood fills my mouth.

"Who taught you how to do that?" she demands.

I touch my face, don't answer.

Mama slaps my other cheek, harder this time.

"Answer me!" Her eyes are wild, her teeth bared like a growling dog's.

I turn and run. Her shouts are cut off as I slam the door behind me. I race down the empty hallway to the exit, then dash madly down the stairs.

When I burst through the ground floor door, breathless and panting, I find the lobby empty. I run outside, the image of Mama's bloodthirsty face blaring in the front of my mind.

I don't want to believe it, but it was there, beaming from her eyes. I felt it to my marrow.

She wants me dead.

Mama wants me dead.

CHAPTER 21

I run down a walkway, directionless and half-blind with tears.

Mama's terrified of me. And it has nothing to do with what the Bullocks could discover about my years at Guzmán's camp. Nothing to do with Guzmán at all. Her fear of me began long before that, when we were still living in the Panhandle. I can see it now, in my memories, like a shadow darkening her face.

But why? She'd slapped me out of her head before I could see the reason behind it.

I trip over an ankle-high streetcleaner bot and go sprawling over the pavement. I get up, my palms and knees smarting. The streets are empty of cars and there are no pedestrians. I'm alone except for dozens of robots, rolling and rambling along the walkways, ignoring me. In the distance I hear the wail of a siren.

I spot the familiar steeple of St. Luke's Hospital a couple blocks away. An image from yesterday pops into my head: Mama's gaze hanging on Steffa's face. The glint of curiosity in her eyes, and with it a growing suspicion.

Steffa.

I break into a run. When I burst into the lobby,

breathless, I find a small crowd pressed together underneath a wall screen. No one notices me. All eyes look upward at the screen, where a jerky feed from a high-altitude drone stretches across the wall. There's a large gathering of some sort, somewhere in the wilds beyond the city.

The satphone rings. My stomach drops as I picture Mama on the other end. I slowly remove it from my pocket, see Rafa's name flashing.

I don't answer. At the edge of the lobby I see a stairway sign above a door. I shoulder through it and sprint up the stairs.

I exit the stairwell on the seventh floor, gasping. At the end of the hallway I throw open the door to Steffa's room. Rafa and Papi stand next to her as she lies on the bed. They turn and look at me.

"Why didn't you pick up?" Rafa asks. He's still holding the phone to his ear. I rush over to him, avoiding Papi's face, and snatch the device from him. I crack open the window and toss both of our phones out into the air.

"What're you doing?" Rafa protests. He presses his forehead against the glass, watches the phones hit the street far below.

"She can track us with those," I say, still breathing heavy.

"Who?"

"Sol, I have to talk with you." I feel Papi's hand on my shoulder. I flinch, pull away.

"Don't touch me," I snap. I keep my eyes down, seeing only his battered, worn work shoes. I'm afraid to look at his face, afraid of what I might see there.

I move to the bed.

"You were crying," Steffa croaks, blinking slowly.

"I'm going to take you out of here," I tell her.

"But my leg."

"I'll carry you."

"What are you doing?" Rafa protests. "You can't just

take her out of here."

"Rafa, I need your help." I pull back the sheets. "I'll explain later. Help me get her out of here." I imagine Mama screaming into her phone, ordering Ministry of Justice agents to find me.

"Why aren't you with your mother?" Papi asks. "Did something happen?"

I ignore him and the suspicion in his voice as I remove the tape holding Steffa's IV in place. She squirms in discomfort.

"I don't want to talk about her," I snarl. Steffa winces, yelps as I remove the IV from her arm. "Press your thumb here," I tell her. "It'll hurt a bit, but that'll keep if from bleeding."

Papi steps around to the side of me. I feel him watching me closely. "My God, *you know*, don't you?" His voice reverberates with surprise, despair. "I knew you'd find out. I *knew* it."

I grab Steffa under the arms and sit her up. Out of the corner of my eye I see Papi with his hands over his face. "Oh, God," he moans. "You know."

Under a light wrapping, Steffa's leg is still swollen. "Do you think you can walk?" I ask her.

She stares at her leg. "I don't know."

"Sol, listen to me," Papi says, sniffing, trying to steady his voice. "You're in danger."

"In danger?" Rafa exclaims.

Papi reaches out to me. "Let me help you."

I slap his hand away. "Get the fuck away from me."

"Sol!" Rafa yells. "What's gotten into you?"

"Look at me, please," Papi insists.

"I told you, I don't want to——"

"Look at me!" His voice strains with desperation, anguish.

I take a breath, swallow. I turn to Papi.

Oh, God. The remorse and regret twist his face into something almost unrecognizable. It's as if his soul's been broken, shattered into a million pieces. Like he's been emptied out of everything except a dark, unbearable shame.

"You don't have to be afraid of me." He says it like a vow. "I want to help."

Not lying.

I stand there frozen as he rushes from the room and returns with a wheelchair. "Here," he says, rolling it to me. "Take the service elevator. There's a side exit on the east side of the building. I'll bring my car around."

He hurries out the door, leaving the three of us alone.

I stare at the empty doorway. Nothing makes sense.

"Are you going to tell me what's going on?" Rafa asks.

"It's like he said. We're in danger." I turn and move to the bed. "Help me lift her."

Rafa looks at me, nods. We ease Steffa into the wheelchair.

I shake my head. "I'm so sorry I got you both into this mess, Rafa."

He grips the push handles, shrugs, manages to smile. "Forget it. A lo hecho, pecho."

I place my hand on top of his and squeeze. Then I turn and poke my head out the hallway, find it empty. "Okay, vamos."

Rafa races to the service elevator and pushes the button. I follow, pushing Steffa in the wheelchair. There's no one around. No staff, no visitors. The hospital feels eerily empty and quiet.

We take the elevator to the ground floor, find Papi waiting for us outside, standing next to a dusty old Jeep. He helps us load Steffa in the back. Rafa and I climb in and Papi drives out of the parking lot.

"Stay out of sight," he says. Rafa and I duck down, squatting on the floorboards. Steffa lies across the seat. "Where are we going?" she asks.

"Someplace safe," Papi answers. Then to me he says, "I have the key to a friend's office a few blocks from here.

We can hide you there while we figure out what to do."

I raise up and peek out the window. A pair of robots pause at a corner, waiting for us to make our turn. The streets are still empty.

"Where is everyone?" I ask Papi.

"Haven't you seen the news feeds?"

"Not enough to know what's happening."

"Everyone's hiding," Papi says.

"Hiding from what?"

"Guzmán's army," he says, his voice thick with dread. "They're about to attack the city."

*   *   *

Papi sets a cup of water on the end table next to the sofa where Steffa lies sleeping. He peers out at the street through the window, then pulls the cord to close the blinds. The office is roomy and comfortable. I still feel the grip of the hierba.

"How do they know it's Guzmán?" Rafa asks.

Papi taps the wall screen to life and the same feed from the hospital lobby appears. "Look at that. That's not some backwoods turf militia out there. Only one person in the Republic has an army that size."

The image slowly pans across a long line of vehicles. Trucks, Humvees, motorcycles, old school buses. A cavalry of steel and guns, a thousand strong.

"Why haven't they sent out drones yet?" I ask, recalling how they broke up the group chasing us.

Papi shakes his head. "Maybe they're holding them back, waiting to use them until they have to."

Right, I think. A few drones might be able to scatter a small chase party, but this is something else entirely: an army.

Papi unzips the bag hanging from his shoulder, removes two pistols from it, sets them on the table in front of me. The Glock 20s we used to take with us on camping trips.

He takes a deep breath. "Take these." I grab the guns, give one to Rafa. We put them in our pockets.

"I've got some body armor at my apartment," Papi says. "Round trip's maybe thirty minutes. You'll be okay until I get back?"

I nod. He turns to leave and I grab his arm. "No, wait," I blurt out. "I have to talk to you."

He motions to the wall screen, his face desperate. "Sol, all hell's about to break loose. We don't have time."

"Por favor, Papi," I plead.

He looks down at his shoes, shakes his head. "Not while you're like that."

"Like what?"

"Your eyes are dilated."

Suddenly I sense he's more afraid of me than Guzmán's invasion.

"Sol," he says, "I'll be right ba—"

"Why does Mama want me dead?" I burst out, gripping his arm tighter. "Why is she so afraid of me?"

"Sol!" Rafa cries. Steffa whimpers and squirms on the sofa, but doesn't wake up. Rafa lowers his voice. "How can you say something like that?"

Papi's face doesn't change. His eyes are still cast downward, avoiding me.

"Look at me," I tell him.

He doesn't move.

"Look," I insist.

Slowly he lifts his gaze and our eyes meet. The hierba's starting to fade, but the effect's still strong enough for me to see the shadow behind his eyes. A hidden, secret shame.

I shiver. *Something about the day they took me.*

"You know, don't you?" I say, my voice cracking. "You have to tell me. Right here, right now."

Something inside him seems to break. His shoulders curve inward, head lowers, the posture of a boxer who's just lost a decision. Finally he nods.

We move to an adjacent room, barely larger than a closet, with two chairs separated by a small table. I close the door behind us; we sit and face each other.

Papi's nervous and his eyes are sad. He swallows, sighs. For a long moment neither of us speaks.

"My first intern's name was Alex," he says slowly. "Do you remember him?"

The name conjures distant memories of a young man with intense blue eyes who sometimes had dinner with us when we lived in Tyler. Or was it Hillsboro? "Kind of," I answer.

"He didn't live with us like Abner did, so you didn't see him that often."

Papi clears his throat. "Alex was nineteen or twenty, a geology student, still in college. He was a nice boy…smart and well-mannered. He also happened to be Rudder Bullock's nephew."

His gaze is fixed on the tabletop. "Corissa saw it as a great opportunity, a way to get in good with the Bullocks. A stepping stone for my career." He exhales tiredly. "I didn't care about all that. I just wanted the kid to learn something."

And then something happened to the boy. He hasn't said it yet, but I feel it coming, sensing the words before he says them. *An accident.*

"He died," I say.

Papi looks up at me suddenly, then nods in understanding. "We were on a survey and Alex was setting up some equipment on a ridge. It was pretty steep and there was some loose gravel. He lost his footing, fell into a ravine."

"He fell and died."

Papi looks down at the table again. I see shame, regret. "Hit his head on a rock."

He takes a shaky breath. "Your mother was beside herself. She said it was all my fault, said when the Bullocks found out they'd blame me too. My career would be over.

They'd make sure of it. We'd be finished."

It's the first time I've heard the story. A chapter in our lives I never knew existed. "So what happened?"

Papi struggles to continue. "Your mother was so smart, so beautiful. I never understood why she married someone like me. A poor scientist with no connections, no money. I did everything I could not to disappoint her. I tried to be the man she wanted me to be, but..." His voice trails off.

"What happened after Alex died?"

Papi closes his eyes, pinches the bridge of his nose. "It's possible to love someone too much, did you know that? It blinds you, makes you do things you never thought you'd do in a million years."

"Tell me what happened." My heart races. I feel myself getting closer to the truth.

"Your mother and I went back out there." He grimaces at the memory. "We beat up the body, shot it up, tried to make it look like a robbery. Then we reported Alex missing with the university. Told them he didn't show up for work that day."

My stomach lurches. "You covered it up."

"I told your mother it would never work." He shakes his head. "But damned if it didn't. The investigators blamed it on freelancers, just like your mother said they would." He snorts. "The Bullocks even thanked me for making his final months happy ones. The night before he died he'd told them how much he loved doing survey work. Imagine that. They actually *thanked* me."

We sit without speaking for a while.

"Afterwards, we never brought it up again, never discussed it," Papi mutters.

Until...

He doesn't give voice to the word, but it's there. And with it, the rest of truth. The line connecting me and Mama and the boy's death. The answer to all my questions.

"Until when, Papi?" I prompt.

He shakes his head, squeezes his eyes shut. "I can't."

"Tell me," I insist, hammering my fist on the table.

"It's so horrible," he whimpers.

I push my awareness into him, violent like a punch. The edges of my vision blur, then everything goes black and I feel as if I'm falling. Flashes of our life on the plains race through my head. Goats and chickens. A wide sky, cloudless and perfectly azure. Endless fields of prairie grass, rippling like ocean waves in the summer wind. Then the smell of Mama's chicken curry fills my nostrils, makes my mouth water. I'm standing in the kitchen of our home in the Panhandle. Mama glares at me, furious. No, not glaring at me. *Glaring at Papi.* It's his memory of an argument.

The argument. The one he can't take back, the one that's haunted him for years.

I can't make out words, but I feel the strain of violent, vicious shouting. Mama leans forward into Papi's face. He turns away, crying. He doesn't want to do it, but he doesn't have the energy to fight anymore. She's already convinced Abner—Papi suspects how but doesn't want to admit it, even as he pictures Mama and Abner in bed together—and now she won't stop until she breaks him too. She's been working on him for months, slowly wearing him down. Now he's exhausted, now he can't take any more. He lowers his head in surrender, tells her all right, all right, let's just do it and get it over with.

Get what over with?

I snap back to myself. My forehead's wet with cold sweat.

"I was weak," he confesses. "I'm sorry, I'm so sorry." He covers his face with his hands. "Don't see me," he sobs. "Don't look at me."

I grab his wrists, lower them to the table. He doesn't resist. Whatever it was that Mama beat out of him, he never got it back. He's broken, lost.

Again I push inside his mind. The darkest corners of his consciousness begin to unfold.

The universe disappears around me. Finally, the hideous truth reveals itself.

I see it all now. Everything. The pieces of a cruel puzzle come together, move into place. I see the thing that was always there, like a low hum in the background I never heard until now. The dark undercurrent of our final months of life on the plains.

It was my power.

My ability to see more than lies. That's where it all started. When Mama became aware of it, she knew one day I'd find them out, one day I'd uncover the secret of the intern's death and what they did about it. Papi tried to tell her she was wrong, that even if I found out I'd never tell anyone. I'd never hurt my own parents. But Mama wouldn't listen. She stopped my lessons for fear of being found out. She grew suspicious, paranoid. And then one day she came to him with the solution.

A solution he told himself he'd never agree to…

I recoil from it, pulling myself away from Papi's mind. He looks at me with the face of a condemned man. "What kind of a woman forces a man to choose between his wife and his daughter?" His eyes glisten with tears. "And what kind of a man actually makes that choice?"

I'm stunned beyond words, numb with disbelief.

"Those men that took me," I manage, my voice barely above a whisper. "The freelancers. They were supposed to kill me, weren't they? That's what Mama hired them for, what she talked you into going along with." I swallow against the sickening churn of my stomach.

He shakes his head. "I couldn't go through with it. I just couldn't. That morning I gave them extra so they'd take you to Guzmán instead of…doing what your mother wanted. I knew he'd take you in. Then at least you'd be alive."

"And Mama and Abner never knew. All that time I was with Guzmán they thought I was dead."

He doesn't answer, doesn't need to. I saw it all in his

head, the entire sham. He paid off the freelancers in secret, told them I was a reader, told them if they delivered me to Guzmán they'd get paid a fortune for me. Then when the day came, when they captured me and threw me over the horse, they fired off a few rounds from inside the house so I'd think they were all dead, so I'd never get the idea to come looking for them. And to make the story even more legit, Papi had the leader pretend to find me out by sniffing the hierba on my breath and connecting it with some invented folklore he'd heard as a child.

I sit there, barely able to fathom it all. The lies and deceptions. Their crimes and their cover-ups. What she wanted to do to me. What he allowed to happen.

I stare at him, at this man who allowed his only child to be sold into slavery. Everything I ever felt for him suddenly falls away.

I stand up and glare at the stranger in front of me, rage coursing through me. "You should have saved your money," I sneer. "You should have let them do the job Mama hired them for."

He looks up at me. Shame tinged with confusion.

"Do you know what they did to me?" I growl. "After they took me away?"

He drops his head. Tears fall to the table. "No," he whimpers, but it's a lie. He knows.

"They didn't deliver me to Guzmán right away," I tell him. "They waited a few weeks…until they got tired of me."

My father covers his face. "No, no," he sobs. "I don't want to hear it."

"There were ten of them. They took me every day, every single one of them. Some would go twice, even three times a day."

"No, no. Please stop."

"That's what I said," I seethe. "Stop, please stop. But they didn't. They just kept doing it. And you paid them. You *paid* them to do that to me."

Images and sensations from those nightmarish weeks come back with horrible clarity. The pain between my legs, the stink of their breath. I squeeze my eyes shut, press my palms to my forehead, trying to force the memories out.

Moments pass and I find my breath, feel my heart slow down. I open my eyes and look down at him, a tear-stained, snotty mess. I take a last look at the broken man, sensing his despair. He doesn't know how he'll live with what he's just heard. It's going to haunt him forever. *As it should.*

I reach out my hand, palm up. "Give me the keys to the Jeep."

CHAPTER 22

I stand next to the window, looking out at the empty street. The hierba's effect is gone. I feel detached, untethered to this place, to my body.

"Sol, close the blinds," Rafa says, concern in his voice. "Someone might see you." He walks over to me, speaks softly. "What happened in there?"

"We can't stay here," I mumble.

"Why not?"

I shake my head slowly. "We can't trust them. Neither of them."

He places his hand on my shoulder. "What do you want to do?"

I want to burn Dallas to the ground, that's what I want to do. I want to drop a nuke on it, take it off the map. This place that gives my father a living, that my mother idealizes as heaven on earth. This too clean, too perfect jewel of a city sitting atop a pile-of-shit failure of a country.

I turn and look at the closed door, picture him behind it, still weeping. On the screen the drone's feed pans across countless vehicles.

"It's really happening," Rafa ponders as he watches the feed. "I never thought he'd try to take Dallas so soon. I figured he'd win over a few more towns, take more time to recruit more fighters, build up his forces."

"That actually *was* the plan," I say, remembering don Flaco hunched over his map, carefully working out which towns he'd take and in what order.

"Wonder what changed his mind."

I stare at the screen. *Oh, Jesus.* I raise my hand to my mouth. "I'm an idiot."

"What?"

"Christ, why didn't I see it before?"

"See *what* before?"

I tap my chest with my finger. "He's coming now because of *me*. Guzmán knows I'm here, remember? He must think I've sold him out, told the Bullocks all his plans and secrets."

Rafa's mouth drops open.

"I've forced his hand," I say.

Rafa nods, looks at the screen. "What do we do?"

Steffa snoozes on the sofa. I reach up and wrap my hand around the Virgin pendant, squeezing it.

I never should have left camp, never should have dragged Lela and Rafa and Steffa into this mess, never should have let that gringo off the hook when I caught him lying.

The gringo!

"Rafa," I blurt out, "we have to go back to the hospital."

He looks at me like I'm crazy. "¿Estás loca?"

I hand him the keys to the Jeep. "I'm serious. I'll explain on the way. We have to hurry."

Steffa stirs but doesn't awaken as I gather her up and carry her out. I pause and look back at the door to the adjacent room, still closed, then I turn and go outside.

On the way to the hospital I tell Rafa what I have in mind. He listens as he drives. In the rearview I see his eyes moving back and forth like he's doing a complicated math problem.

"It *might* work," he answers, his voice slow and cautious. "*If* no one spots us, and *if* we can actually get past security, and *if* the tech turns out not to be a dud."

I look down at Steffa. She's asleep, lying across the seat next to me.

Rafa sticks out his lower lip, shrugs. "But, yeah, it could work."

Moments later he parks the Jeep near the side exit, the same spot where Papi picked us up. A pair of robots roll down the sidewalk in the falling light of dusk. The sun hangs low in the west, halfway down the horizon. There's no one around, nothing but ten meters of manicured grass between the Jeep and the exit door.

I gently rock the girl's shoulder. "Steffa, Steffa." Her eyes crack open. "Rafa and I have to leave for a few minutes. You wait for us here, okay?"

Her eyes pop open. She wriggles to a sitting position, looks at me suspiciously. "Where are you going?"

"We'll be right back," Rafa says, exiting the vehicle. "We'll lock the doors to keep you safe."

She notices him adjusting the Glock in the back of his pants, then furrows her brow at me. "Why can't I go?"

"Because we might have to run," I tell her. "And your leg's not ready to run yet."

She frowns. "We won't be long," I insist, reaching for her. "You have to stay here, and you need to get down so no one sees you."

She pushes against me as I lower her to the floorboard. I close the door, hear the locks engage. Through the window she scowls at me.

"Come on," Rafa calls. He's already at the exit door, holding it open and waving me over. I take a last look at Steffa—she's still glaring at me for leaving her alone—and I press my palm against the window. Then I turn and hurry into the building.

The stairwell's empty and quiet. "Patient rooms start on the second floor," Rafa whispers.

We pad up the stairs, crack open the door. The hallway runs the length of the building, doors lining each side. At the far end there's another exit door, and beyond it, another stairway. A supplies robot rolls down the hallway. "Not this one," I tell Rafa.

We try the third floor, find it empty. Fourth floor, an orderly making rounds.

On the fifth floor there are two guards wearing Ministry of Justice uniforms at the far end of hallway, near the other exit. I shut the door, careful not to make any noise. "This is it," I whisper.

Rafa nods. "You ready?"

I nod back.

"Okay," he says, "give me two minutes." He turns and bounds down the stairs, then pushes through the fourth floor door.

Breathe.

I count the seconds, imagining everything that could go wrong, until a couple minutes have passed. I straighten my jacket, wipe the flop sweat from my forehead, try to harden my face into a scowl.

I kiss the Virgin pendant, tuck it into my shirt, and push through the door.

"Halt!" One of the guards calls out, then takes a couple steps toward me. "This floor's off limits." His partner watches me, but stays at his post in front of the door.

I stride toward him without pausing. "Bullock-Melville wants that freelancer moved to a secure location across town. They're bringing a car out front in two minutes."

He places his right hand on his holstered gun, shows me the palm of his left. "Ma'am, stay right where you are."

I fight the instinct to stop, forcing myself to keep moving forward until I'm right in front of him. He unbuttons the holster, grips the butt of his gun.

I glance at the pistol, then glare at him. "What are you going to do, shoot me for doing my job? I'm with the Ministry of Justice."

The second guard steps beside his partner. "What the hell are you talking about? Nobody from Min of J called us."

I shrug. "Take it up with my boss."

As they stand shoulder to shoulder facing me, behind them the exit door slowly opens. Rafa quietly creeps toward them and raises the Glock. "Don't move," he growls as he cocks the pistol.

They both turn toward the sound, and I rush forward, taking out my Glock and reaching them in two quick strides. I press the muzzle into the closer one's neck, my hands trembling. He stiffens, then they both slowly lift their hands.

"We need to have a chat with the trader," I say.

*   *   *

For once, we're lucky. They haven't removed the rogue AI yet.

"You can't do it," the gringo protests from the bed. "You just can't." *Caaaiiint* do it. Jesus, if I ever get out of this I'll never hear an East Texas accent again without thinking of this cockroach.

Rafa stands next to the bathroom, where we have the two guards disarmed and locked inside, his gun trained on the door. Outside dusk fades into darkness and the lights of the city come to life. Streetlamps glow incandescent and the bright circus colors of building lights blink on.

As Rafa helps me put the wrist and ankle restraints on blond ponytail, the gringo tries to bargain with us.

"I'll give you half. My hand to God. Fifty percent. That'll set you up right nice."

"Quiet," I shush, tightening the restraint's buckle. I raise the gun as if I'm going to hit him with the butt. He winces and shuts up. Somehow I resist the urge to follow through with the motion.

I move to the bedside cabinet and open the top drawer,

emptying it of its contents. Swabs, bandages, tongue depressors fall to the floor.

I look at Rafa. "How long?"

He shrugs. "I don't know."

We stand there, waiting and saying nothing. I shift my eyes from Rafa to the gringo. A minute passes, then another. Nothing. I picture Steffa hiding in the Jeep's back seat. Scared and alone.

"Maybe it's not coming," I say. "What if it doesn't come?"

Before Rafa can answer, the door to the hallway slowly starts to open. I hold my breath, point the gun at the doorway.

A supply bot rolls into the room. I exhale and step out of its way.

It moves around the bed and stops on front of the supply cabinet. I nod toward a finger-sized depression on the top of its casing. "I think that's it," I tell Rafa. He reaches down and places his finger in the depression and the bot stops moving. On the bot's side panel red letters flash on and off, reading UNIT PAUSED.

Rafa opens a small flap labeled with a connection icon and runs out a long adapter cord. I lift up the gringo's hospital gown, revealing the bulge in his thigh and the two trodes dangling from it. Rafa passes me the cord.

"Seventy-five percent," the gringo begs, his eyes wide in terror, fixed on the cord in my hand. "How can you say no to three quarters? Deal of a lifetime, right here, right now. How can you say no to something like—"

Something snaps inside me. I smash his face with my forearm, the same way I once saw Lela do it. I feel his nose crunch and break. He yelps in pain and blood starts to pour from his nostrils.

I lean over the trader, the sickening smell of blood and sour breath wafting up. I take the Glock, wedge it into his mouth. He squeezes his eyes shut.

"Sol," Rafa warns behind me.

I click off the safety, thinking of Lela.

"Sol, don't," Rafa begs. "They'll hear."

Goddammit. I remove the Glock from his mouth, glare at him. "Shut up and don't move."

I take the adapter cord, connect it to the trodes coming from the gringo's thigh. A pair of beeps tell us the connection's good.

Rafa looks at me. "That's it?"

"That's how he explained it back in San Angelo. The rogue can penetrate the grid from any point. From there it spreads out and takes over the whole system, corrupting it."

"*If* it can get past their countermeasures," Rafa adds.

I nod toward the gringo. "He believed it could, whatever that's worth." I exhale. "We'll find out soon enough."

"So suppose it gets past the countermeasures," Rafa says. "What happens then?"

We both turn to the gringo. His nose is already swelling and turning purple; the bottom half of his face is a mess of blood and snot. He turns his head, spits blood on the sheets. "Nobody knows."

I recall what he told me about rogue AIs, how they're like crazy people. There's no way to predict what one might do, how it might behave.

A bell tone sounds from the supply bot. I look down and see its side panel flashing green: TRANSFER COMPLETE.

I disconnect the trodes.

For a moment nothing happens, then all the robot's supply compartments slide open. It slowly reaches inside with its four arms, removes some plastic packages, and drops them on the floor.

Rafa and I exchange looks.

Then the machine's arms erupt into a frenzy, sending supplies flying into the air. Bandages and hand towels and plastic gloves fly around the room, bounce off the walls and ceiling. The bot looks like some mechanical spider gone berserk.

A glove hits Rafa on the side of the face. "Come on, let's get out of here."

I nod. "Yeah, vamos."

Rafa shoves a chair up against the bathroom doorknob, then rushes past me out of the room. I move to follow him, but then pause in the doorway.

I look back at blond ponytail, holding the Glock at my side. The bot's run out of supplies and the room is suddenly still and quiet. I run my thumb along the ridges of the pistol's grip.

The trader stares at me, bloody and defeated, the life gone from his eyes. It's almost as if he's asking me to do it.

Not worth the bullet. I shove the Glock into my pants and turn to leave.

"You just killed the city," the trader groans.

I walk into the hallway, shutting the door behind me. I pull out the pendant, kiss it.

I follow Rafa to the exit, smiling to myself. "I sure did. And won't my parents be disappointed?"

CHAPTER 23

Steffa clambers up onto the seat and glowers at me, her face splotchy and red with anger.

I open the door and reach for her. She pulls away. "I'm sorry we took so long," I tell her, but she keeps scowling at me.

Rafa drives a few blocks, then parks the Jeep on a side street. He turns on the dashboard screen, the soft white glow illuminating his face.

"My God," he gasps.

"What is it?" I lean forward, look at the screen. It's the same drone feed from before, but now switched over to nightview. Far below there's a chaos of explosions and green tracers flying in every direction.

"It's started," Rafa mutters.

There's a sudden splintering sound behind us. Steffa shrieks and dives to the floorboard. I turn around and see two large spiderweb cracks in the rear window. Behind us in the alley, there's a black Humvee. A figure leans out the passenger side, arms extending a pistol toward us.

"Get down!" Rafa floors it and I tumble backwards against the seat.

I scramble down into the floorboard, shielding Steffa

with my body. The vehicle lurches as Rafa accelerates out of the alley.

Another shot hits the Jeep with a loud thud. The engine revs and whines, tires screech. We fly around another corner.

"How many?" I cry. More shots ring out behind us.

"I don't know," Rafa yells. "A lot."

Jesus.

"How'd they find us so fast?" he shouts.

"I don't know." Maybe the gringo's guards busted out of the bathroom as soon as we left and called the cops. Or maybe Mama's had Min of J agents looking for us since the moment I ran out on her. It's hardly worth worrying about, I instantly decide, now that the bullets are flying all around us.

"Where should we go?" Rafa cries. Then he shrieks in pain and I know he's been shot.

"Stay down," I tell Steffa, then I rise up and throw myself into the front seat. Rafa's hunched over, gripping the wheel with one hand. His right arm hangs limp at his side. On the back of his right shoulder there's a large bloodstain.

We're barreling down a wide street. I glance behind us, keeping my head down, squinting against the headlights, counting six pairs. The Jeep veers toward the walkway, then jolts back to the middle of the road. I look at Rafa. He coughs, winces in pain.

"Switch places with me," I yell. He looks at me, his face knotted in agony, and nods. The back window shatters. Steffa screams as glass rains down on top of her.

I climb over Rafa's lap into the driver's side and he moves over, slinks down onto the passenger floorboard. Blood on the seat soaks through my shirt, dampens my back.

Ahead of us on the left, I see a pedestrian path. "Hang on," I shout.

We slam against the walkway's grassy incline with such

force the front wheels come off the ground for a sickening moment. Then we're speeding up a hill, flying over its crest and down the other side. The Jeep jerks around madly as I weave it between the rolling, grassy mounds. I check the rearview. Headlights bounce and hop about in chaos. Muzzle flashes, popping sounds.

It's a miracle they haven't shot out the tires yet. I toggle the grid map on the dashboard, noticing how far south we are. The mud and grass beyond the city limits are only a couple clicks away.

"We've got to get out of the city," I shout.

"Out of the city?" Rafa yells. "Where?"

"To the south."

"*The south?*" Rafa toggles the dashboard to the drone feed, where images of Guzmán's assault flash on the screen. "You want to drive into *that?*"

It's not like we have a lot of options.

"Staying in the city's suicide," I say, whipping the wheel over. "At least out there we'll have room to move around."

I glance over at Rafa. His eyes are squeezed shut and he grimaces with every lurch of the vehicle. A shot hits the door mirror on Rafa's side. It explodes off its housing, skitters across the hood and disappears.

South.

We come around a tall ridge. In the small moment when we disappear from view, I brake hard and make a sharp turn, pointing the Jeep south, then I stand on the gas. Seconds later, in the rearview I see red taillights speed past the ridge. They didn't turn and follow us. I push the Jeep hard, putting distance between us and our pursuers, but I can already see their taillights flashing red as they brake, turn around, and pick up our trail again.

The tires squeak against the pavement as we exit the walking paths. I turn a corner and head down a narrow street, barely wide enough for the Jeep to pass through. Shop windows and brick walls blur past us. Tiny glass shards cover the seat cushions, sparkling like diamonds in the storefront lights. I turn the wheel over hard and we exit onto a wider avenue. Gunfire crackles. The rear passenger window shatters.

A few blocks ahead, the rainbow glow of the city ends. Beyond it, darkness. I press the gas harder.

We speed forward. I hunch over the wheel, trying to will the Jeep faster. I reach down and turn off the dashboard screen, then the headlights. Outside the city, we'll be almost invisible out there in the dark.

"What are you doing?" Rafa yells.

"So they won't see us."

"They might have nightview gear, you know."

"Shut up, Rafa."

We reach the end of the street, the edge of the city. The Jeep's shocks bounce and the vehicle sags as the surface changes from hard pavement to soft earth. We lose speed though I haven't taken my foot off the gas. We're in a thick patch of wet grass.

The Jeep slides, then finds traction and we race forward. The interior of the vehicle darkens as we distance ourselves from the city lights. In the rearview a group of headlights reaches the city's edge, then follows us beyond it. I turn southwest, hoping they can't see our change of direction.

We slip and slog through the grassy muck.

A few moments pass, then Rafa turns and looks behind us. "They've stopped shooting."

I listen. The only sounds are the whine of the engine and the slosh of the tires. The rearview reflects no headlights behind us, only the lights of the city, growing more distant with each moment.

"Did we lose them?"

"They're still heading south," Rafa says. "They haven't turned to follow us."

"Steffa, are you okay back there?"

No answer. A surge of panic shoots through me.

"Steffa, are you hurt?" I shout.

"I'm okay," she calls. "Can I get up now?"

I exhale. "Not yet. Just stay down."

Rafa watches behind us, still clutching his shoulder. "How bad are you hit?" I ask.

He lifts his hand, examines the wound. "Went straight through. But it's bleeding bad."

In the corner of my vision, the horizon flashes yellow once, then again, then a third time in quick succession. Seconds later the sounds of the explosions reach us, low rumbles like thunder. It's several clicks south of us. Right about where a tower compound would be.

I point and say, "Over there, look. That's where they're fighting."

"You think they've gotten past the towers yet?" Rafa groans.

"No," I answer. If they'd already fought their way past the tower perimeter, these fields would be swarming with vehicles speeding toward the city.

I steer the Jeep due west. "We'll try to go around it," I tell him.

The chase party still hasn't turned in our direction.

"But the towers," Rafa says. "We'll never get past them."

I grip the wheel tighter. And even if we do manage to slip past the towers without getting shot to pieces, what then?

We drive on through the muddy, dark expanse. A minute passes and Steffa asks again if she can get up onto the seat.

Still no headlights in the rearview. "Yes," I answer. "Careful with all the glass. And if something happens you go right back down, you hear me?"

"Okay."

I ease up on the gas, try to come up with something. Dallas on our right, a war raging on our left, a pack of Humvees out there in the dark somewhere, hunting us like wolves. We're safe for the moment, but the moment won't last. There's nowhere for us to go.

"Look!" Steffa cries. "Someone turned off the city."

I look toward the city and gasp. Dallas has gone dark.

It's as if the entire city has disappeared. Not a single light shines where a second before there was a rainbow's spectrum of color from buildings and streetlights, vivid and brilliant against the darkness.

"You think that's the rogue?" Rafa asks through clenched teeth.

"Maybe." There's no way to know for sure. "It could be a civil defense thing," I guess. "Some emergency measure."

Our attention snaps ahead of us, where an explosion illuminates the night into sudden orange and yellow. Steffa shrieks and a moment later the shock wave hits us.

"Get down," I shout, braking and turning the Jeep away from the blast.

"Holy shit," Rafa cries. "You see that?"

"See it? That strike almost hit us!"

Rafa's watching behind us. "No, it wasn't a drone strike. It was a drone *crashing.*"

A second explosion erupts, this one close enough to rock the Jeep. My ears ring and flash spots fill my vision.

Rafa points. "Look!"

As I steer a wide circle around the burning patch of grass, I get a good look. I can make out the smoldering remains of a wing and a portion of the fuselage. It's a surveillance drone, like the one we saw out west.

A third drone falls from the sky, far to the south of us. Then another half a click ahead of us.

"Matamoscas?" I ask Rafa.

"Those were spy drones," he answers. "They never fly them low enough to be hit."

We exchange a knowing look.

"The rogue?" I ask.

Rafa nods. "Has to be."

Something catches my eye in the rearview. Headlights.

Shit. The chase group's found us.

The pinpoints of light quickly grow larger as they close the distance. We trudge through the wet terrain, losing ground with each moment. South of us the light show of Guzmán's invasion continues, faraway explosions and the faint crackle of gunfire.

Then a second chase group appears in front of us. A row of headlights bobbing up and down, bearing down on us fast.

Rafa slumps in the seat, holding his shoulder. "Christ, they've got us."

I whip the wheel over, spraying a rooster tail of watery mud high into the air. I point the Jeep south and stand on the gas.

"What are you doing?" Rafa protests, pointing at the raging battle in the distance, now directly in front of us. "We can't go into *that*."

But there's nowhere else to go, no other direction to turn. "Maybe there's a way through," I say, hearing the desperation in my voice.

The Jeep speeds southward, the battle growing larger in the windshield. Green and red tracer rounds appear, flying in all directions like mad fireflies. In the distance the cab of a semitruck burns, flames shooting high into the night sky. Then it blows up into a brilliant ball of orange light.

Behind us the chase groups converge, gaining on us. A bullet strikes the Jeep with a popping clang.

"Stay down, Rafa," I shout.

I hunch over, trying to make myself a smaller target. The chaos of the battle grows nearer, louder. Now I can make out armored cars, buses with mounted guns, semitrucks with war gear. Guzmán's army.

Bullets rip through the Jeep. Red warnings flash, lighting up the dashboard.

Suddenly there's a motorcycle next to us, no more than an arm's length from my window. One of Guzmán's motoboys. The rider looks over at me through his goggles, then levels a shotgun at my head.

Light and sound explode and time stops. The Jeep lifts into the air and turns sideways. The ground slowly rotates until it's below me, then time speeds up again. Violent spins and the sound of crunching metal. Ground sky ground sky ground sky.

Then I'm out of the Jeep, flying through the air, my arms and legs flapping like a doll's. When I finally tumble to a stop, I'm not sure if I'm dead or alive. The first thing I'm aware of is the cold, wet ground against my cheek. I raise my head and look around.

I'm lying in a bog. Around me cars and trucks speed through the mud, tracer rounds zip back and forth. Soundless images to the ringing in my ears.

I try to lift my head, but everything goes blurry and my field of vision narrows like I'm looking through a tunnel. Then the tunnel goes dark and everything disappears.

CHAPTER 24

My head throbs with blinding pain and my eyes are squeezed shut against the shock of bright daylight.

Where am I? What happened?

I crack my eyelids open and the space around me takes shape.

I'm on a cot, in a tent, alone. I'm wearing different clothes. Loose cotton shirt and pants, no shoes. There's a pair of hiking boots on the plastic tarp floor next to the cot.

I remember the chaos, being thrown from the Jeep, passing out. I look at the tent around me.

Guzmán. His people must have picked me up, brought me here.

I sit up and the world lurches around me, sickening my stomach. I rub my temples, take deep breaths. Then I look at my hands, arms. My skin is raw, covered in scrapes and small cuts.

A head pokes inside the door flap. I look up, see a woman I don't recognize. She withdraws and closes the flap.

Every muscle in my body aches, joints hurt with every move. I swing my legs off the cot, put the shoes on. I can barely tie the laces. Even my fingers hurt.

The door flap flies open and Chavez enters. He stands there, huge and silent like some clothed gorilla, and looks me over. "Bruja," he announces, shaking his head. "Never thought I'd see you again."

I'm too tired to react, too exhausted to be frightened. "Sorry to disappoint you." My head pulses in pain with each heartbeat.

"He wants to see you," he says.

"Where's Steffa?"

"¿Quién?"

"The girl. She was with me. And where's Rafa?"

Chavez shrugs. "Boss told me to come get you, that's it."

I stand. My head swims and my knees buckle.

Chavez rushes over and grabs me around the shoulders, saving me from falling to the floor. "Easy," he says. "Take it slow."

We exit the tent into brilliant sunlight. I squint as Chavez leads me through a boggy field. The sun's already high overhead; it must be around noon, which means I've been out of it for a long while. With each step my boots make sucking sounds in the mud. There are hundreds of tents all around. People bustle back and forth. The familiar buzz of Guzmán's camp, though right now it seems heightened, more excited than I remember it.

We stop in front of a large tent. Chavez lets go of my arm, motions to the door flap. "Go on."

I look at him, confused. "Just me?"

He nods. "Just you."

I stare at the door flap for a moment, then push my way through. On the other side I find myself in the familiar surroundings of Guzmán's office. Worn photographs of revolutionaries pinned to the walls, children's drawings, a wide table with a mess of papers. And behind it sits don Flaco, puffing on his pipe.

"Siéntate," he says, motioning to a chair. He looks

calm, relaxed.

The sudden familiarity of don Flaco's tent, his gravelly voice, the smell of his tobacco overwhelms me. It's hard to fathom, after everything that's happened, that I've ended up right back here. I grab the chair arms and slowly lower my aching body.

"The girl's fine," he says. "Bruised up, but nothing bad."

"Y Rafa?"

"Broken leg and a couple ribs. But he'll be all right."

I sigh. *They're alive.*

"You've been asleep a long while." He puffs thoughtfully. "How's your head?"

I rub my temple. "Feels like someone's hammering the backs of my eyes."

Guzmán juts out his lower lip. "All three of you were damned lucky. I saw what was left of that Jeep. Puta madre."

Lucky. Maybe Rafa, who if he's smart already came up with some 'she kidnapped me at gunpoint' story. And definitely Steffa. She's lucky to find herself in a place where she'll be taken care of.

But me? I murdered one of don Flaco's guards, kidnapped the trader, corrupted Lela, got her killed. No, lucky doesn't describe my circumstance at all.

My mind wanders to how he'll do it. Will he do it like the Fundies and make some public spectacle out of my betrayal, maybe a hanging? Or will he simply have Chavez walk me out of camp and take care of me in some muddy field? Chavez would like that, I think. I picture him eagerly waiting outside the door flap, gun in hand.

"We found the gringo in the desert when we came after you," he says. "Freelancers robbed him, left him dead."

"Abner?"

"Sí."

I nod. It's a small consolation.

Don Flaco scratches his beard. "The boy told me

everything already. The tech in that gringo's leg, the Fundies, what happened in Dallas." He pauses for a moment. "Y Lela," he adds.

I fidget. "So if you already know everything, why'd you bother with cleaning me up and bringing me here? You miss my company or something?" I've seen people killed for less rudeness, but I'm too exhausted to censor myself. And what would it change, anyway?

Guzmán smiles, taps the pipe on the edge of the table. Tobacco falls to the dirt floor, still smoking. He smothers it with a twist of his boot heel.

Then he reaches into his jacket pocket. I take a breath, prepare myself.

Instead of a gun, he removes a small plastic bag. He places it on the table.

Hierba.

He leans forward. "After I tell you what I'm going to tell you, you're going to have questions for me. And you'll want to know if my answers are the truth."

I stare at the bag.

"That gringo Abner," Guzmán continues, "he offered me a lot of money to make you disappear."

I don't react, my eyes fixed on the hierba.

Don Flaco tilts his head. "This doesn't surprise you?"

I shake my head. Mama coerced her husband into having his own daughter killed. It's not a stretch to imagine her bullying her lover-conspirator to finish the job. Don Flaco's news comes as no revelation, moving nothing inside me.

"I said no, of course." He slides the bag closer to me. "Take it," he urges.

"I don't want to."

"There are things you should know."

I shrug. "So tell me."

"Chew the hierba first."

"I won't."

He stares at me, curious. "Why not?"

For a moment I don't say anything. Then I look into his eyes. "Mama always told me what I have is a gift, but that's not true." I swallow. "It's a curse, this thing I have. A birth defect." I lean forward. "Do you know what it's like to see the truth, to really see it? It's horrible, hideous. The truth's a terrible monster that ought to be kept locked away and hidden. I never want to see that monster's ugly face again."

Don Flaco furrows his brow, seems to struggle for something to say.

Behind me the door flap ruffles as someone enters. Chavez appears and sets a plate down on the table in front of me. Steaming eggs, beans, tortillas. He places a fork and cup of water next to the plate.

"Provecho," he says, then turns and leaves.

My mouth waters as the smell of the food hits me.

"Eat," Guzmán orders.

I look at him, bewildered.

"You handed Dallas to me," he chuckles. "I owe you much more than a breakfast."

Owe me? I narrow my eyes at him. He seems amused by my confusion. "Go on, eat," he insists.

I'm too hungry to ask questions. I shovel a forkful of eggs into a tortilla, roll it up, take a large bite.

"I'm not going to punish you," he says. "You don't have to worry about that. Same for Rafa."

I stop chewing and look up at him, study his face. The tips of his mustache curl up as he grins. "¿Ya ves? I told you. Don't you want to know if I'm telling the truth?"

I glance at the hierba, then scoop more eggs into the tortilla.

"After the city went dark, all their defenses and combat tech went down, even out at the towers." He snaps his fingers. "One minute they're holding their own, the next they're helpless and blind. Couldn't see us, couldn't talk to each other. Running around like chickens with no heads, as the gringos say. After that we rolled right in. The

Dallasites are still hiding, thinking we're going to kill their men, rape their women. Same as every other town. Eventually they'll come out."

"And the Bullocks?" I ask.

"Long gone. They choppered out before we hit the city. Probably on some ship in the Gulf by now, taking a nice cruise to some friendly Caribbean dictator's turf."

I swallow a mouthful of beans, wondering if Mama got out with them, feeling a strange detachment, a void where both she and Papi used to be. It's an odd realization, knowing I no longer care where my parents are or what's happened with them. The world's turned itself inside out. The possible futures I'd imagined for myself only days ago are gone, and I don't know what's supposed to replace them or what comes next. All I can think of is what I've lost. Who I've lost.

I place my fork on the plate and sigh, thinking of Lela.

"Sol!" I whirl around and Steffa's there, standing in the doorway. Rafa's holding open the flap, leaning on a crutch under his arm.

She rushes to me. I drop out of the chair to my knees and she throws her arms around my neck. I squeeze her tight, a flood of tears blurring my vision. I look up at Rafa, reach out my hand. He hobbles inside the tent, takes it, squeezes.

The three of us stay there like that for a long time. Finally I hold Steffa by the shoulders and move her back a step.

"Let me get a look at you." Her face is full of small cuts and abrasions, and there's a purple swelling under one eye.

She shrugs. "It doesn't hurt too bad."

"And how's your leg?"

"Feels better." She takes a little hop on the injured leg to prove it.

I look up at Rafa. He smiles, nods.

We're safe, all of us.

Then a twinge of doubt tickles the back of my mind.

But I've thought that before, haven't I?

I turn toward don Flaco, moving my gaze between him and the bag of hierba on the table.

"So all right," I tell him as I reach for the bag. "I do have some questions."

CHAPTER 25

I promise Steffa I'll see her soon, and Rafa takes her, leaving me alone with Guzmán.

Don Flaco sits across the table from me, studying his map, taking notes, tallying up his natural gas empire. It's a familiar scene, as familiar as the bitterness filling my mouth as I wait for the hierba to take hold.

The smells hit me first, as always. The burnt-charcoal odor of the ashes in his pipe, the sour, sweaty stench of the clothes he hasn't changed in days.

I'm ready.

"Is Steffa safe here?" I ask him.

Guzmán snaps his attention up from the map, ponders the question. "Yes. I'll do my best to keep her safe."

Not even the slightest waver. It's the truth.

"What about Rafa?"

He chuckles. "If he doesn't go on any more aventuras with you, he'll be fine."

"Just yes or no," I tell him, studying his face, listening to his voice. "Will Rafa be safe here with you?"

"Yes. I won't punish him for helping you. He'll be as safe as anyone else in camp."

Truth.

I pause, take a breath. *Thank God.*

"And what about me?" I ask.

"Same for you. No venganza, no punishment. As long as you're in my territory, you'll be as protected as I can keep you."

Truth...but there's something else.

"But...what?" I prompt.

"But you don't have to stay in my territory if you don't want to. You're free to go where you want."

I blink and run my finger over the tracker scar on my arm. Guzmán notices the gesture. Shame emerges like a shadow over his face. *Shame.*

It's hard to believe his words, even though I know he's not lying. "You're serious?"

"I've taken enough of your life already, don't you think?"

I watch his face carefully, pondering this new found generosity, wondering how this conversation would be going if he hadn't taken Dallas so easily. For a moment, I consider extending my awareness to try and see more, but then I decide against it. Whatever horrors lurk in the dark corners of his mind, he can keep them to himself.

"It's not about Dallas," he offers, as if *he's* reading *my* mind.

"What do you mean?"

He pauses, clears his throat. "We always knew about your parents, ever since the day the freelancers brought you to us."

I shiver, the tiny hairs on my arms stand up. "Knew *what* about my parents?"

"Your mother wanted the freelancers to kill you, and your father paid them so they'd bring you to us instead. We knew they were still alive. We knew all these things from the start."

"We meaning who?"

"Lela y yo."

I can't find words. "But...how...who told...?"

"Lela asked them. She had a special way of asking, if you remember. She got it out of them."

It's the truth, every stunning word of it. They knew about Mama and Papi all along.

Lela, why didn't you tell me?

I feel numb. "Why didn't you say something?" I manage.

Guzmán shifts in his chair. "Lela said you'd suffered too much already. More than anyone should have to. She wanted to protect you."

"*Protect* me?" I blurt out. "Like how you protected me with tracking devices, eyes on me all the time, and no freedom to even take a piss on my own?"

"That's not what I meant."

I shut my eyes, rub my temples. I don't want to believe what I'm hearing.

For a long time neither of us speaks. I stare at the floor.

"Maybe I'd do it differently if I had it to live over again," he confesses, his voice resonating with sorrow and regret. "Maybe she would have too. All she wanted was to keep you safe. That was her whole life, the only thing that mattered to her. So if you want to stay, I'll keep you safe. That's my promise to you...and to her."

Not lying.

I stand, legs shaking, my mind trying to bend itself around everything I've heard. I turn to leave.

"Where are you going?" Guzmán calls out.

I don't answer.

*   *   *

I sit on the edge of the cot in my tent, staring at the plastic tarp floor. Outside there's the bustling din of camp. Engines sputtering, workers hammering, children shouting. Shadows pass back and forth across the canvas wall. People in a hurry, doing things, living lives.

I take out the Virgin pendant, absently run my finger

over the folds in Mary's dress. I sit there, my thoughts turning to the past, what I thought it was, my place in it.

She could have dragged me back to camp at any time, but she didn't. She thought she could talk sense into me before we got to Dallas.

I'm so sorry, Lela.

I stare at the floor for some time, I'm not sure how long, when Steffa comes in.

She scowls at me. "You said you'd come see me soon."

"I'm sorry," I say, staring at the floor.

She steps forward. "Were you crying?"

"A little bit."

"About what?"

"Nothing." I wipe my eyes.

She notices the tracker scar on my forearm, touches it cautiously. "What's that?"

"I used to have something in there so people could find me."

"Like in case you got lost?"

I run my finger over the scar. "Yes. In case I got lost."

"But now you don't need it?"

"No, not anymore."

"Are you going to stay here?" she asks. "With Señor Flaco?"

"I don't know."

I look up at her, the effect of the hierba still lingering. I see her doubt, her worry that this camp might be like her last one.

"It's safe here," I assure her. "I promise."

She wavers. I sense she wants to believe me, but after all she's been through it's no wonder she doesn't trust anyone's words. She wants to ask me again, but holds back.

"Yes, I'm going to stay," I say, answering her unvoiced question. Some of the anxiety fades from her face, but not all of it.

I slide off the cot and kneel in front of her. "Here, I've

got something for you."

I remove the Virgin pendant and place it around her neck. She holds it in her hand, runs her finger over the image.

"It'll bring you good luck," I say. "It's very special to me, so I want you to take care of it."

She turns it over in her fingers. Sunlight comes through the tent's door flap, shines on her face.

"It belonged to my mother," I tell her. It doesn't feel like a lie.

"Did she die?"

"She did."

"Were you sad?"

"Very sad."

"Are you still sad?"

"Yes."

"Was she a good mother?"

"She took care of me, always looked out for me."

"So she was a good mother?"

I reach out and touch Steffa's cheek.

"Yes. She was."

ACKNOWLEDGEMENTS

It's almost embarrassing for me to have my name as the only one on the cover when so many contributed to this book. First, for my friends, fellow writers, and first readers—otherwise known as the Space City Critters— many thanks for the consistently thoughtful feedback.

Para mi Clau, mil gracias por todo tu apoyo. Te quiero muchísimo.

A special thanks for the beta readers who invested their valuable time to help me work through the final drafts: John Husisian, Robin Shackelford, Cheryl Nelson Deariso, George Wright Padgett, Holly Walrath, Jason Kristopher, and Kristin Mireles. And a huge thanks to Betsy Aoki for her wonderful insights and feedback.

To my editor Juliet Ulman: you were a godsend! I'm so grateful for your red-penned guidance. Thanks for everything.

Finally, I'd like to call out a few people who do wonderful, thankless work nurturing the SF&F writing community in my home state. Pat Hauldren, Keri Bas, and Dominick D'Aunno. Your support and generosity have been invaluable to me and countless other writers. Thank you for everything you do.

ABOUT THE AUTHOR

D.L. Young is a Texas-based author. His stories have appeared in many publications and anthologies.

He's also the founder of the Space City Critters Writers Workshop, a member of Mensa, an English football fan, and a cigar lover.

For new release updates and subscriber-only discounts and exclusives, visit his website at www.dlyoungfiction.com.